Holmes the Hunter

and other Sherlock Holmes Mysteries

by

Susan Knight

Edited by David Marcum

Hardcover ISBN 978-1-80424-743-3
Paperback ISBN 978-1-80424-744-0
ePub ISBN 978-1-80424-745-7
PDF ISBN 978-1-80424-746-4
Published by MX Publishing
335 Princess Park Manor, Royal Drive,
London, N11 3GX
www.mxpublishing.com

Cover Design by Awan

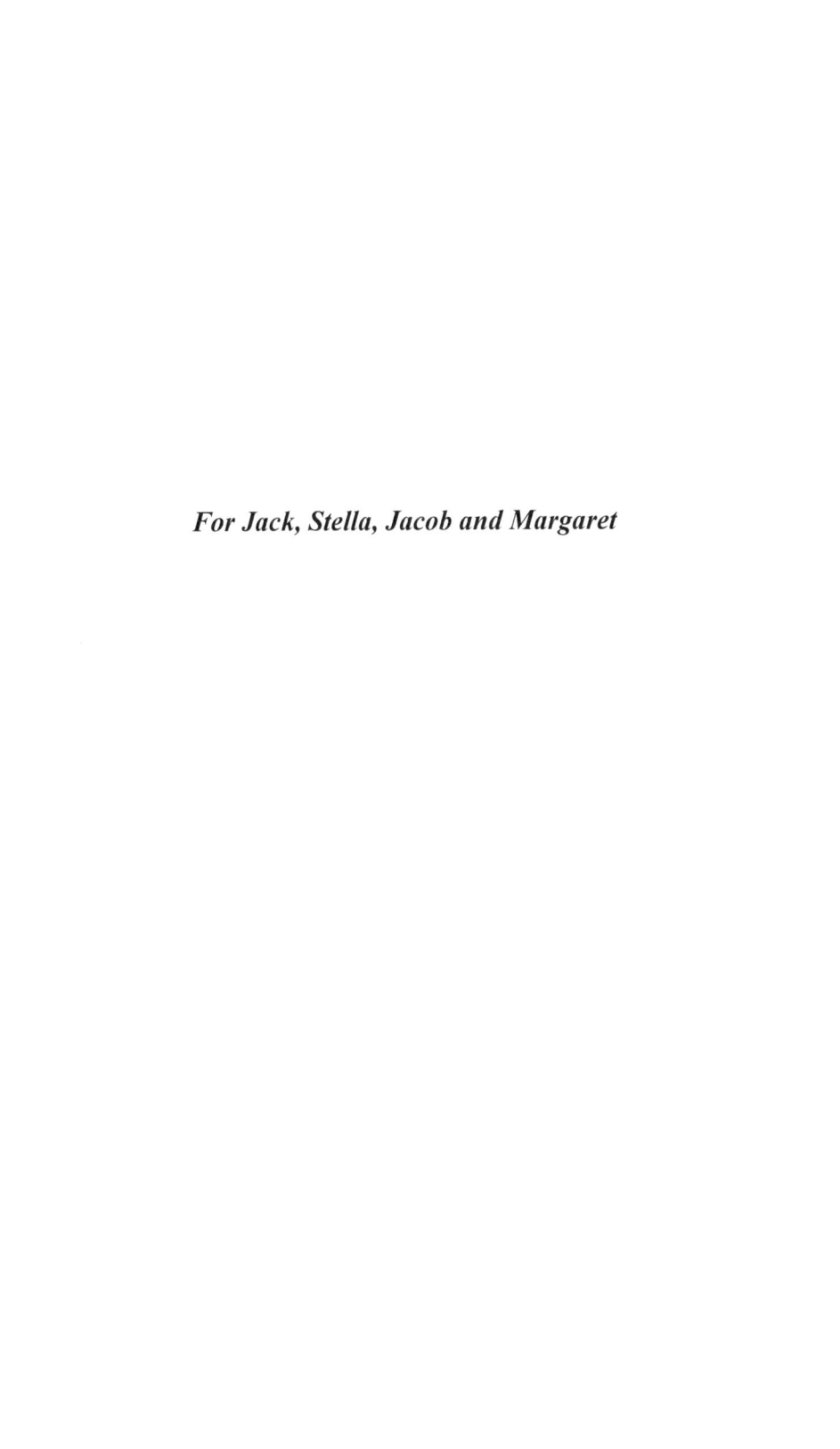

For Jack, Stella, Jacob and Margaret

Introduction

Most of these stories first appeared in various volumes of the *MX Books of New Sherlock Holmes Stories*, from 2023 to 2025, as follows: *The Adventure of the Old Russian Woman* (Vol. XL), *The St Pancras Puzzle* (Vol. XLII), *The Other Woman* and *A Matter of ABC* (Vol. XLIV), *Inspector Gregson at Bay* (Vol. XLVII), *Sherlock Holmes and the Female Detective* (Vol. LI), and *Holmes the Hunter* (Vol. LII).

Sadly, there will be no more of these anthologies, since their inestimable editor, David Marcum, has decided after ten years hard slog to turn his attention to other projects, including his own writing. His legacy remains, however, in that all royalties from the sales of the books go to support Stepping Stones, the school for special needs children based at Sir Arthur Conan Doyle's former house, Undershaw, in Surrey. I was privileged to visit there in May 2025 to celebrate David's achievement at a terrific event organised by Steve and Sharon Emecz of MX publishing, and attended by local dignitaries and several celebrities, as well as other Sherlockian writers.

The brief David gave us was to write in the style of the Canon, with no deviations into, for instance, the supernatural, unless Holmes could find a rational explanation for the mystery. Use of Smart phones or other pieces of modern technology were, of course, totally banned. Most of us took on the challenge of reproducing Dr Watson's voice to the best of our ability, something I have found most enjoyable, and a change from my usual literary persona of Mrs Martha Hudson.

I have also included one new story, *The Case of the Fatal Flowers,* as well as a few of the short light pieces I wrote for my blog, featuring Holmes and Watson at their dining table, discussing Mrs Hudson's adventures and literary endeavours, and the subsequent disconcerting (to Holmes) changes they made to her culinary offerings. I hope they will amuse, after all the murders and grisly deaths.

SK

Contents

Holmes the Hunter   1

Sherlock Holmes and the Female Detective   33

The St Pancras Puzzle   61

The Other Woman   97

The Adventure of the Old Russian Woman   126

A Matter of ABC   154

Inspector Gregson at Bay   194

The Case of the Fatal Flowers   217

Titbits from the Dining Table of 221b Baker Street   239

Holmes the Hunter

"I have been thinking, Watson." Holmes was adding something unspeakably rank to the concoction brewing in the flask suspended over his Bunsen burner. "A few days in the countryside, enjoying the fine spring weather, would do us both a power of good."

I had been absorbed in the latest intelligence from South Africa, where the Boers were continuing to wage war against our boys, but I now gazed at Holmes over the top of my newspaper, in no little astonishment. When had Holmes ever expressed delight at the prospect of uprooting himself from Baker Street, unless it be in pursuit of a criminal?

"The countryside?" I queried. "Where?"

He turned to me then.

"An old acquaintance in Sussex has been invited for the weekend, and is hoping we might accompany him. I thought it would make a pleasant break."

I was even more astonished.

"A weekend in Sussex!" I exclaimed. "What old acquaintance is this?"

"Someone from years ago. The invitation is to a house party."

I threw down my paper. A house party, indeed! The prospect of which would usually make my friend run twenty miles in the opposite direction.

"Come now, Holmes," I said. "There's must be more to this than a social engagement."

He grinned merrily at me. "Ah, Watson, there is no fooling you. In fact, I barely know the fellow. It's a chap my brother went to school with. Mycroft has kept in touch with him over the years."

I began to see the light. There was certainly something afoot if Holmes's brother, who held a powerful but mysterious role in the government of the country, was involved.

"The invitation," Holmes continued, "was, in point of fact, initially made to Mycroft, but, as you know, he is exceedingly loath to venture beyond the isosceles triangle that comprises his apartment, his place of work and the Diogenes club. He suggested to our friend that you and I might attend the party in his place, to which the gentleman was most agreeable."

"So what is it all about?"

"For many years, this Frederick Jansson worked abroad, in various embassies..." Holmes paused, and gave me a significant look. I understood this to mean that the man was a spy. "He has connections, let us say. And certain of these have led him to intelligence of a plot, by a group of people opposed to our current government's activities abroad, to assassinate a number of key individuals."

"Good Lord!"

"Suspicion points to the hosts of this party, neighbours of his, as being involved."

"So is this not rather a matter for the police?"

Holmes sighed. "Would it were so simple. No, Watson, Jansson has no firm evidence to lead to a prosecution. He fears an attempt will be made over this weekend to eliminate at least one of the men on the list."

"So we would be walking into a lion's den?"

"Not for the first time, Watson. Come, now, man, things have been desperately quiet since we returned from Constantinople with Mrs Hudson[1]. What do you say?"

"I shall pack my revolver."

Thus it was that the following Friday afternoon saw us on the Brighton train, our destination Coombe Hall, a country house on the banks of the river Ouse. We alighted at Haywards Heath, where Frederick Jansson was awaiting us with a carriage. He was a jolly, chubby man in his late forties, of small stature, with a baby face that spoke of an innocence, which I suspected, from the little I had heard of him, hid a shrewd, if not devious mind.

"Holmes," he said in a high-tenor voice, grasping my friend's hand the while and shaking it heartily. "I am delighted to see you again after so many years. And to meet you too, Dr Watson. I have followed your accounts of this rogue's exploits most avidly."

As he drove us from the station, he explained how he considered it wise for us not to reveal our true identities to our hosts, something we had already decided upon.

"I told them that you are my house guests for the weekend, whereupon Metcalfe insisted I bring you along as well."

To my amusement and Holmes's dismay, Jansson had already taken it upon himself to assign us new names. I was to be Dr John Willoughby, while Holmes was newly styled Stanley Hunter.

"Stanley!" Holmes expostulated (the only verb powerful enough to describe his outburst!). "I abhor the name."

"Then blame your parents," Jansson replied drily. "If anyone tries to check you out, they are the names of two most respectable gentlemen of my acquaintance, buried alive in the backwaters of Norfolk."

---

[1] See *Death in the Harem: A Mrs Hudson & Sherlock Holmes mystery*, MX publishing, 2024.

He then described our hosts. Vernon Metcalfe was a man who had made his fortune in the diamond mines of South Africa. His wife Helene was of Dutch descent.

"A Boer?" I asked.

Jansson nodded his head. "It's probable. Metcalfe is British, but his sympathies, though concealed, certainly lie, I understand, with the Boers, particularly their notions of the right to keep slaves from among the indigenous population. He is deeply religious, but someone who believes in the God-given superiority of the white man."

"Surely," I said, "a man like that would not wish to shed the blood of others, would not be involved in any assassination plot."

Jansson laughed. "You might think so, Doctor, but, in my experience, it is common for people who claim the highest principles to be able to condone, for whatever reason, the most unspeakable acts. In fact, the very notion that they are chosen of God, seems to them to justify anything they want to do, in His name, of course. Their enemies are God's enemies."

It was a depressing thought, but one with which, from my own experience, in Afghanistan and elsewhere, I had to agree. If this Metcalfe was to be our host for the weekend, I rather dreaded the experience.

After about forty minutes of a drive, we found ourselves skirting high stone walls, the estate, as Jansson told us, that was Coombe Hall.

"It seems," Holmes said, "that they value their privacy."

At last, we arrived at the heavy metal gates that marked the entrance to the property. These were padlocked shut, so it proved necessary to ring a bell to summon the gatekeeper from his lodge to open for us. This the humpy-backed old fellow did willingly enough, recognising Jansson, though squinting rather suspiciously at Holmes and myself. With some effort, he caused the gates to swing open with a loud squeal, like an animal in pain. I wondered aloud that no oil had been employed to ease the hinges and lessen the noise.

"But you see, Watson," Holmes replied, "no one can come and go through these gates without being heard."

That explanation did nothing to relieve my anxieties.

A long driveway led up through an avenue of lime trees, opening out eventually to the manor house, in front of which, a circular pool sported a three-tiered fountain. The house itself, of pale brick, was handsome in the formal way of a Georgian mansion, stone steps leading up to an exterior landing surmounted with high pillars and a mansard roof. The many windows glinted in the afternoon sun. If anyone was watching us from behind them, they could not be seen.

As we approached, a young groom appeared from the side of the house. The three of us having descended from the carriage with our travelling cases, the lad sprang into the driver's seat and caused the horse to trot away, presumably to the mews. I watched it reluctantly, as if our last hope of escape had gone.

My fears, however, were soon dissipated by the emergence from the house of a tall, well-built, genial man in, I surmised, his late sixties, along with a truly beautiful blonde woman, many years younger than himself. They welcomed us effusively, with what seemed sincere warmth. If this was Vernon Metcalfe and his wife, Helene, then, I felt sure, Jansson's suspicions were misplaced.

"Delighted to meet you, Dr Willoughby, Mr Hunter. Any friend of Freddie's is a friend of ours." Metcalfe said. "By the way," addressing Holmes, "are you one?

"I beg your pardon?" Holmes replied.

"A hunter… We are rather given to the pleasures of the chase, here, d'you see." The man rubbed plump hands together. "Only sadly, it is not the season just now. However, you would be very welcome to return in the autumn, if your tastes are in that direction."

Holmes smiled. "A very generous offer, sir. I shall certainly consider it."

Holmes the hunter? Perhaps. But never of game. I hadn't discussed it with him but I imagined his opinion concurred with that of mine and Mr Oscar Wilde, who described hunting as "the unspeakable in pursuit of the uneatable".

"Now Vernon, don't keep our guests on the steps." Helene Metcalfe spoke with a very slight, attractive accent, which I assumed must be Dutch. "Please follow me, gentlemen."

She led the way into the house, into an airy hallway with a pale marble floor and ionic pillars, painted white. Servants divested us of our outer garments and we proceeded through to a reception room, where several people sat or stood, conversing. The older, seated, couple were introduced to us as Lord and Lady Tonbridge, unimpeachably respectable, evidently, and rather conscious, I felt, of their own superiority. Or perhaps I simply received that impression because of the way Lady Tonbridge viewed us through the lorgnette she held up to her long aristocratic nose, as if afflicted by a bad smell.

Gretta, the Metcalfe's daughter – but surely Helene was far too young to have a daughter in the forties – was bony, pallid and too thin for good health. She immediately apologised for the unavoidable absence of her husband, of whom we knew nothing until that moment, so were unlikely to care one way or the other.

"Darby would have so much liked to meet you both," she twittered.

"Perhaps another time," Holmes replied.

I noticed that Vernon Metcalfe was frowning slightly.

"Your husband, Gretta," he remarked, "might have made an effort to turn up for once."

"Oh, dad's the absolute limit, grandfather!" a lively young girl of about seventeen piped up. "Always too busy to enjoy himself."

This was Veronica, or Ronnie as everyone apparently called her, the Metcalfe's bubbly granddaughter. A solemn boy stood beside her - her brother Aubrey.

Lounging on a couch was a somewhat flash-looking man who turned out to be Gretta's younger brother, Philip. He didn't bother to get up, just nodded at us in an off-hand manner.

"Is Sybil ever coming down, nunc?" Ronnie asked him. "She's been an absolute age."

Philip laughed with something of a sneer. "Oh, she's probably getting herself all dressed up to meet our venerable guests."

Was that us? Venerable? He wasn't much younger than we were.

"And what about Bertie?" Ronnie turned to the Tonbridges. "And his friend, Winnie? Where are they?"

"Oh, you know Bertie," Lady Tonbridge replied. "Always late."

"Bertie," Lord Tonbridge explained, for our benefit, "is our scamp of a son."

"Well, they'd better be here in time for tennis tomorrow," Ronnie said. "I've been looking forward to a return match for an absolute age. I quite intend to give Bertie a good thrashing."

A merry smile accompanied these rather violent words.

"I sincerely hope they'll be here by dinner time," Helene Metcalfe said. "Cook will be really put out otherwise. She's preparing Bertie's favourite mess."

I was beginning to feel distinctly uncomfortable, as if we had intruded on a family get-together, and a rather dull one at that. However, here we were, with a job to do, even if the present company appeared to be the least likely nest of conspirators that we were ever likely to come across. At least the sherry we were served was excellent, and I was happy to sit myself down and quietly take in more of my surroundings.

The drawing room where we found ourselves was decorated in luxurious good taste, walls hung with pale green silk, surmounted here and there by unremarkable paintings of country scenes in heavy gilt frames. A white marble chimney piece in the style, if not the work of Robert Adam, stood below a ceiling festooned with moulded plasterwork. The chairs and couches were upholstered in shades of green slightly darker than the wall hangings, and a pale rug covered the parquet floor, the whole lending the room a charmingly light atmosphere, enhanced by the view through French windows, out over the back lawn of the estate, where the setting sun was turning the distant river Ouse to a ribbon of molten gold. Surely an unlikely setting, I mused, for sinister goings-on.

After a decent interval of polite conversation, Holmes and I excused ourselves to go to our rooms and change for dinner. On the stairs, we met a young lady hurrying down. This had to be Sybil, all decked out in snowy frills and unseasonal puffs of white fur.

"Oh Lordy," she exclaimed. "Am I too late?"

I could not help but be reminded of the white rabbit from Mr Carroll's charming tale of Alice in Wonderland. There was certainly something of the bunny about the girl, who was petite but prettily plump, with big scared eyes, a twitching snub nose, and a prominent overbite.

We assured her that the company was still assembled below, so she gave us a quick smile and scampered on down.

"Curiouser and curiouser," I remarked, but I am afraid Holmes missed the literary reference.

Dinner was a dreary enough affair. The company was wrapped up in their own interests, which involved extensive discussions of local people Holmes and I did not know – and showed no curiosity concerning us, which I suppose was quite useful for our incognito, if rather discourteous. Perhaps Jansson had spun a confection which told them all they wished to know. At least the food was delicious, if very rich: mulligatawny soup, stewed eels, saddle of mutton with redcurrant jelly. A Nesselrode pudding for dessert, followed by Stilton cheese. All washed down with excellent burgundies and port.

Of the two young people yet to arrive there was no sign, so whatever Cook's mess consisted of – and I could not hazard a guess – was wasted.

After dinner, we gentlemen withdrew, in the traditional way, to what Vernon Metcalfe called "the smoking room." There we were expected to smoke, drink more port, but also to sit down to a game of poker.

"I trust, gentlemen," our host remarked to us, "you have no objection to a little wager."

The smile that accompanied his words was, I have to say, somewhat wolfish. For the first time, I suspected a ruthless side to the man.

I had no great liking for the game which I had only played once or twice before, and tried to beg off. Metcalfe wasn't having it.

"Come now, Willoughby. Only a little fun among friends," he insisted.

I sat down with the others, Holmes giving me a wink. I rather dreaded what would happen next. At first, however, all went well. Our host had the upper hand, as he no doubt expected, greedily pulling the heap of coins towards himself each time.

"I fear, gentlemen," he said happily, "that I am quite cleaning you out of your small change. What say we up the stakes just a little? It might sharpen the competitive spirit."

"Count me out, Metcalfe," Lord Tonbridge remarked. "Your fine port has my competitive spirit quite blunted."

I, too, made my excuses, hoping Holmes would do the same. He, however, agreed to play, as did Jansson and Philip, the latter, I am afraid, looking rather the worse for the drink which he had all too freely imbibed.

The new game having started, it soon became clear that the tables had turned. Holmes, unable or unwilling to restrain himself, started to win. Philip soon dropped out, followed by Jansson, leaving Metcalfe facing Holmes (or Hunter, as I had to remember to call him) across the green baize. The stakes rose each time, and our host, while still smiling fixedly, was clearly infuriated at losing. I glanced across at Jansson, who raised his eyebrows and pursed his lips. Antagonising our host was the last thing we should be doing.

It was the last turn of the cards. A sudden grin of triumph lit up Metcalfe's face. His hand beat Holmes's. I knew, of course, that Holmes could have won, that he had lost deliberately.

Metcalfe, suspecting nothing, was become generous in victory.

"My dear fellow," he said gathering his spoils, "you are a worthy antagonist."

"I sincerely hope so," Holmes replied.

Preparatory to retiring, Holmes and I, along with Jansson, briefly discussed our impressions so far in the privacy of the latter's bedroom. Our new friend had perhaps over-indulged in fine wines as well, for I noticed that his words were become slurred and his reactions seemed sluggish.

"I wonder," he remarked, sinking into a chair, "if I have brought you here on a wild goose chase, gentlemen. My information came from a seemingly impeccable source, and yet so far nothing has occurred to bear out our fears."

I said that I had been wondering the same thing.

"Let us wait and see," Holmes replied. "This evening, Metcalfe displayed another side to his character. A man who plays poker as relentlessly as that is capable of anything."

"Rather like yourself," I added.

"I am capable of many things, Watson, including winning or losing at poker, but for me, it is incidental how a game like that turns out, while for him to win is everything."

"Hmm." I could not remember Holmes ever being resigned to losing in any situation, but did not voice this aloud.

"There's a certain document I must show you. I need your help with it," Jansson said. "I should have explained to you before, but we are all tired just now, and it can surely wait until tomorrow."

I could tell that Holmes was avid to see it at once, but he rather reluctantly acceded to Jansson suggestion, since the man was clearly on his last legs.

The next morning, I awoke early. Distant, strange noises had roused me, along with a bright sun shining on my face through a crack in the curtains. I resolved to break my fast and then venture out to explore the parkland surrounding the house.

Down in the breakfast room I helped myself to a fine dish of eggs and devilled kidneys with fresh rolls, my only companion there being young Aubrey, who viewed me shyly. I smiled to encourage him, and asked how old he was (nine) and if he attended school. He named a small public establishment, grimacing somewhat.

"You don't like it?" I asked.

"It's all right," he replied. "Only the other fellows make fun of me."

Oh dear. "Why's that?" I asked.

He shrugged. "I don't know, sir. Maybe because I am good at my lessons and like to do well. They say I am stuck up, and regularly give me a pasting for it." He paused. "I have asked Mama if I can come home and have Miss Everdale teach me again."

"She was your governess?"

"Yes. I love Miss Everdale and will marry her when I grow up." His earnest face lit up briefly. "But grandfather says I should stop behaving like a spoilt cry-baby, and that school will make a man of me... Mama always does what Grandfather says."

"What about your father? What does he say?"

The boy just shook his head, which spoke volumes.

"Well," I said, "stick it out, old chap. It's not for ever, you know."

He looked back it me doubtfully, then said, "Have a crumpet, sir. They're jolly good. We don't get spreads like this at Highfields."

I obligingly took a crumpet, smothered in melting butter, and agreed that they were delicious.

"Hey," Aubrey said, after polishing off another, "would you like to see the Imaginary, sir?"

"The what?"

"The Imaginary. It's jolly good."

"Where is it?"

Aubrey waved at the window. Since I had been planning a walk anyway, I agreed, much to his delight.

What had I expected? Some childish haunt, I had reckoned, but the reality, as I now discovered, was quite different. Aubrey had led me to a walled enclosure in a distant part of the estate, containing a quantity of animals in cages. A Menagerie! Now I realised whence emanated the strange sounds I had heard in the night, whether it was monkeys chattering, wolves howling, foxes barking, parrots squawking, owls hooting, or the sawing call of an angry leopard, prowling restlessly in his tiny enclosure.

This was clearly Aubrey's favourite place. He excitedly described each creature to me.

"Do you know what that is?" he asked, pointing to a large black bird, with a viciously curved beak, and what looked to be a horn on its head.

I replied that I did not.

"That," he replied importantly, "is a cassowary… It's very wary." He laughed at his own joke. "But do you know something peculiar, sir, it can't fly. What kind of a bird is that, sir, that can't fly?"

I told him about ostriches, which can't fly either. "But they can run very fast."

"So can I run fast," he boasted.

Back at the house, we found four young people heading off to the tennis courts. Ronnie and Sybil were accompanied by two young men, one I supposed being Bertie. But where was Winnie? I had assumed by the name that Bertie's friend was another young lady.

"That's him." Aubrey assured me.

"Winnie? Or Willie?"

"I don't know. Winnie, I think. He writes for the papers and escaped from prison." Aubrey obviously considered this very impressive.

"Goodness gracious!" I exclaimed.

"Yes, he had to run like a... like an Austrian to get away."

"A what?"

"That bird you said."

We drifted over to the tennis courts to watch the play. I have to say the new young man, whatever his name was, looked to be a most unlikely jailbird. Slicked-back fair hair, a smoothly polished complexion, a healthy tan: he was for all the world like every other young man of a certain class that I had come across. Aubrey must have got it wrong.

Also watching the play, with a somewhat jaundiced eye, was Philip Metcalfe.

"I say, you're a doctor, aren't you?" he exclaimed. "What can you give me for a splitting headache?"

Advice not to drink so much, I could have said. However, I recommended plenty of water.

"Or a tea made of feverfew might prove helpful," I added. "It's a well-tried herbal medicine. Perhaps Cook..."

"Feverfew be hanged!" Philip exclaimed. "I need the hair of the dog."

And before I could reply that another drink was the last thing he needed, he stomped off.

"He's just cross because Winnie is paying attention to his girl," Aubrey opined wisely. "And she likes him, too."

Truly, the young people seemed to be enjoying themselves immensely, and I enjoyed watching them. Of a sudden, however, Holmes was at my side. He drew me away from the boy.

"Jansson is gone," he said in low tones.

"Gone where?"

"I was told he was called away early this morning by an urgent message. I don't believe a word of it, Watson. He would have informed me first."

"Good Lord!" This was disturbing news indeed.

"Did you notice how confused he seemed last night? I put it down to the late hour and the heavy drinking. However, I am now wondering if he was drugged."

"Well, yes," I replied. "That would fit the symptoms."

"In addition, I didn't hear the gates squeaking open, which would have happened if he left that way."

"As to that," I replied, "you might have slept through the noise. We are far enough distant from the gates, after all."

Holmes turned a cold gaze upon me.

"I was awake with the dawn, Watson. And, as you should know by now, I am a light sleeper and possess preternaturally acute hearing."

I decided to let that pass. God forbid I should attribute any physical weakness to the man.

"But surely," I said, "him being gone, for whatever reason, leaves us in a most invidious position."

"Metcalfe has assured me that we are most welcome to stay on, remarking that it is a long way back to Norfolk."

"Norfolk?"

"Which is where we are supposed to be from, Watson, in case you have forgotten."

"Oh yes, of course."

"However, I fear friend Jansson may have met with some mischief. If he didn't leave through the gates, there is only one other way. Let us take a stroll down to the river."

"You think...? Oh, God!"

"I think nothing, Watson. I look for evidence."

Aubrey regarded us somewhat sorrowfully as we left him. While I am no great companion for a small boy, I felt for his obvious loneliness. Maybe, among the new people, due to arrive in the afternoon for tea, there would be some children of his own age.

The Ouse wound past the lower edge of the estate. Under other circumstances, I should have appreciated the gentle beauty of the scene, willows dipping their new leaves into the slow flow. However, I was conscious of Holmes's attentive examination of the area, and tried to emulate it.

"Look, Watson," he said, pointing down at the ground.

I could see nothing but grass. Holmes shook his head and sighed.

"Look again."

Now I discerned a deeper imprint, and saw that it had created a faint furrow.

"Something has been wheeled down here recently, possibly in a barrow," Holmes said, and started following the trail.

"A boat house!" I exclaimed, indicating a wooden structure ahead of us. Of course, Holmes had noticed it already, and was pacing towards it.

Within, I could see nothing to arouse my suspicions. Just two boats in a boat house. No sign of a body or evidence of a struggle.

Holmes however made an exclamation of satisfaction.

"Ha!" he said, pointing to one of the craft. "Someone has taken this boat out very recently, and bearing some sort of a heavy weight, at that."

"How can you tell?" I asked.

"The oars are wet." He indicated those same implements, hung up on the wall of the hut. "They are still dripping. And look at the side of the boat. Now it floats high, but the waterline reveals that it was recently very low."

I could see that: a darker area very near the gunwale.

"It doesn't mean…"

"No, Watson. It doesn't. But admit it is suggestive."

He climbed into the boat and examined it with the forensic thoroughness so characteristic of him.

"Ha!" he exclaimed again, picking up something from one of the seats. He put it on the palm of his hand and held it out to me. "What do you make of that?" It was a thread of some sort that had caught on a splinter.

"It looks rather like the blanket on my bed," I replied, dismayed.

"Exactly… Come, Watson. Let's get out of here before we arouse suspicion."

"If it's not too late for that."

Holmes decided he now needed to gain access to Jansson's bedroom in the hope that the chambermaid had not already tidied everything up. The company being occupied outside, either watching the tennis or strolling in the grounds in the late May sunshine, left, we hoped, the coast clear. I was to stand guard on the landing, should anyone happen along. Unluckily for me, it was Helene Metcalfe herself who made an appearance. She was hurrying, as if on a mission, but stopped short at the sight of me.

"Dr Willoughby," she exclaimed, "whatever are you doing here? Why aren't you out enjoying yourself with the others?"

"I was just on my way down, madam," I said in a loud voice, "when my eye was caught by these striking pictures." I indicated the very mediocre set of hunting prints hanging there.

She regarded them, and me, dubiously, and made to pass me. I feared her destination was Jansson's room.

"No news of our friend?" I asked, my voice still raised. "I was most astonished to learn he had gone away without a word to us. Nothing serious, I hope."

She smiled as if to reassure. Really, she had the most charming smile. And dimples.

"Some domestic issue, I understand, that required his immediate attention."

"Well, I hope he will be able to return soon."

She regarded me steadily. "As to that," she said, "I cannot say. Now I must check on the state of his room. In case he left anything behind, you understand... Excuse me, please." And, before I could delay her further, she slipped past me quickly and entered Jansson's room.

I waited on tenterhooks, expecting another exclamation of surprise or even anger from her. But nothing of the sort. I slipped into my own room, to await her departure, agonising as to Holmes's whereabouts. After ten minutes or more, I heard the adjacent bedroom door open and shut, and light footsteps hurry down the passage. I waited a little longer, to make sure the coast was clear. Stepping, finally, out of my room, I found Holmes just quitting Jansson's. He placed a finger on his lips and indicated we should go back into my room.

Once there, I asked, "What happened? She didn't see you?"

Holmes was dusting himself down.

"Luckily – and thank you for that – I heard you talking to her, and had time to hide under the bed, where, it seems the maid has long neglected to sweep."

I chuckled at the image of Holmes's long frame in that confined space, trying not to sneeze.

"Could you see what she was doing there?"

"Not exactly, but Helene Metcalfe wasn't engaged in housework. She was clearly searching for something. This perhaps." He held up an envelope. "Jansson had hidden it under the bedframe. Had I not had occasion to hide there, it would have taken me longer to find it."

"Thank goodness, she didn't think to look there. But what is it?"

"Let us see."

He opened the envelope and took out several sheets of paper, scanned them briefly, then tossed them to me with a short laugh.

"It's in code," I said.

"Of course it is. Good old Jansson! This must be the document he mentioned last night. Well, it will take me a while to decipher it, but that's for later, I'm afraid. We mustn't stay absent from the party any longer or questions will surely be asked."

As we headed down the stairs together, he added, "And, Watson, I regret to say there was a blanket missing from the bed."

Under the circumstances, it was hard to play the part of the carefree weekend guest, but the arrival on the lawn of a picnic lunch was a good distraction, especially as the fare was excellent: juicy joints of beef and lamb, roast fowl, crusty pies of pigeon and veal, plenty of ale and cider, or lemonade for younger people. Heaps of sandwiches packed with Cheddar cheese or cress or slices of meat. As for the desserts, young Aubrey's eyes were out on stalks at the sight of so many apple turnovers, cheesecakes, blancmanges, sugared buns and iced biscuits.

"It's difficult to know where to start," I said to him.

For Aubrey, that posed no problem at all.

"Jolly smashing," he said, through a full mouth.

My eyes drifted to the river where our quartet of merry young people had taken to the canoes. But what if they found something unspeakable in the river?

"Nunc won't like that," Aubrey remarked, following my gaze.

"What?"

"His girl off with the others again. Ronnie says Sybil has a bit of a pash for Bertie. Still," he thoughtfully bit into a jam puff. "Nunc has loads of girlfriends. Don't suppose he'll be too bothered."

I peered across to where Philip Metcalfe was standing, by the drinks table. He also was gazing down at the boat people, a fierce glower on his face. He didn't seem exactly unbothered to me.

"And I reckon," Aubrey continued, still chewing, "Ronnie has a bit of a pash for Winnie. I like him, too. I hope they get married."

"Was Winnie really in prison?" I asked.

"Yes." The boy's voice thrilled. "He escaped with his life. I expect they're still after him."

"The police, you mean."

"Yes, but not the bobbies here. In South Africa, you know."

"South Africa… Ahh…"

Now that was very interesting. So was this Winnie, who seemed to be such a pleasant and unobjectionable young man, a Boer supporter, in fact, and part of the plot? I needed to talk to Holmes as soon as possible. Once again, I abandoned young Aubrey, only to be waylaid a moment later by his mother, whom I only knew as Gretta.

"Dr Willoughby," she said, "thank you so much for taking time to talk to my son."

"He's a charming young lad," I replied. "You must be very proud of him."

"Yes," she replied uncertainly. "I am, of course. But… but… I worry about him… Can I confide in you?"

"Now?"

"If you don't mind."

How could I refuse? She led me away from the throng, many of them still eating and chatting, some making their way to the Menagerie to gape at the caged animals, some wandering down to the river. Seclusion was to be found at last at the side of the house in a formal garden of tightly clipped box hedges, that enclosed flower beds in a geometric design beloved of the Italians. It is a style I, who prefer the abundance of the English cottage garden, can admire but not love. A sundial stood in the midst of all, Gretta leaning on this as if needing support.

"I feel," she said, "that I can talk frankly to you… as a doctor."

"Of course."

What poured out was typical of the neurasthenic personality I suspected her to be: all manner of anxieties more related to herself than to her son. I gathered from hints she dropped, that her absent husband was not only uninterested in his offspring, but also in her.

"How I wish," she sighed, "that I had a mother to confide in."

"But you have… don't you?"

She laughed a little wildly.

"Oh, really, Doctor! Helene is not my mother. Mine died years ago, when Philip was small. Papa only married that woman a few years ago."

"My apologies."

That woman! I could tell from Gretta's tone that Helene Metcalfe wasn't her favourite person. "Did he meet her in South Africa?" I continued. "I only ask because I assumed she was from there."

"Yes…" She turned a plain anxious face up to me. "She has changed my father dreadfully, Dr Willoughby."

But before I could find out how, the very subject of our discourse swept into view. I wondered was she keeping an eye on me.

"There you are at last, Gretta," she exclaimed. "Now, charming as the company of Dr Willoughby must surely be, you are neglecting your duties as a mother… Aubrey has just been violently sick."

Oh dear. I felt quite guilty. I should have stopped the child from stuffing himself so much, although it was hardly my place to do so. Gretta rushed off with cries of alarm, while Helene Metcalfe remained, studying me quizzically.

"I suppose she was pouring out her silly little heart to you, Doctor." She chuckled. "I am afraid Gretta tends to behave that way in the company of gentlemen. Her wretched husband isn"t a very satisfactory spouse, you see. And then, of course, she has reached that certain age."

Laughing merrily, dimples and all, she tripped away from me.

Well, beautiful she might be, elegant she might be, while, let it be admitted, of a certain age herself – though she bore it well – but the woman was cruel and quite likely dangerous. I made my way back, to find Holmes, and briefed him on what Aubrey had told me.

"Escaped from prison in South Africa! You don't think the boy was making it up?"

"I'm not sure. He seemed definite about it. It would be an odd thing, wouldn't it, for a child to say unless it was true?"

"That depends on what he has been reading… or hearing. Still, let us bear it in mind."

Aubrey himself had evidently recovered well, and was even having to be restrained from further indulgence in sweetmeats. The party otherwise was still in full flow. I suggested to Holmes that we might take a turn in the Menagerie, but he replied that it gave him no pleasure to see wild creatures caged up. So, sometime later, after we had managed, without offending our hosts, we returned to our rooms - Holmes to try and decipher the code left by Jansson, I to take a nap, since all the food I had consumed lay heavy on me.

Perhaps I was overly suspicious, but it seemed to me that my room had been searched. Of course, the chambermaid had visited, had made up the bed and tidied, but things that need not have been moved were in a slightly different place than before. I had concealed my revolver, but not so thoroughly that a search among my belongings might not have discovered it. Now I wondered, and decided to find out if Holmes had received the same impression.

"Yes, someone has been here," he said. "I was very careful to leave everything in a certain way and, although the searchers tried to put it all back in place, they did not quite manage. However, good luck if they hoped to find anything. I kept the papers on me."

I explained about my revolver. Holmes frowned slightly, and I was expecting him to chastise me for my negligence. However, he just remarked that it would not be unusual for a gentleman visiting the countryside to bring with him a gun, for sporting purposes, whether it was hunting season or not.

"The very fact that it was not well-hidden actually stands in your favour."

I hoped he was not just being kind.

"Now, leave me to my labours," he continued. "And take some rest. If anything is to happen, it may well be tonight and we need to be alert."

He turned back to the sheets of paper left by Jansson. I was dismissed.

Although afflicted with fatigue, the moment I laid myself down, I could not sleep for the thoughts and concerns buzzing around in my head. Where was Jansson? Was he alive or had he – horrible thought – been got rid of? Was there a simple explanation for the condition of the boat? Had Jansson taken it himself for some reason? Had Aubrey been fantasising? Was young Winnie involved? And what was the role of the Metcalfes in the business?

The dinner that evening resolved nothing in my mind. The experience was as normal and almost as dreary as before, though lightened somewhat by the presence of the two young men, Bertie and Winnie, and by the continuing excellence of the fare. No mention was made of Winnie's incarceration or escape, so I was inclined to think that, after all, Aubrey's imagination had run away with him. Everyone expressed pleasure at the way the afternoon had gone, although at one point Vernon Metcalfe remarked, "A pity Freddie missed it."

"Have you had any word from him?" Holmes asked in innocent tones. "Any notion of if or when he might return?"

"No," Metcalfe replied. "I was as astonished as you were, Hunter, to find he had done a moonlight flit." He sounded genuine. "But I suppose," he added, "a man in his line of work has always to be prepared to drop everything, and obey instructions."

In his line of work, indeed. Now what, I wondered, did Metcalfe assume that to be? I also knew, because Holmes told me that he had made very discreet inquiries, that no telegram or other message had been received the night before that might have summoned our friend away.

We gentlemen withdrew as before to the smoking room, although poker was not offered this time. I rather felt that Vernon Metcalfe had no wish to face Holmes again across the baize. For myself, I had been hoping to engage young Winnie in conversation, to try and assess what sort of a man he was. However, both he and Bertie slipped away before I had to chance to speak to them, whispering about some secret scheme they had. The rest of us seemed destined for an early night, especially since Metcalfe was most insistent that we attend chapel before breakfast, the next day being a Sunday.

"Chapel?" I asked.

"We have our own here, situated in the east wing," Metcalfe replied, looking at us sharply from under sun-bleached eyebrows. "A simple place of worship, with no graven images to distract. No priests here, either. I myself lead the service, and trust that is acceptable."

We all murmured that it was, although I distinctly heard a sigh from Lord Tonbridge, who perhaps perforce had attended such ceremonies before.

I would never consider myself a fanciful sort of man, but, since that frightful business in Devon regarding Sir Henry Baskerville and the legend of the hound, I had on occasion been afflicted by nightmares in which I was pursued by a giant beast. Now, drifting into slumber, I found myself once again on that boggy moor, running for my life, except that this time I was suddenly dodging between the box hedges of a formal garden, the creature gaining on me with every step, a creature with the body of a gigantic cat and the face… the face of Helene Metcalfe.

Did I cry out? I woke with a start. Someone was bending over me. I was about to cry out again, when I heard familiar tones.

"Hush, Watson." It was Holmes.

I endeavoured to pull myself out of sleep. It had to be the middle of the night.

"What is it?"

"There's not a moment to lose. Come quickly and bring your revolver. Evil work is afoot here."

I threw my overcoat on over my nightwear, since Holmes would not even let me pause to get dressed.

"And take care."

We made our way out into the grounds. The bright curve of a gibbous moon illuminated what to me looked to be a quiet enough scene. Holmes stealthily led the way down towards the river, under the cover of a line of trees, pausing occasionally to listen. I paused too, but could hear nothing except a light breeze rustling the leaves.

Then a terrible scream rent the air.

"Too late!" Holmes exclaimed, and started running towards the sound.

I followed after, my pistol cocked at the ready.

Had my dream mysteriously and horribly foreshadowed what was to happen? For here was Holmes again, rushing back towards me this time, while behind him, a great beast charged, body of a big cat, and the head... the head... Oh God, no!

I shot it. What else could I do? Two shots, and it gave a great howl and rolled to the ground, panting in its death throes. Now, by the pure light of the moon, I could see it was no supernatural creature woven of dreams, but the leopard from the menagerie. And tumbling from its mouth... a head.

Later, huddled together in the green salon, the occupants of the house were trying to make sense of what had happened. Vernon Metcalfe sat cradling a large glass of brandy, Gretta nearby, watching him. Philip had a protective arm around Sybil, while Ronnie sat apart, white with shock. Lord and Lady Tonbridge, wearing their nightclothes like suits of armour, held themselves upright, fearsome expressions on their faces.

"How ever could this have happened, Vernon?" her ladyship asked. "To think of that great beast roaming free. I have never been more shocked in my life. It could have been any one of us. It could have been me!"

She gathered her robe tighter round her large frame.

"No, madam, that it could not."

She looked askance at Holmes. Had this man really dared contradict her?

"No, madam. It was a carefully planned scheme, even though it has so frightfully backfired."

"My wife loved the leopard, Hunter." Vernon Metcalfe spoke up. "She raised Lola from a cub, you know." He turned to me. "Did you really have to kill the poor creature, Dr Willoughby?"

"I had no choice, sir," I replied. "It was coming for us."

He nodded sadly.

I closed my eyes, the horrid vision of that head held between the drooling jaws of the maddened beast would, I was sure, never leave me.

"You speak of some sinister scheme or other, Hunter," Lord Tonbridge remarked. "What is the evidence, I ask you, for this preposterous claim? Clearly it was just a terrible accident. When the police arrive, I suggest we get them to arrest Briggs for negligence." Briggs being the gatekeeper, who clearly had other duties as well.

"Yes, yes. The senile old fool must have left the cage door unlatched when he last fed the animal," his wife added.

Holmes smiled. "That won't do, Lady Tonbridge, as you very well know…"

Before he had a chance to explain, the French windows opened, and Bertie came in, looking distraught.

"The damned leopard has escaped and is on the prowl." he said. "And now I can't find him."

"The leopard?" asked Gretta.

"No, of course not."

"Winnie?" This was Ronnie. "You can't find Winnie?"

"Yes." He looked around the room. "Why are you all up? Has something dreadful happened?"

Holmes stood up. "I am afraid, Bertie, I have bad news for you."

"He's dead, isn't he? I heard the scream, although..." He frowned.

"Although it didn't exactly sound like your friend."

"Well, no..."

"That's because," Holmes said, "it wasn't."

Everyone stared at him. I suddenly realised that they didn't know. They hadn't seen what we had seen.

"I have to inform you that things haven't worked quite how some of you intended," Holmes said. "Has it, Winnie?"

On cue, that same young man entered in the room, having, as it turned out, remained waiting outside the door until Holmes summoned him in. All eyes now turned to him, surprise and, yes, shock, written on several faces. Not on Ronnie's, however. She looked genuinely happy.

"Oh, Winnie, you're all right," she cried. "You're alive. Lady Tonbridge said..."

"Yes, I most certainly am alive, and I'm not sure I understand what's been going on here. Please someone tell me."

He looked around the room, expectantly.

"But if not Winnie... then who?" Bertie asked.

"Shut up, Bertie." That was Philip.

"Vernon, where's your wife. Where's Helene?" Lady Tonbridge spoke again, in urgent tones.

"She's asleep... isn't she?" Metcalfe replied. "I didn't want to wake her..."

Holmes shook his head.

"I'm afraid not, sir. Helene went outside to let loose the leopard. It has attacked her."

Metcalfe shook his head. "No, no, you're wrong. It can't be. Lola loved my wife. Helene raised her from a cub, after I... after the mother was shot."

"A wild creature has no love, especially one confined like that for years to a small cage." Holmes softened his tone. "She's dead sir. Your wife is dead."

"No!" A terrible wail of anguish. "No!"

Before our eyes, Metcalfe aged into an old man. His trembling hand reached for his glass of brandy and he swallowed the lot in one gulp. Then he started muttering what might have been a prayer... or a curse. Gretta hurried to his side, showing herself of sterner stuff than I might have imagined, ministering to him, whispering consoling words and holding his hand. My evil thought was that she was even a little pleased.

Winnie was evidently confused.

"I still don't understand what's happened. Mrs Metcalfe dead... and you all thought it was me?"

At first no one replied. Then Ronnie burst out, "That's what... what they said."

"I suppose it very well might have been," Winnie replied thoughtfully, "had not Mr Holmes warned me earlier not to go out."

"Mr Holmes?" exclaimed Lord Tonbridge. "You mean Mr Hunter."

"No, sir. This is Mr Sherlock Holmes and that's Dr Watson."

Someone gasped. Lady Tonbridge gripped the arm of her chair so hard that the knuckles showed white.

"Sherlock Holmes!" Lord Tonbridge had turned dangerously red with fury. "This is preposterous, sir, coming here under false pretences. How dare you, sir?"

"I dared, in order to save a life. Or rather, more than one. I regret that Mrs Metcalfe has died, but she is hardly the innocent victim, is she?" Holmes turned back to Winnie. "Please continue."

"Very well." Winnie looked shaken, but complied with Holmes's request. "I explained to Mr Holmes how Bertie had suggested we go out late and do a bit of star-gazing: there's supposed to be some sort of a meteor shower tonight. Why not, I thought, I'd like to see that, and there's a lovely clear sky for it." He paused, then continued. "Bertie told me to meet him near the Menagerie. However, Mr Holmes later instructed me under no circumstances to venture out, and not to say a word about it to Bertie, which, I must say, I thought strange and a bit mean. But Mr Holmes said it was very important I do as he told me, and even made me promise."

"I actually stood guard outside your room. To make sure." Holmes smiled at him.

"Did you, indeed?" Winnie looked somewhat offended. "Quite unnecessary. My word is my bond, Mr Holmes... Anyway, I stayed in as you said, and now it seems all hell has broken loose out there. Poor Mrs Metcalfe." He looked around. "Bloody hell, what are you doing?"

His supposed friend had drawn a pistol and was pointing it, with a shaking hand, at Winnie.

"Bertie, no!" This was Ronnie again.

"Don't be so stupid, Bertie." This from his mother.

"Come now, young man." Holmes said. "That's not going to work, is it?"

Meanwhile, I leapt forward, knocking the gun from Bertie's hand, and grabbing it before anyone else could. I have to say I was utterly confused, but trusted that all would become clear in due course.

It did, but not until after the police had arrived in the welcome and familiar shape of Inspector Lestrade, whom Holmes had alerted by telephone earlier in the evening. A couple of burly constables were delegated to guard the occupants of the salon, while we, including young Winnie, decamped to the smoking room.

"I am afraid," Holmes remarked after we had settled ourselves down, "that it took me an unconscionable time to decipher the incriminating code. It did not help that it was in Dutch, a language I know but inadequately." He shook his head. "It proved to be the outline of a plot against a list of targets, including young Winnie here."

"Me! Why?"

"I understand you were captured and imprisoned by the Boers in South Africa while working there as a journalist. You managed to escape – quite ingeniously – and made your way to Portuguese East Africa. But later, you returned to South Africa, as an army lieutenant, and were present at the Siege of Ladysmith. You ruffled Boer feathers, young man, making them something of a laughing stock, to the extent that a group of them decided to get rid of you."

"But Mr Holmes, that doesn't make sense. I admire the Boers. I have spoken out against British prejudice against them, and called for them to be treated with generosity and tolerance."

"Sadly, these people here were not inclined to extend the same generosity to you."

Winnie put his head in his hands. "I thought they were friends. My God, I thought Bertie… Oh, how could he?"

The conspirators, as it turned out from the incriminating papers Holmes had deciphered, consisted of Helene Metcalfe (though not Vernon, surprisingly), Lord and Lady Tonbridge and their son Bertie. Helene was of Afrikaner stock and nurtured a deep hatred of the British in South Africa, while the Tonbridges owned a gold mine in Transvaal and bitterly resented the restrictions imposed on them regarding the treatment of their black "slaves" by the colonial administration. Bertie was simply besotted with Helene and would do anything she asked him to. They had lured Winnie to Coombe Hall, with the express intention of getting him killed in a way that would look like a tragic accident. Apparently, Lord Tonbridge had joked how appropriate it would be to use a South African leopard to do the deed.

As for Frederick Jansson, he too had fallen victim to their deadly plot.

Helene Metcalfe knew full well that he was on to them. It was she who had cut his throat as he lay in a drugged sleep, and who, with Bertie, had taken his body, wrapped in a blanket, down to the boathouse in a wheelbarrow (the signs of which Holmes had noticed). From there, with Jansson tied up and his body weighed down with stones, Bertie had rowed a good distance before tipping the unfortunate man into the river. This we only found out fully, when the corpse surfaced a week later, and Bertie confessed all.

"How did you manage, Mr Holmes, to evade suspicion?" Lestrade now asked. "I mean, with you on the case, they were mad to go ahead with it."

Holmes explained about our pseudonyms.

"They suspected us, of course," he said, "as associates of Jansson, but checked our credentials as Hunter and Willoughby, and found, as they supposed, that we were harmless friends of his from Norfolk. In addition, were we the country bumpkins they took us for, we would have been invaluable as witnesses to the "accident"." He gave a grim smile. "Once I had deciphered the code, I knew there was no time to be lost. The attempt on Winnie here had to be tonight, for he would be leaving early on the morrow. So, when I overheard," (presumably, I thought, with those preternaturally sharp ears!) "the young men planning their nocturnal excursion, I had to make sure that Winnie would not venture out. Subsequently, a sudden burst of noise from the direction of the menagerie indicated to me that something had disturbed the animals. That's when I woke you, Watson, to go and investigate."

"So, Mr Holmes," Lestrade remarked, "you can't even enjoy a nice few days away in the countryside, without getting into trouble. Still, you've saved this young man's life, and those of the others you found on the list. A good weekend's work, I'd say."

All well and good, and Mycroft would be pleased enough, despite the loss of his old friend. I knew, nonetheless, that it would be impossible to erase from my memory the image of the leopard charging towards us, the head of Helene Metcalfe in its mouth, an expression of sheer terror frozen on to the dead woman's face. Indeed, I still occasionally have those recurrent nightmares.

The conspirators having been arrested, Holmes and I were packing up to leave Coombe Hall. Outside, I found Aubrey tossing pebbles into the fountain in front of the house.

"They say it brings good luck," he told me.

"Who does?"

He shrugged his shoulders.

How much did the child know of what had happened?

"Poor leopard," he said after a while.

Not poor grandmother.

"We're going to stay here now," he went on. "Mama will be looking after grandfather."

What she always wanted, I thought.

"And will you go back to school?" I asked.

"Yes, but not to Highfields. Somewhere local, Mama says," adding proudly, "Grandfather wants me here."

"A new start," I told him. "Always a good thing."

"Yes, jolly good." And he threw in another pebble.

Later that day, back in the reassuring comfort of Baker Street, I ruminated on recent events.

"I was quite wrong about Winnie," I said to Holmes "I thought he was the rotten egg,"

"Mm," Holmes replied.

He was intent on another of his evil-smelling experiments, and, I could tell, was hardly listening to me.

Nevertheless, I continued my train of thought. "He seems to be an excellent young man with a lot of promise," I went on, reaching for another of Mrs Hudson's delicious drop scones. "You know

something, Holmes, I can't help wondering if Great Britain's future history would be much different,
had that plot to kill Mr Winston Churchill succeeded."

"Mm," said Holmes, turning up the flame on his Bunsen burner.

Sherlock Holmes and the Female Detective

Holmes was wool-gathering, staring disconsolately out of our upstairs window, in the hope, I suppose, that a new engrossing puzzle was about to arrive on our doorstep. He had been like this for nigh on an hour, and I feared that all too soon his glance would stray to the box where he kept his cocaine and syringes. If the day had been in any way clement, I should have suggested a bracing walk in the Regent's Park. But it was damp, with that November chill that seems to seep into one's very bones.

"You should get a hobby, Holmes," I said, raising my head from the article I was reading on the intriguing new science of psychology. "Chess, perhaps."

"Chess!" he snorted. "And whom, pray, would I play with? You? I'd beat you every time, so where would be the challenge in that?"

I ignored the insult, attributing it to the frustrations of inactivity.

"You could always play against yourself," I replied. "Then you would have only a fifty-fifty chance of winning."

"Pah! Watson. I suppose you consider that very witty."

I grinned, but before I could think up a suitable response, a light tap sounded on the door.

"I didn't hear anyone arrive below, Watson," Holmes said. "Did you?"

"No," I replied. "It's probably Mrs Hudson asking when we want our tea."

It was, indeed, our estimable landlady, but her request was not as expected.

"Mr Holmes," she said. "My seamstress is here, and she has a problem which perhaps you might help her with."

"Your seamstress!"

I am afraid Holmes's disdain sounded all too clearly in his tone. Or did he imagine he was about to be asked to help with hemming a skirt?

"It's a distressing matter but not without interest for you, I think," Mrs Hudson continued. "If you would only consent to meet with Lottie and hear what she has to say."

"Let her come then." Holmes waved a hand, sighing. Anything to dispel the boredom of the afternoon.

The woman in question must have been lurking on the stairs right behind Mrs Hudson, for she stepped forward immediately: a small, worn-looking person in her thirties, someone you would not look at twice if you passed her in the street, plainly dressed in a grey serge jacket and skirt.

"Thank you so much for seeing me, Mr Holmes," she said in a surprisingly deep, melodious voice, that shook a little. "You see, I am driven mad with worry for poor Mrs Flowerdew."

"Before anything else, please be seated," Holmes said, somewhat brusquely, "and Mrs Hudson, perhaps you would be so kind as to bring us all a pot of tea. It is already nearly four of the clock and Watson is parched."

Quite untrue, though tea is always welcome. Our landlady withdrew, closing the door behind her.

"Now," Holmes continued, the woman having perched herself on one of our harder chairs, "please explain."

"It's rather delicate." She glanced at me.

"Dr Watson is my friend and colleague and utterly discreet. You may speak freely in front of both of us."

I smiled reassuringly at her, my curiosity, I confess, already a little aroused.

"Very well. Best if I start from the beginning, Dr Watson, Mr Holmes, sirs. My name is Charlotte Booth and I am, as Martha... Mrs Hudson... told you, a seamstress by trade, and in that capacity have been engaged on several occasions by a Mrs Alfred Flowerdew, of the borough of Lewisham. However, I am a widow, and the income generated by such work is insufficient to support myself and my young son, and so I supplement it by helping out the police."

"The police?" Holmes sounded surprised. "In what capacity?"

"I sometimes work as a searcher, sir. You see, when women suspected of theft are arrested, they have to be searched. Of course, male officers cannot possibly with propriety conduct such examinations, so they call on the likes of me." She paused and her face lit up in a rare smile. "You'd be astonished, gents, at the some of the places where such women conceal their loot. In their hats and hair, in their mouths, in their garments – puff sleeves are much favoured for ease of concealment – even in their stays and other under-garments."

I nodded. I had heard of the practice of employing women in this capacity before.

"That was how I started off, as a searcher, but since those early days I have been more often engaged to follow known miscreants, to try and catch them perpetrating a criminal act. The police like me because I look ordinary and can pass unnoticed through a crowd, or enter a shop without arousing suspicion. In that way, I have brought several vicious folk to justice."

"It sounds quite dangerous," I said.

"Yes, Doctor, it can be," she replied. "I have been struck several times and stabbed once, although happily only in my shoulder."

A brave young woman!

"Most interesting," Holmes remarked, with a yawn. "But how is this relevant to the case of Mrs ... er...Flowerdew?"

"Not directly, although I have also been engaged by a certain well-established private detective agency, when they require the gathering of information to be used in divorce or similar cases of a domestic nature. As a seamstress, you see, it is easy for me quite legitimately be admitted to households where I can keep my eyes and ears open."

"And it is in this regard that you have attended Mrs Flowerdew?"

"Oh no, sir. Mrs Flowerdew simply wished for me to make a dress for her. As I mentioned, this was not the first time she has requested my services. If I say so myself, gents, and as Mrs Hudson can tell you, I'm a skilled and prompt worker and my gowns are of the highest quality. In addition, you know, I charge less than many others."

"Yes, yes."

I could see that Holmes was getting impatient. Would the woman ever come to the point? And no need to advertise her services to us, for, after all, we were hardly likely to be ordering garments from her, now or in the future.

"Well, you see, sirs, Mrs Flowerdew," she continued, "is a pretty little lady of maybe forty or so years of age. Maybe nearer fifty, to be exact. She has always been very pleasant to me and, in the past, as I thought, happy enough with her life, although childless. However, when I visited her this last time, three weeks ago, I was quite shocked by her appearance. Wan and thin, the roses drained from her cheeks. I asked her if she was all right but she merely said that she hadn't been well. I noticed, too, that a new housekeeper had been appointed, a flashy-looking person to my eye, one I should rather have seen flaunting herself on the stage in some low theatrical establishment than working in a respectable home in the suburbs. When I asked what had happened to the previous housekeeper, a homely, comfortable body named Elsie Chambers, Mrs Flowerdew simply said that Alfred – that's Mr Flowerdew – had found her work deficient and that this Alice Penn was like to prove much more satisfactory."

Charlotte Booth paused. She was clearly trying to master her emotions.

"When I returned, two weeks later with the finished garment for her to try, I was met at the front door by this same Alice Penn. She was quite rude and abrupt, and would not admit me, saying that Mrs Flowerdew was indisposed and not able for visitors. She almost snatched the dress from me, telling me that she would give it to her mistress and that payment would be arranged. I explained that it needed to be fitted on the lady herself in case minor adjustments had to be made. She just muttered "Another time" and almost slammed the door on me. I didn't like it, Mr Holmes. I didn't like it at all."

"Is that it?" Holmes asked, lying back in his chair, his eyes closed. "Is that what is worrying you?"

"There's more," she answered, perhaps a little put out by his attitude. "This morning, I attempted another visit but with the same result. Dismissed on the doorstep – and still not paid, by the way – so I decided on a ruse I had employed before, when investigating possible... pardon me... marital infidelities. I concealed myself in an alleyway opposite the house and waited. Luckily, I have learnt patience and was not inclined to abandon my vigil even after two hours in the cold and damp. The wait was rewarded at last when I observed Alice Penn leave the house. To my dismay I saw that she was wearing the very dress I had made for her mistress."

"My God!" I exclaimed. "Something's very wrong there."

Charlotte Booth nodded. "You may well say so, Dr Watson, sir," she replied. "So, when I was certain she was gone, I approached the house again, but this time made my way to the back, where I knew the kitchen door to be situated. I was ready with an excuse to give to the cook or to any servant I should meet, but to my astonishment there was no one about, even though the back door stood open. Moreover, the place showed strong signs of neglect. Dirty dishes and empty bottles of beer and gin were strewn everywhere, and there was a rank smell. I'd be mortified if I let my place fall into rack and ruin like that." She paused, no doubt reimagining the shocking scene.

"Please continue," Holmes said.

"Yes, sir... I'm getting there. I cautiously made my way into the body of the house, but again met with no one. I thought that very strange, Very strange, indeed. Wouldn't you think so?"

I nodded encouragingly.

"So then, having climbed the stairs to the room I knew to be Mrs Flowerdew's, I knocked on the door and called out her name. At first there was no reply. I knocked again and this time heard a faint murmur, which I understood to be permission to enter. However," she paused for dramatic effect, "the door was locked fast."

At that moment, a tap on our own door caused us all to jump. Well, I did at least. However, it was only Mrs Hudson with a tray of tea, and, I was delighted to observe, some freshly made drop scones.

"It's a shocking tale, isn't it?" she remarked. Clearly the seamstress had already apprised her of the circumstances regarding this Mrs Flowerdew.

"Had the lady locked herself in?"" I asked.

"Not at all. She managed to creep to the door and spoke to me through the keyhole. It seems she had been imprisoned in the room by her husband and the fearsome Alice. Imprisoned, sirs!" She shook her head. "All the other servants had been dismissed. 'They are trying to poison me, Lottie,' the poor lady told me. 'I have stopped eating what they give me, but fear I am not long for this world anyway.' "

Charlotte Booth shook her head some more. "You can imagine how horrified I was to hear that. I tried to find a key to open the door and, having failed, to break it down, to no avail. All I could do was to promise her to return with help. That is why I have come to you, Mr Holmes. Mrs Hudson is always singing your praises."

"I am most gratified to hear it," Holmes replied, nodding an acknowledgement to our landlady. "However, Mrs Booth, this is surely a matter for the police."

"You would think so, wouldn't you?" The seamstress gave a bitter smile. "The trouble is that Mr Alfred Flowerdew *is* the police. He is the District Inspector at the station in Lewisham. No use reporting it there, Mr Holmes. I've seen over and over again how the members of the force stick up for each other. They wouldn't pay attention to the likes of me."

"But in a clear case of at least marital cruelty such as this…" I ventured.

"Mrs Booth is right to be wary, Watson." Holmes interjected. "Alfred Flowerdew has only to say that his wife is mad, which, pardon me, madam, may well be the case." He was sitting straighter now, his interest excited at last. "But that, of course, cannot justify inhumane treatment."

"I don't think her mad, sir, or, if she is, he and his trollop have made her so," the seamstress remarked shortly.

"You'll look into it, won't you, Mr Holmes?" Mrs Hudson said, offering round the plate of drop scones. I was the only one to partake.

"If your suspicions and those of the lady concerned are correct," Holmes told the seamstress, "then there is no time at all to be lost. Mrs Flowerdew says she is not eating, but, while the body can sustain life for several weeks without food, as I know from my own researches, she will die very quickly if she is not taking liquids. And if she is drinking anything at all, then of course poison can be administered that way as well as any other." He frowned. "Of course, the whole business may yet be a figment of a troubled mind…"

Charlotte Booth looked to interrupt but Holmes held up a finger to restrain her.

"Nonetheless," he continued, "in the light of what you have told me regarding the dismissal of the servants and the neglected state of the house, plus the very telling fact of this Alice Penn having the impudence to wear the very same dress you made for her mistress, I am inclined to believe that evil deeds are afoot in the Flowerdew household." He stood up. "I shall therefore ask you, Mrs Booth, to accompany myself and Dr Watson to Lewisham." He turned to me. "I particularly wish you to be present, Watson, in your capacity as a doctor, so bring your medical bag with you."

I nodded.

"It is too late this evening, I fear," Holmes continued. "Inspector Flowerdew will no doubt be on his way home shortly and I particularly wish him not to be there when we arrive. Let us meet early tomorrow morning at Charing Cross station. Say just before eight, since I seem to recall that the Lewisham train leaves on the hour."

Good heavens! Had the man even memorised the suburban train timetables!

"Oh, thank you, sir," Charlotte Booth exclaimed. "Thank you so very much." Whereupon she at last helped herself to a scone.

It was a strange-looking trio that made the journey the next morning from Charing Cross to Lewisham. Myself – the professional man of means, the doctor with his leather case; the seamstress in her plain and slightly shabby grey suit; the labouring man in his filthy greatcoat, sporting an equally dirty brimmed hat and big scuffed boots. Charlotte Booth had to look twice or thrice at this apparition before realising that it was Holmes.

It proved impossible to discuss our plans just then, however, for, although we had found a compartment to ourselves, at the very last minute a prosperous-looking middle-aged gentleman and his wife joined us. At the sight of Holmes, they clearly wished to withdraw again, but too late. The train was already in motion. The wife cowered against her husband, who shot reproving glances at my friend and muttered about a waste of a first-class ticket when forced to travel with those persons who by rights merited only third-class.

Holmes grinned at them, baring long stained teeth, which made the lady wife cower even more. At the next stop, the couple hastily alighted, no doubt to find more acceptable travelling companions.

When the train started up again, Holmes, having already discussed the matter with me, conveyed his plan of action to Charlotte Booth.

"In case the whole matter is a simple misunderstanding, Dr Watson will first attempt to gain access to the lady, on foot, he will say, of concern about her well-being. If the housekeeper is caring of her mistress, she may admit him. At least her attitude can be judged from her response."

"She will not admit him. I would bet my life on it," Charlotte Booth replied.

"Your life!" Holmes smiled. "That's quite a wager, my dear."

"You will soon see." The seamstress folded her arms, a grim expression on her face.

"In that case, I shall call to the house offering my services as a handy-man."

"Do you think that will work, sir?" She looked sceptical.

"Holmes has quite a way with the ladies, when he wants to get round them," I remarked.

Charlotte Booth looked even more sceptical, but Holmes laughed.

"Well, thank you, Watson," he said. "I am flattered. But even if Alice Penn proves unimpressed with my undoubted charms, I am sure that I can inveigle my way into the house somehow."

"So what do I do?" Mrs Booth asked.

"You will wait patiently, as you have told us you have often had occasion to do before. Then, if we have to force the issue, your presence will be invaluable in reassuring the poor lady."

If the seamstress was disappointed in her reduced role, she did not show it, but nodded agreement.

The Flowerdew residence in Wivenhoe Place was a medium-sized, end-of-terrace house with a sizable garden to one side. Apart from the somewhat overgrown nature of this latter, the place looked perfectly respectable. One could hardly conceive of anything shocking occurring behind those unimpeachable red bricks. When I expressed surprise that a policeman, even a District Inspector, could afford a house like this, the seamstress replied that she understood the money came from Mrs Flowerdew's inheritance.

"Of course, with her gone, it would be all his," Charlotte Booth added drily.

"Which it is anyway under current law," I added.

She shook her head. "Such injustice. A woman's wealth should be her own."

I agreed heartily. However, this was neither the time nor the place to discuss the rights of women.

Walking up to the front door, I rapped firmly upon it with a brass knocker in the somewhat tarnished form of a lion's head. There being no answer, I tried again. Eventually, a young woman opened it. She looked as if I had roused her from sleep, even though it was already past nine o'clock. Her dress had been hastily donned, the bodice half-buttoned, and her fair hair was unkempt. Attractive in a slatternly way, she regarded me through heavy-lidded, unfriendly eyes.

"Yes?"

"Good morning," I said, politely raising my hat. "My name is Dr Sacker. Apologies for calling unannounced but I have been approached by a friend of Mrs Flowerdew, who, understanding her to be unwell, is most worried about her. She requested me to see if I could assist in the lady's recovery in some way."

Alice Penn, for assuredly it was she, looked puzzled by my speech.

"Who did you say you are?" she asked.

"Dr Sacker," I repeated, Holmes and I having judged it safer for me not to use my real name. It was admittedly unlikely that the young woman would be acquainted with my published accounts of Holmes's adventures, but no need to take the risk.

"Mrs Flowerdew has her own doctor." Spoken uncompromisingly.

"I see. I am very pleased to hear that. But, to reassure Mrs Flowerdew's friend, may I request the name of my colleague?" I asked.

"You may not," and Alice Penn slammed the door shut in my face.

It was no more than we had expected and as Charlotte Booth had predicted. We would have to employ the next stage of the plan.

I removed with the seamstress to a nearby pastry shop while Holmes, not wishing to call too soon after my visit, in case it aroused the housekeeper's suspicions, engaged to keep watch on the house. With any luck, Alice Penn might decide to go out, as she had done before.

It was a long and dreary wait in the shop. Despite my fondness for sweets, there is a limit to the number of jam tarts that even I can comfortably consume, while Charlotte Booth sat rather miserably over a single cup of cold tea. I am sure the little waitress, who hovered hopefully at our table, was most intrigued. Maybe she took me for a member of that class of well-heeled gentlemen who prey on young women, although the seamstress, with her worn looks and plain garb, would hardly fit the usual type of victim.

Although distracted with worry for her friend, with nothing else to talk about, she opened up to me about her life, and about the little boy, Matthew, who was the centre of her world, a rascal, she said fondly, of seven years. Her late husband had been a police constable, who had died young of consumption.

"All those nights in the wet, the fog," she complained. "I reckon that's what did it for him, Dr Watson, sir."

It was through her connection with the force that she had been recruited as a searcher.

"They've been good to me, Doctor, I'll say that for them. Without the extra work, I don't know how I should have managed."

"But I think you told us that you've also been employed by some private detective agencies."

"Yes, indeed. Though I have to say that I am not always happy with what I have to do. Spying on unfaithful wives to provide evidence in divorce cases, and the like. Quite often the poor woman is trapped in a horrible marriage to start with, so you can well understand her wanting to find a bit of happiness elsewhere, can't you?"

I made a non-committal murmur.

"No, Doctor," she continued, "I prefer hunting down the real villains, the thieves and cutpurses. The really rotten eggs."

"You're quite the lady detective," I said, laughing.

She blushed and suddenly became quite pretty.

"Oh, I'm no lady, I'm afraid, sir. I wouldn't presume. As for being a detective, I suppose I am in some small way. After all, I have brought quite a number of blackguards to justice." She paused, thoughtfully. "Monty Crowe, the forger, Mrs Casper, the fraudulent fortune-teller, Belle McGregor, the baby farmer, Sam Briggs, the butcher's assistant who murdered his employer and chopped him up into prime cuts."

"Good heavens," I said, startled.

"Yes, that Sam Briggs was a really nasty piece of work. It was him as stabbed me in the shoulder, trying to make his escape, but we caught him anyway." She smiled at the recollection. "You know what, Doctor, in my opinion, it would be no bad thing if the police force allowed women to be officially employed. One day, perhaps."

I nodded. I do not share the prejudice that deems women too delicate or mentally unfit for police work. Many females of my acquaintance are at least as able, enterprising and practical as males, and often, more so. The young woman in front of me was certainly a case in point.

Eventually, after two or more hours, the pastry shop door opened to admit Holmes, even more disreputable-looking than before, if that were possible. The little waitress was wide-eyed when he sat himself down at our table. Her head shook like a nodding doll's as she took his order for a big pot of tea – "scalding hot, if you please" – and a portion of pie and mash.

The seamstress and I were of course impatient to hear what had transpired but Holmes held up a hand to forestall our questions.

"All in good time, Watson. I am in dire need of some sustenance first," he announced, much to my astonishment. Food is usually incidental to his investigations, if he even remembers to eat at all.

A steaming plate having been set down in front of him, he set to with an unwonted appetite and relish.

"A fine pie," he even called out to the little waitress, who bobbed and blushed.

At last, with a sigh, he sat back in his chair and shook his head.

"That woman," he said. "A vampire if ever I saw one."

"Alice Penn?" I asked.

"Who else? I was lucky to get out of there alive."

He recounted how he had called to the house in the guise of an odd-job man, informing Alice that some tiles were loose on the roof and that it was also probable, given the autumnal weather and the abundance of trees near the house, that the guttering would need clearing of dead leaves.

"It had occurred to me that, if I could get a ladder, I could perhaps see into Mrs Flowerdew's bedroom and find out if all was well with her."

Alice had studied him for a few moments and apparently liked what she saw. After all, despite the rough clothes, Holmes was still a fine-looking man, with, at that moment, a touch of the gypsy about him. I could understand how a woman like Alice Penn might find him attractive.

"I don't know if we have a ladder, Jim," she had said (Jim being the name Holmes had given her), "but I expect I could find something for you to do."

She brought him into the house, then, into the kitchen, where she offered him some beer. He could see that she was glad of company, while he was happy to draw her out, in case he should learn something of note.

It soon transpired that she was not at all content with the situation in which she found herself.

"I'm not used to domestic work, Jim," she had said. The state of the kitchen alone attesting the truth of that. "I never thought it would be skivvy stuff like this when I gave up the job at the Alhambra."

So Charlotte Booth had been quite correct, imagining Alice to have been on the stage. Apparently, she been a singer and dancer in one of Shoreditch's notorious establishments.

"Fred and his mates turned up one night." She had laughed. "We thought it was a raid at first, but they was just punters like the others. Fred took quite a shine to me, and kept coming back. Then he suggested I come and live with him here. Well, I thought it would be a good move, seeing as how life in the theatre is uncertain, "specially when a girl starts getting on a bit."

She had looked at him coyly and expectantly, so Holmes had felt obliged to insist that, in his eyes, she was a fine young piece of work.

"What about... er... Fred's wife?" he had ventured.

"Oh, her." Alice was dismissive. "He told me she was on her last legs…"

"And is she?" Holmes had asked.

"The old bitch is hanging on and on and meantime, here am I stuck with Fred and no nearer being his new missus than ever." She had sighed and offered him some more beer, partaking freely herself, Holmes only pretending to do so.

"So," he had asked, "where is the woman of the house now? Is she home?"

Alice had smiled lasciviously at him.

"Why d'you want to know? Want to know if the coast's clear, is that it, darling?" She had leaned forward and stroked his hand. "You don't need to worry about her none, Jimmy."

Her intention could not have been clearer, and I chuckled at Holmes's patent horror in recalling it.

"How did you escape?" I asked

"Barely. I suggested I return later with a ladder, as a cover in case of suspicious neighbours. "Good idea," she had said. "And if the old man comes back unexpected, you can use it to climb out the bedroom window." Laughing heartily."

"So you found out nothing," Charlotte said, somewhat tight-lipped.

"I wouldn't say that, Mrs Booth. The fact that Alice is bored to death might well prove useful to us. I noticed several dog-eared copies of yellow-backed sensational literature lying about, a translation of Paul de Kock among others – sign of someone who craves excitement in her own life. If necessary, we might play on this susceptibility of hers."

"But what about Mrs Flowerdew?" Charlotte was clearly frustrated at Holmes's lack of progress. "The poor woman might be at death's door."

"I could hardly force the issue just then." Holmes replied. "What! Would you, have had me knock Alice unconscious and search the house?"

Charlotte Booth shrugged.

"So will you go back?" I asked. "With a ladder?"

Holmes shuddered. "I suppose I must. However, Watson, I rely on you to save me if necessary. In any case, I shall insist on clearing the gutters first. With luck, that way I shall learn all that is necessary regarding Mrs Flowerdew."

Applying to the little waitress, who was still hovering, all agog, he discovered the location of the nearest ironmonger's shop, from which he was hoping to hire a suitable ladder for the afternoon. This time, we accompanied him, and it was lucky that we did, for the available ladder was of such an unwieldy height and weight, it was impossible for one man easily to carry it.

Once again, heads turned in the street to observe the strange procession that we made, the scruffy labourer and the respectable gentleman manhandling a long wooden ladder, followed by the seamstress, carrying my doctor's bag.

Having arrived at Wivenhoe Place, Holmes had to struggle alone the last part of the way, while Charlotte Booth and I ambled slowly past the house. From a discreet distance, we observed how Holmes dragged the ladder round the back, where Charlotte had told him Mrs Flowerdew's bedroom was situated.

It was not long, however, before we heard a female voice raised in shrill anger. To intervene or not? The plucky seamstress made the decision for me.

"It'll be quite in order for me to call in, Doctor, since I have not yet been paid for the dress I made." Whereupon she took herself off hot-foot, while I lingered uncertainly on the front doorstep.

I was endeavouring to hear what was happening, and so did not notice a giant of a man approaching until he was upon me.

"What the devil are you doing here?" he asked.

From his uniform and general demeanour, I assumed this must be District Inspector Alfred Flowerdew himself, inopportunely returned.

"I am Dr Sacker," I spluttered as he loomed above me, burly and red-faced. "I have been asked to examine your sick wife."

"Examine my wife! Who asked you? Not me anyway. Some meddling nosy parker, I suppose."

"A friend of Mrs Flowerdew's." I replied. "Hearing of her indisposition, she was worried about her."

"A friend? My wife has no friends. Not anymore." He shook his head, as if sorrowfully. "You're wasting your time, here, Doctor. She's gone quite barmy. Locked herself in her room."

"If I could just see her…"

"She won't admit you. Mad as a hatter, I tell you."

Shouts and cries from the back of the house drew his attention from me, and he hastened thither, muttering "What the devil!" again. I followed after.

Rounding the corner of the house, a bizarre sight confronted us. Holmes was holding for dear life on to an upper window frame, while Alice Penn was shaking the ladder he was on, and Charlotte Booth was trying to pull her away.

"Alice!" shouted the District Inspector. "What in hell's name's going on here!"

"I caught a thief for you, Fred, trying to break in," she called back to him. She glanced at me. "Blimey, there's a whole bleedin' gang of 'em."

"No, no," I said. "I can explain."

Flowerdew rounded on me.

"You're in it, too, are you?"

Over his shoulder, I saw Holmes shake his head at me.

"No," I said. "Nothing of the sort. I know nothing of this man. As I said, I am a doctor that Mrs Booth here asked to check on her friend."

"And I'm no thief, neither," the seamstress piped up. "If there's a thief around here, it's her," pointing at Alice. "Wearing the dress I made for her mistress and not paying for it neither."

Alice left the ladder be and advanced threateningly on the seamstress, now standing next to me.

"Say that again! Say again that I'm a thief, if you dare."

She raised her hands as if ready to claw Charlotte's eyes out.

"Now, now, Alice," Flowerdew said. "Calm down. There's quite clearly been a misunderstanding here…" His tone was suddenly appeasing, "See, Mrs Booth, my dear, my wife gave the dress to Alice… Poor Florrie. She's bedridden, now and won't be wearing dresses ever again, I'm afraid." He sniffed as if overcome with emotion. So if we have forgotten to pay you, Mrs Booth…" He reached into his inside pocket and drew out a wallet." How much?"

"You going to pay her, Fred, after what she said about me?" Alice's voice was hard.

"Just leave it be, woman." He took out a coin. "Here's a guinea for you."

"A guinea!" Alice screeched. "Far too much."

Charlotte Booth took the money.

"Thank-you, sir," she said with dignity.

"As for the other matter…" Flowerdew spun round. "What the hell!"

For Holmes was nowhere to be seen.

"That was a near thing!"

The two of us safely back in Baker Street – Charlotte Booth having returned home to her little son – Holmes was chuckling over a pipe and a restorative glass of single malt whisky.

"Good you were able to provide a distraction, Watson, or I'd be languishing in Lewisham prison by now."

"I'm just sorry for the poor ironmonger, missing his ladder. You realise that you are a de facto thief, after all, Holmes?"

"I'll make sure the ladder is returned to the shop. But we have more urgent business to attend to. I wasn't able to see into Mrs Flowerdew's bedroom, for the curtains were drawn closed, and before I could attempt an entry, Alice Penn arrived on the scene like a vengeful Fury."

"So we still have no notion as to the true condition of the lady?"

"Unfortunately, not... Did you feel that Flowerdew's grief was genuine, Watson?"

"Crocodile tears, to my mind. He changed his tune too quickly, yet still would not admit me to see her."

"There is no alternative, then. We shall have to enter covertly."

"Break in, you mean, Holmes."

"Precisely."

I sighed. "One of these days you'll go too far."

"No, Watson. One of these days *we'll* go too far... Have some more whisky. It's very good. Glenlivet as drunk by Queen Victoria."

The following morning saw Holmes, Charlotte Booth, who had insisted on being present, and myself with my doctor's bag, back at the pastry shop. The little waitress was pleased to see us but frowned in puzzlement at the sight of Holmes, now dressed as himself. I could almost guess at her thoughts, that he looked vaguely familiar but that she could not quite place him.

We had watched Flowerdew depart for work earlier, but Holmes reckoning that Alice Penn would not rouse herself quite so soon, we had retreated to the comfort of the shop. This time, not leaving things to chance, the woman was to be lured from the house by a ruse we reckoned she would find irresistible.

"Here he comes," Holmes said with satisfaction, as a grimy urchin entered the pastry shop, one of the Wiggins clan from among the Baker Street Irregulars.

The little waitress started to shoo him out, but Holmes told her with a reassuring smile that the boy was with him and asked her to bring over a big plate of jam tarts and a mug of tea. She shook her head wonderingly as she piled the pastries on to a plate.

"Well?" Holmes asked.

"Went like a dream, guv," young Wiggins reported. "I telled 'er like wot you said. That a fine gentleman 'ad given me a penny to deliver the note and the rose. She tooked both, smelt the rose and read the note and smiled and said, 'Tell the gent, Yes.' "

"I knew she would fall for it in her vanity," Holmes told us. "In her boredom and thirst for adventure."

"Whatever did the note say?" asked Charlotte Booth, who had not been present when Holmes and I – Holmes more than I, in truth – had hatched the plan on the previous evening.

"It purports to be from a secret admirer, who observed her on stage at the Alhambra and who has long wished to make her further acquaintance," I told her. "He writes that if Alice is willing to meet him, to learn something greatly to her advantage, he will send a hansom forthwith to pick her up. To avoid compromising her in the sight of the neighbours and to reassure her as to his honourable intentions, a lady in his employ of irreproachable character and mature years will accompany her to his office."

Charlotte looked confused. "What lady?"

"Mrs Hudson, of course." I laughed. "She was delighted to be involved in the enterprise and is prepared to lead the woman a merry dance."

"I hope Martha will be safe?" Charlotte said. "That Alice Penn is not a woman to be trifled with. If she suspects anything it'll surely go bad for poor Martha."

"Don't worry," Holmes replied. "The hansom driver is in on the plot as well. He will be ready to rush to Mrs Hudson's rescue if necessary, though I am sure it will not come to that."

"I sincerely hope not," the seamstress remarked.

We waited in the pastry shop until a certain cab passed by, slowing slightly. This allowed us to observe Mrs Hudson nodding almost imperceptibly at us through the window, to signal the all clear. We paid the little waitress, forthwith. She seemed sorry to see us go and urged us to "Come agin soon, won't you, gents and lady."

Young Wiggins answered that he would if there were any more tarts going begging.

"Cheeky," the little waitress said.

Now there were four of us, making our way to Wivenhoe Place, including the boy, whose face was become even more grubby, smeared as it was with a considerable quantity of raspberry jam. His job now would be to keep watch and warn us if anyone approached the house. To this end, he sat himself down by the garden wall and played jacks with pebbles. Meanwhile, Charlotte and I went up to the front door, as before, to see if anyone else was home, I rapped sharply with the brass lion knocker. There being no answer, we followed Holmes round to the back of the house. This time, the kitchen door was locked fast. The ladder, meanwhile, was lying flat on the ground.

"What now?" asked Charlotte Booth. "Will we have to give up? Or climb up?"

"Not at all," I said, as Holmes removed a little case of instruments from his pocket, his housebreaking kit.

"Oh, my Lord!" the seamstress exclaimed. "We'll be sent to prison, the lot of us."

Holmes worked quickly and skilfully, and soon the door creaked open.

"Don't worry, Mrs Booth," he said. "As you can see, the door is open and, if anyone should ask, that's how we found it."

We entered without stealth, as if we had every right to be there, just in case there happened, after all, to be someone in the house. However, all was quiet. Too quiet for my taste, and I hoped we were in time to save poor Mrs Flowerdew.

I had been prepared for disorder but the state of the kitchen utterly appalled me. Clear it was that no effort had been made to wash or tidy for a long time, or even clear away the rotting remains of meals. Droppings indicated the presence of mice, or worse. I wondered that the District Inspector could bear it until I mused that he probably never set foot in that part of the house. Indeed, as we progressed further, the signs of neglect were less evident, though a film of grey dust coated most surfaces. Up the unswept stairs, we climbed, Charlotte Booth leading the way.

"This is her room," she said, and tried the door handle. It was still locked.

"Mrs Flowerdew... Florrie..." she called. "It's Lottie. Are you there? Can you open the door?"

Silence.

She called again.

Still silence.

We looked at each other. Holmes again extracted his wallet of instruments and set to work. A satisfying click at last, and the door opened on a wave of fetid air.

We were greeted by an unearthly yowl, bulging green eyes shining out at us from the darkness. What devilment was this? Poor Charlotte Booth clutched at my arm in terror, and, I have to confess, I rather clung back.

Of course, it was nothing supernatural, after all. Our eyes adjusting to the gloom, we soon discerned a ginger cat standing there, its hair on end. The creature was skin and bones and clearly starving.

"Oh, the poor thing!" Charlotte said.

Beyond this apparition, darker blocks in the general murk signalled furniture, and the seamstress hastened to what had to be the bed.

"She's not here," she said, dismayed.

Holmes stepped forward and pulled open the heavy curtains, letting a sulphurous light illuminate the room through filthy windows. It was true, the bed, sheets stained and tossed, was empty. No Mrs Flowerdew.

"Watson, quick, over here," Holmes called.

What I had taken to be a heap of rags, proved, on examination, to be a tiny woman huddled under the window ledge.

"Is she alive?" Charlotte asked.

"Just about," I said, examining her "Fetch some water, if you please."

"Not that," Holmes added sharply as Charlotte reached for a jug on the dresser. "Fresh water from the kitchen."

I pulled the stinking sheets from the bed and then gently picked up Mrs Flowerdew and laid her on the mattress, which thankfully was not in too horrid a state. I chafed her limbs to restore some circulation, muttering reassuring words until Charlotte returned with a mug of water. I dipped a clean handkerchief into it and then wetted the lady's mouth. At first, she failed to respond, but, finally, to my relief, she licked her lips and half-opened anaemic eyes.

"Here's Lottie, my dear," I said to her in soft tones, "and I'm Doctor Watson come to look after you. You are safe now."

I gave her more water, in small sips. She murmured something.

"What is it?"

"Cl.. Cleo…pat…ra …"

"Cleopatra? Queen of Egypt."

She nodded. Mad, after all. I looked at Holmes.

"I imagine," he said, "that she means the cat. There is a C emblazoned on the disc hanging round its neck."

Mrs Flowerdew nodded again, clearly agitated.

"Cleo will be just fine," Charlotte told her. "I'll get her something to drink and eat, and you too, Florrie dear."

"Not from that kitchen," Holmes replied, reaching again into his pocket and drawing out a small paper package. "Here is one of Mrs Hudson's drop scones. That will do, won't it, Watson?"

"Perfect," I said, taking the scone and breaking off a tiny morsel. "Too much at once could be harmful, but it was foresighted of you to bring it, Holmes."

I chided myself that I had not thought to do the same.

Suddenly we heard a thunderous noise on the stairs and two large constables rushed into the room.

"The game's up, me boyos," one shouted, brandishing his truncheon.

"Whatever do you mean, officer?" Holmes replied, calmly and languidly.

The two men, taking in the scene before them at last, looked confused.

"We was told there was thieves breakin' in," the other said.

"Do we look like thieves to you?"

Young Wiggins crept in behind the constables.

"I couldn't stop 'em, Mr 'Olmes," he said. "They come in like greased lightnin', so they done."

"No harm, Wiggins," Holmes said. "I was about to call for the police myself."

"Sherlock 'Olmes, is it?" said the first constable. "I've 'eard of you."

"No doubt," my friend replied.

"I've 'heard of 'im," the constable repeated to the other, younger man. " 'E's a detective, 'e is, but not with the po-leece. Private geezer."

"So what you up to then, Mister Private Detective?" the younger one asked. "This 'ere's our Super's place, in case you don't know it."

"I'm well aware of that, constable," Holmes replied. "And I trust you will return forthwith to Lewisham station and arrest your Super at once."

The men stood with their mouths hanging open.

"Wha'?"

"For the attempted murder of his wife. He has imprisoned her here, and, having failed to poison her, has been letting her starve to death."

"It's a joke," said the younger one.

The other looked at Mrs Flowerdew (I was still allowing her morsels of scone and sips of water), the state of her, of the bed, of the room.

"Well, I'll be…!" He was lost for words.

More thunderous steps sounded on the stairs. This time it was none other than Alfred Flowerdew himself. Despite what they had just heard of him, the two constables stood to attention.

"What the devil is going on here?" The man looked about to explode with rage, his apoplectic complexion purple. "They told me my place was being robbed!"

"We got a call at the station from a neighbour who saw people entering illegally," the younger constable told him.

"And you didn't think to convey that information to me?" Flowerdew growled.

"We couldn't find you, sir, so we come over as fast as we could… and found… these people."

Flowerdew looked at me, eyes so narrowed that they all but disappeared into his fleshy cheeks. "You, Doctor! Don't you ever give up? Didn't I tell you my wife was mad? Told you that she locked herself in and refused to eat."

"If she locked herself in, where's the key?" I asked. "If she's refused to eat, why's she eating now?"

"Because she's mad, that's why," He pushed his face up close to mine. "She's probably hidden the key." He looked round as if the thing might suddenly materialise. "Where's Alice?" he added.

"Gone out," I told him.

He grinned, suddenly relaxed. "So that's why my wife's locked in. For her own safety, d'you see. We can't have her wandering about the house by herself in the state she's in, can we?"

"You're changing your tune," Holmes said. "And just look at the state she's in."

We all did. At the poor shrunken woman, in her filthy night dress, trembling in terror.

"She needs calm and quiet," I said sternly. "Please all go downstairs and continue your discussion there. And Mrs Booth, perhaps you could call for an ambulance. Mrs Flowerdew is in a very bad way. She must be taken to hospital as quickly as possible."

"By what right...?" the District Inspector started to say, but, catching the cold eyes of his constables upon himself, never finished his sentence, and, instead, meekly took himself out of the room with the others.

"Thank you, doctor," his wife spoke softly. "Thank you ever so much." Then she grinned triumphantly. "Know what I did?" she asked. "I licked the window."

"What!" I exclaimed, fearing again for her sanity.

"They didn't know... There was water on the window and I licked it."

Condensation! That's why we found her where we did. I smiled back at her.

"Clever girl," I said, and she giggled.

Upstairs with my patient, I missed the excitement below, although some of the ruckus was faintly audible. It was only later, however, after Mrs Flowerdew had been safely dispatched by ambulance to my old alma mater of St Batholomew's, that I received a detailed description of what had transpired. Holmes, Charlotte Booth and I had returned to Baker Street with Mrs Hudson, who was bursting with news of her own adventure.

Our landlady recounted how the impatient Alice, at first full of anticipation and questions about her supposed secret admirer, which Mrs Hudson had fielded as well as she could, all too soon became suspicious.

"We were already on the Sevenoaks road when she demanded to be brought home," Mrs Hudson recounted. "At first, I tried to cajole her into continuing on, but she became quite aggressive, accusing me of kidnap, and, to be honest, gentlemen, I quite feared for my safety, so I instructed Higgins, the driver, to bring us back. At least Alice seemed to accept my claim to know nothing very much, that I was some simple old soul who had been hired to escort her."

"While you were upstairs, Watson, she burst in on us in a red rage," Holmes said, clearly relishing the memory, "though I think she was too angry to be fully aware of our presence. She made for Flowerdew and started punching and scratching him, accusing him of organising the note, the hansom and the whole wasted journey. 'I suppose,' she screeched, 'you wanted to get rid of me, the way you've got rid of your wife.' She really thought Mrs Hudson was taking her to be killed and disposed of in the hop fields of Kent... The product of reading too much sensational fiction! Always a bad idea."

"But how did Flowerdew react when she accused him like that?" I asked. "In front of his constables, too?"

"He shouted back that he knew nothing about any of it, that it was all her doing, that he was ignorant of any plot to kill his wife, having assumed her to be under Alice's tender care. Nothing, he claimed, could have shocked him more than seeing his wife's abject condition..." Holmes smiled sardonically. "Of course, no one was taken in for a minute by that, not even his dim-witted constables. But while they were arresting him, Alice tried to slip away. Only for the quick-thinking of Mrs Booth here, she might even have succeeded. Charlotte chased her out into the garden and flattened her into the briar patch."

"That I should have liked to see," I said.

"You should have, Doctor," Mrs Hudson said, glancing fondly at her friend. "Lottie was the heroine of the hour."

"All the same," the seamstress responded, "I could have wished to have avoided the briars. Apart from being scratched to pieces myself, it ruined the lovely dress Alice was wearing. The one I had made for Mrs Flowerdew."

One month later, recovering well, and with her husband and the dreadful Alice locked away, the lady herself was back home in Wivenhoe Place. Sterling work had been done in cleaning and freshly decorating the house in advance of her arrival by the previous housekeeper, Elsie Chambers, and the rest of the reinstated staff. There was one addition to the number. Charlotte Booth had moved in as Mrs Flowerdew's companion, with little Matthew become the surrogate grandchild. Charlotte has continued to work as a seamstress, but only for favoured clients such as Mrs Hudson. As for her other role, she has virtually retired from that, though I overheard her mention to Holmes that if he was ever in need of a female detective to help in his investigations, he would know where to come.[2]

---

[2] This story was inspired by an absorbing study, *The Mysterious Case of the Victorian Female Detective* by Sara Lodge (Yale, 2024)

The St Pancras Puzzle

"Is anyone a doctor? A doctor! We need a doctor!"

A frantic porter in the uniform of the Midlands Railway was accosting passengers arriving at St Pancras station, Holmes and myself among them. We had just returned from the smoky midland city of Birmingham, where my friend had been instrumental in foiling a vile blackmail plot: Mrs N need no longer fear that a girlhood indiscretion would ruin her life as a devoted wife and mother.

"I am a doctor!" I informed the porter.

"Thanks be to God, sir," he replied, grabbing my arm. "It's a nasty business and no mistake."

He pulled me through the crowds to a distant and deserted platform where two others of his ilk – one short and fat, the other young and white with shock – were standing guard over a prone figure. As we approached, I saw that the man lying there, a burly individual of middle age, was wearing the uniform of a police constable. Blood that had flowed from a wound on his head, now pooled and congealed around him.

"I am very much afraid," I said, after examining the man, "that he is quite beyond my help."

The first porter must have been of the Catholic religion, for he made the sign of the cross over his breast.

"We thought as much, sir," he replied. "The poor fellow. Did he fall, do you think?"

I shook my head. "This was no accident."

Even a casual view of the injuries would indicate that someone had bludgeoned the man many times with some heavy object.

"Oh lawd," the fat porter said, shaking his head, "Mr Wright won't like that. Not one bit, he won't."

"Who is Mr Wright?" I asked.

All three men looked at me with astonishment as if to ask had I really never heard of this illustrious personage?

"Mr Nehemiah Wright. The director-in-chief of the Midland Railways."

"I see. Well, before you inform anyone, even Mr Nehemiah Wright, you had better alert the police."

"If *you* say so, sir," the first porter replied, placing the responsibility for bypassing the director on to my shoulders.

He headed off to make the call.

"And for the love of God," I said to the other two, "find something to cover this poor fellow." For the curious had started to gather as they always will at the scene of anything untoward.

The two porters looked at each other, rather stupidly, I thought, and stayed where they were.

"Or we can use this," I told them, lightly spreading the copy of the Birmingham Daily Post I had been reading on the train over the victim's upper body.

I looked around for Holmes. He was standing a way off, a frown on his brow.

"What do you make of this, Watson?" he asked, indicating an object lying on the ground.

It was a long nightcap of white cloth, just like the one worn by Ebenezer Scrooge in illustrations to the famous story by Mr Dickens.

"Curious, isn't it," Holmes remarked.

"Most odd. I didn't think anyone wore such things these days, except perhaps for some of my more elderly patients."

Holmes sighed.

"The fashion element is hardly relevant, Watson. What is odd is that it should be lying discarded on a station platform instead of neatly folded in someone's bedroom."

He stared down at it as if it were a witness able to reveal exactly what had happened.

"What is also most telling," he continued, "is what is not here, what's missing."

"What?" I asked.

"Surely you don't need me to tell you?" he replied.

I ignored the jibe. I was tired after a very early start, was most anxious to get home after our trip – the Midland railway not being the most clean and comfortable mode of transport – and was not in the mood for one of his conundrums. However, leaving immediately was out of the question. The first porter, having returned, informed us that the police were on their way but wished us all to stay put until they arrived. Sighing resignedly, I observed with a sinking heart, from Holmes's alert demeanour – bloodhound that he was – that he was as keen to linger as I was to leave the poor victim to the attention of the proper authorities.

In the meantime, a small, ball-shaped, choleric gentleman, with a shiny bald head, shiny forehead and shiny cheeks and chins that hung down over a tight starched collar was bouncing towards us as fast as his short legs would carry him. The porters shrank back.

"What exactly is going on here?" he barked at no one in particular. "Another old tramp has croaked, is it?"

He made to lift a corner of the newspaper.

"Better wait for the police," Holmes warned.

The man stared at him through piggy eyes. "And who are you, sir, to tell me what to do?"

"I am Sherlock Holmes, and this is my colleague, Dr Watson, who has ascertained that the man has met a violent end. You, I presume, are Mr Nehemiah Wright."

"You presume correctly, sir." He puffed himself up like a turkey cock.

I wondered who had informed him of the incident. Presumably the porter who had telephoned to the police, terrified to be found remiss, had notified his superior at the same time.

The name of my friend seemed to have made no impression whatsoever on the director, who perhaps was one of those rare beings who had never heard of Sherlock Holmes. He spent the time waiting for the police impatiently tapping a highly polished boot on the platform, while casting venomous glances our way, as if it were we who were responsible for the corpse.

At long last, the familiar lanky figure of Inspector Merivale, together with a couple of constables, could be seen marching along the platform towards us.

"Ha!" he said, when he drew close. "Sherlock Holmes! How do you happen be involved in this business, might I ask?"

"Completely by chance, Merivale. Myself and Watson were arriving from Birmingham when this porter" (indicating the man) "called urgently for a doctor. Watson responded, only to find the poor fellow lying here as you can see him."

"Right you are." Merivale carefully lifted the newssheet. One of the constables gasped.

"It's… it's Jim Walters! From the Islington station."

The Inspector turned to me.

"Was the man still alive when you first examined him, Doctor?"

I shook my head. "No. It was clear that life had let him some time earlier. Not long, mind. Maybe a half hour or so, judging by the temperature of the body. And, as you see, rigor mortis has not yet set in."

Meanwhile, the director was hopping from one leg to another.

"Inspector," he shrilled, "I am Nehemiah Wright."

"Are you, indeed?" Merivale said. "And what have you to do with this sorry business?"

"Well… nothing… Nothing at all. I know nothing at all about it. Of course not. But I am director of the Midland Railway, do you see. To have a dead man, a policeman as I understand it, on my property… I have a certain responsibility, you understand, to the travelling public."

Merivale nodded. "It was clearly a frenzied attack," he said. "Have you any idea, sir, how the constable happened to be here on this particular platform?"

"None at all. This is a seldom used branch line connecting to the lesser inhabited regions of the home counties. I cannot comprehend what your man was doing here. Not at all. No, no, no." Mr Wright shook his head so vigorously that all his chins wobbled.

"He was perhaps in pursuit of some felon, when the man turned on him," Merivale suggested.

Wright nodded. "Yes, yes. That must be it. Assuredly."

"Which raises the question as to where this supposed felon was heading," Holmes said.

We all cast our eyes to the limit of the platform, the empty rails stretching beyond it.

"Did any train leave from here in the past half hour?" Merivale asked.

Nehemiah Wright took a large fob watch from his waistcoat pocket and proceeded to consult it, as if the answer lay within its silver case.

"No," said the first porter. "Last train…"

"Yes, yes, yes, Sullivan," the director interrupted. "As I was about to say, the last train from here was at a quarter past nine. It now being eleven thirty…."

"So that rules out the possibility that anyone escaped that way," I said, while Wright glared at me. "As I said, the man has only been dead around a half hour."

"In any case," added Holmes drily, "if a dead body were lying on the platform when the train pulled in or out, someone might possibly have noticed."

"Then the assailant probably simply and coolly made his way back up the empty platform and out through the station," Merivale said. "I assume, if no train was due, there would be no one guarding the barrier."

"Of course not," Wright remarked. "That would be a sheer waste of manpower."

"So how come," Merivale addressed the porters, "you lot went on to that platform, if no trains were due in or out?"

The men shuffled, embarrassed, glancing at Wright.

"Did you hear an altercation?"

"I wish we did sir, then this poor fellow might still be with us," the first porter said. "No... me, Fred and Garrick here just popped down to check... er..."

"You came for a quiet smoke," Holmes said.

The porter looked at him astonished. "How d'you figure that, sir?"

Holmes pointed to a large pillar. It provided a convenient hiding place for anyone not wishing to be observed. At its base, at the side facing away from the main station was a heap of cigarette stubs as well as an empty box that promoted a particularly noxious brand of the weed.

Nehemiah Wright looked about to explode with rage. Indeed, his face had turned to such an intense shade of purple that I quite feared a stroke might be imminent.

"Smoking on duty!" he roared. "That's cause for immediate dismissal!"

"Come now, sir," Holmes said. "We surely have more pressing matters demanding our attention. Had these men not left their duties for a five-minute break, this Jim Walters might not have been found for hours."

"It is against the rules, Mr Shercock." Nehemiah Wright retorted, still purple. "These men know that full well. No smoking at work."

"Be a little flexible, sir," Holmes went on. "Have you never enjoyed a fine cigar in your office? In fact, I see from the light dusting of ash on your waistcoat that you have very recently smoked... what...?" He approached Wright and, to that gentleman's amazement, sniffed at his jacket. "A Flor de Cano, if I'm not much mistaken."

The director fell back, his mouth open.

"What trickery is this, sir?" he exclaimed.

"Mr Holmes has written a monograph on the subject of cigar ash," I explained, though I am afraid this did not appease the man, who continued to gaze on my friend with superstitious horror.

"That's all well and good," Merivale said briskly, "but it hardly advances our investigation into poor Walters" demise. Thank you for your help, Dr Watson. However, I think you and Mr Holmes might now leave the rest to us."

I could hope for nothing better, but Holmes delayed.

"I should be inclined to agree with you," he said, "were it not for two or three odd elements to the case."

"Whatever are you talking about?" Merivale asked.

"First of all, the man's head has been caved in. Why was he not wearing his helmet, and where is it now? Moreover, where is his truncheon?"

"Hm," Merivale said, scratching his jaw. "Well, I expect they'll turn up, once we start searching."

"And then," Holmes continued, "there's that."

He pointed to the nightcap, lying a little way off.

Merivale laughed. "Are you suggesting Constable Walters was wearing that instead of his helmet? Oh, Mr Holmes, you'll be the death of me, you surely will."

"I am, of course, suggesting no such thing. I just wonder how to account for its presence," Holmes retorted, rather huffily.

"All right. Let me borrow your deductive powers for a moment, Mr Holmes..." Merivale frowned thoughtfully. Then clicked his fingers. "How about this? An elderly gent – for only an elderly gent would wear such a thing – staying in the Midland Grand Hotel, wakes late, and rushes for his morning train, quite forgetting in his haste that he is still wearing his nightcap. When he does, he tears it from his head, casting it from him, before jumping on the train."

"Really, Merivale?" Holmes shook his head. "A forgetful elderly gentleman? Is that the best you can come up with?"

"Well, or some other totally innocent explanation. Nothing to do with the matter in hand, anyway. Or perhaps," chuckling, "you reckon our felon was wearing it when chased by PC Walters here. Perhaps it's Wee Willie Winkie we should be looking for." He paused. "All right. It's curious, I'll grant you that. So if you really want to look into it, be my guest."

Holmes smiled. "Thank you... May I take the nightcap, then?"

Merivale nodded, smiling indulgently. However, for Nehemiah Wright this would not do.

"It's lost property," he said. "Suppose the elderly gentleman comes back to ask for it? What then, sir? What then?"

"Then you contact me, sir, and I shall return it forthwith. But I don't imagine it will come to that." Holmes turned to the three porters. "I may have some further questions for you later. With Mr Wright's permission of course."

That personage nodding grudgingly, Holmes took the names of the porters, Sullivan, Whalley and Jessop. He then picked up the nightcap carefully and carried it away with him, while I followed, having nodded farewell to Inspector Merivale and the others.

"Did anything strike you as unusual about all this?" Holmes asked me, once we had settled in the hansom taking us back to Baker Street.

"Nothing at all," I replied. "I frequently trip over dead policemen when at main line railway stations."

He viewed me through narrowed lids.

"Facetiousness does not become you, Watson," he said. "Think, man!"

I knitted my brow in an attempt to satisfy my friend. However, apart from the presence of the nightcap, and the absence of the helmet and truncheon, I could not recall anything that jumped out at me. I said as much.

"Yes, this cap is most enlightening," he replied. "As for the helmet and truncheon, they are key, I think. But there is more."

"I am afraid you must explain, Holmes."

"What brought this Walters to a pillar on a deserted platform? He was hardly on a random patrol."

"Well, if he was chasing someone…"

"Surely people would have noticed a pursuit through the main body of the station. No one seems to have done so."

"Perhaps the constable also wanted a quiet smoke."

"Tut! There you go again, making light of it. No, Watson, I rather believe Walters had gone there for a specific purpose, even maybe to meet someone." Holmes sat back.

"The person who killed him?"

"Quite possibly, Watson. Moreover," he continued, "there was no forgetful elderly gentleman."

He held up the nightcap, and, like Maskelyne performing a magic trick, turned it inside out, returning it, in fact, to its proper configuration, for now a ball formed of cut wool was revealed to be on the pointed tip of it. Holmes held it out for me to examine. There were bloodstains upon it.

"This was used as a weapon," Holmes said.

"Death by pompom," I commented.

"Really, Watson!"

"I'm sorry, but I still don't see…."

"Clearly some hard object, a rock or brick perhaps, was placed inside the cap which was then swung with considerable force, to hit the constable's head."

"Bludgeoning him to death."

"Hm…" Holmes considered the matter. "But in that case, surely there would be more blood on the thing. Rather more likely, isn't it, that the man's own truncheon was used to finish him off. Perhaps this was used to surprise him, knocking off his helmet and laying him flat."

He squeezed the fabric of the cap.

"Ha!" he exclaimed. "How very interesting!"

"What, Holmes?"

He held out his hand on which a few tiny glistening particles lay.

"Glass? But what does it mean? That a paperweight was used?"

"As to that, at the present moment, we can only speculate, something, as you well know, I am not inclined to do, preferring to rationalise from hard evidence…Hello, what's this?" He scraped a few darker particles off the side of the cap, and examined them closely. "Glue, I think. I can't be sure until I examine this under the microscope. But meanwhile… yes… I must go back immediately."

He called to the driver to stop.

"Shall I accompany you?" I asked, somewhat aghast at this sudden change of mind.

"No, Watson," he said, climbing out of the vehicle. "I should like you to go to Islington police station forthwith, and make enquiries regarding Constable Walters, his family, friends and so on. Find out, if he was the sort of man likely to confront a suspect on his own."

Seeing my hopes of dozing at home over a restorative glass of tonic wine fading fast, I gave new instruction to the cab driver, and then settled back, musing on the case into which we had just fallen. I have to say that I was not inclined to accept Holmes's notion that Walters had gone to meet someone. Much more likely that he had seen something suspicious and, diligent in his duty to investigate, had walked to his doom.

The constable on the desk was a large man in his fifties, with ginger whiskers and a florid complexion. High blood pressure, for sure. He was suspicious of my enquiries at first, but when I mentioned Inspector Merivale and Sherlock Holmes, he became more forthcoming.

"Very shocked I was to "ear what 'appened." he said. "Very shocked I was, sir."

"Yes, indeed. A sad business. But I am hoping you can tell me more about Walters?"

"What d'you mean, sir?"

"Family man, was he?"

The constable shook his head. "Not at all. A confirmed bachelor, 'im. Lived with his old mum. Invalid she is. It'll be a terrible shock to 'er, poor soul."

"Walters got on well with his colleagues, I suppose?"

"Well, now..." There was a perceptible pause. "Don't get me wrong. Jim Walters was a decent enough chap..." Another pause. I could almost hear "speak no ill of the dead" going through the man's mind. "Decent enough,'e was. Though to tell the truth, we got the feeling 'e thought 'isself a cut above the rest of us. Kept 'isself to 'isself, if you know what I mean."

"Did his job and then went home."

"That's exactly it, sir. Never any complaints about 'im doing what was asked for, though "e never put 'isself out, neither... But no interest in coming for a pint after "is shift with the rest of us lads. Always said "e "ad to get back to mum. Still, you'd think once in while, wouldn't you, sir?"

I nodded. "You would, indeed. It's only comradely."

"You've 'it on the 'ead again there, sir. Comradely. Yes, indeed."

"I suppose," I continued, "he was the sort of man likely to pursue a possibly violent criminal on his own."

The constable's jaw dropped open under his gingery moustache. Then he burst into a great wheezy laugh. "Jim Walters! An 'ero! Not at all, sir. Steered well clear of anything that might get 'is 'ands dirty, if you gets my meaning."

"Hmm."

"Walked 'is beat, and if anything looked dodgy, 'e was first to call in the troops."

"I see."

"Don't get me wrong, sir. I don't mean to put 'im down. It's just funny that Jim of all people should be kilt like that. They must 'ave jumped out at 'im, unexpected, like."

"Yes, it's very strange." I smiled at the constable, whose ruddy face suddenly looked almost comically downcast.

"So might I ask," I continued, "where does Walters's mother live? I'd like to pay my respects."

The obliging constable promptly gave me the address and directions, and, the house being nearby, I set off on foot, soon reaching a road of modest little dwellings.

Inside number fifteen, I found Mrs Walters, a very old and feeble person indeed, sitting in the small front parlour, a crocheted shawl in evil shades of purple and sulphur over her knees, even though the heat in the room from an open fire was already oppressive. The lady was not alone but in the capable hands of a neighbour, one Mrs Biggs, who took me aside and informed me, in a stage whisper that must have reached the old lady if she wasn't deaf, that "she keeps askin' for Jim. Don't unnerstand when I tell 'er 'e's gorn. Poor old soul." Her ample bosom heaved with a deep sigh. "Don't know what she'll do now. " 'E done everything for 'er, 'e did. I can 'elp out, o' course, but I've mine to mind, too, unnerstand me, doctor?"

"I do indeed, Mrs Biggs," I replied, adding, "Do you think I might I have a quiet word with Mrs Walters? Perhaps if I explain…"

"O' course. Though much good it'll do you, the way she is." She smiled briskly. "Keeps rambling on, she does. I can't make 'ead nor tail of it… Anyways, I'll put the kettle on. I'm sure we'd all like a nice cuppa tea."

"That would be most acceptable," I said, and, as she left the room, I turned to Mrs Walters.

She looked up at me with milky eyes that showed advanced signs of cataracts.

"Are you Mr Chance?" she asked.

"No, I am Dr Watson. How are you Mrs Walters?"

"I thought you was Mr Chance. Jim told me Mr Chance would be coming our way soon," she said, her voice quavering.

"Do you understand what has happened to Jim, Mrs Walters?"

"Jim. 'E's a good boy, 'e is. Said Mr Chance would sort all our problems."

"I'm afraid Jim has had an accident." I took her hand, bluish skin stretched over bone. "Jim won't be coming back, Mrs Walters."

"Oh you," she said, with a toothless grin. "Mr Chance. My Jim always comes back. 'E's a good boy, 'e is."

Mrs Biggs returning with tea cups on a tray laden also with a big brown china teapot, milk jug and sugar bowl, all mismatched and chipped, I sat with the ladies for a while, drinking my boiled and bitter beverage, and wondering what else I should do. Mrs Biggs gave me a strange look when I asked to see Jim's room, though she raised no objections when Mrs Walters nodded.

"You go on up, Mr Chance," she said.

The room furnished no clues, unless you counted Walters's taste for rather fancy accessories. Thrust into the back of a drawer I found a quantity of rings and tie pins, as well as a fob watch complete with chain and stamp seal. I do not claim sufficient expertise to tell genuine from fake, but they looked rather too good to be mere gilded metal and coloured glass. However, if indeed made of gold and precious stones, such objects would be quite beyond a constable's salary. Perhaps, I thought doubtfully, they were inherited. Otherwise, the room was somewhat lacking in personal effects, although a rather saucy picture of the musical hall performer Marie Lloyd was stuck to the inside of the wardrobe door.

I am afraid Mrs Biggs surprised me as I was studying this.

"Are you quite done 'ere, doc?" she asked. Her face had hardened. "Only I 'ave to get back to the little 'uns."

"Of course," I said, blushing as I closed the wardrobe door. "But I am wondering what will happen to Mrs Walters now. Clearly a busy woman like yourself cannot be imposed on any further. Is there any other family?"

My concerned tone caused Mrs Biggs to relent a little.

"She 'as a niece, what lives in Lewisham. I'll write to 'er. Meantime, I'll be sure to keep an eye on the poor old soul."

"Maybe there will be some sort of pension for the dependants of a policeman killed in the line of duty. I'll make enquiries."

"God bless you, sir." She was utterly won over again.

"Nothing much to report, Watson?" Holmes exclaimed. "On the contrary, you have discovered a great deal."

"Have I?"

It was evening and we were both back, sitting in our parlour in Baker Street.

"Putting it together with my new information," Holmes rubbed his hands together, "I am happy to say we are making excellent progress.

"So what exactly did you find out? The identity of the assassin, I suppose."

"Well, now. Not quite. I need to confirm more details..." He leaned back in his chair, drawing on his pipe, emitting the usual clouds of rank smoke. Really, he was most aggravating.

"What?" I asked. "For the love of God, Holmes, can't you explain."

"I decided to visit the Midland Grand Hotel, and very grand it is, too, Watson. Only those with exceedingly well-lined wallets can afford to stay there."

"I am fully aware of that fact. Now tell me something I don"t know. Why you went there, for instance."

"I suspected a robbery had taken place."

"And had it?"

He waved long fingers in the air.

"They denied it, but I insisted. You know how persistent I can be,"

I did indeed.

No one had reported anything missing. However, the hotel possessed a strongroom, where guests might leave their valuables.

"To the casual eye, the boxes were intact," Holmes continued, "but I examined each one closely and discovered that one of these had indeed been forced open. A quantity of priceless gems gone, property of a Dutch diamond merchant." He sat back the familiar satisfied smile on his face of one proved right.

"The security must have been very lax," I said.

"Judge for yourself. On further investigation, and after rousing the night manager, I learnt that an elderly person had descended to the hotel lobby in the early hours 'in a right state,' as the man informed me, still in his night clothes, which included, please to note, Watson, a white nightcap. Waving the key to his strongbox in the air, he insisted on checking that it was still safely stowed, shouting out that he was sure he had been robbed. The manager, one Smithson by name, after trying to persuade him that all was well, eventually gave in and accompanied the old man to the strongroom. He unlocked its heavy door and then left the guest by himself, as was customary with keyholders. Smithson assured me that the man was alone for a few minutes at most. Soon enough, he reappeared, apparently reassured, and anxious to get back to bed. And no, he wasn't carrying anything that the manager could see."

"But he was presumably in a loose night shirt or dressing gown with pockets. Diamonds are easily concealed."

"Well reasoned, Watson." Holmes gave me a merry look.

"So who was this anxious old man?"

"He gave his name as L. Chance, esquire, when checking in."

"Good Lord!"

"Yes, indeed. The same that Mrs Walters mentioned to you."

"The Mr Chance who was about to change the fortunes of Walters and his mother! But, assuming Chance was the thief, that suggests... does it not?... that Constable Walters was aware of the robbery. Could he even have been part of it?"

"Now we are perhaps getting somewhere. What you have told me about the man's tastes and habits suggest that Walters was a man dissatisfied with his lot in life. A man perhaps easily seduced into crime. Quite possibly the fob watch and so on that you found hidden away in the drawer were not mere trinkets but rather the fruit of earlier thefts." He sighed. "It is a shame, Watson, you do not share my ability in distinguishing fakes from the real thing."

I decided to ignore the barb.

"But by God!" I exclaimed. "If Walters was involved, that changes everything."

"We mustn't jump to conclusions, Watson. Let us give the man the benefit of the doubt unless and until the facts prove otherwise. Meanwhile, tomorrow, we return to the hotel. Part of the solution must lie there."

I was most gratified to hear that "we", since the case was starting to intrigue me considerably.

At that moment, however, before he could expatiate further, we were interrupted by a light tap on the door. It was Mrs Hudson with supper. I suddenly realised that I was very hungry. It was, after all, only that same morning we had come from Birmingham before being plunged into this new adventure, and I had hardly broken my fast since an early breakfast. Our good landlady placed before us plates heaped with chops, potatoes, peas and carrots, enhanced with some home-made mustard. I set to with appetite.

"I am glad to see you have your priorities, Watson," Holmes remarked drily, picking up a pea on the tine of his fork.

"Sorry, Holmes, but I find I am ravenous. And my brain works better when I am well-fed. Of course, I wish you to continue your discourse. What happened to Chance? Has he been apprehended?"

"Ah, the elusive Mr Chance… I am afraid, on checking his room, the hotel found that he had quite vanished."

He popped the pea into his mouth.

"Vanished! Leaving the contents of his strong box?"

"Oh, Watson! Use what brains you have, man. There was nothing in his strong box."

"He had already emptied it, then."

"My friend, there was never anything in the box. It was simply a ploy to give him admission to the strongroom, in order to rob the gems."

I clapped a hand to my forehead. "Of course. Forgive my slowness."

"Eat up your chops, Watson. They *may* help speed you up."

"So anyway," I cut a juicy portion of meat from the bone, "you were wrong to some extent. There is an elderly man in the story after all."

Holmes smiled patiently. "Mr Chance vanished, as I said. Leaving behind a night shirt, false whiskers and other bits and pieces. I am apparently not the only person to resort to disguises from time to time. By the way, that was indeed glue on the cap, as I informed Merivale. Goodness knows what he will make of it all." He laughed.

"I see…" I chewed slowly, not really seeing anything at all. "So the thief made his escape, but for some reason, still wearing his nightcap. That would surely make him stand out in a crowd."

Holmes sighed.

"Are you deliberately being obtuse tonight, Watson? Of course, the man wasn't wearing the cap at the time. No, I imagine it proved a handy receptacle for the fruit of his theft."

"Oh, yes. The diamonds, yes, of course."

It was true. My brain wasn't working properly, at that moment. The wine with the meal, along with a post-prandial glass of brandy left me, I am sorry to say, so sleepy that I dozed off in my chair. My only excuse: it had been a long and eventful day. When I roused myself, maybe half an hour later, it was to find Holmes staring out into the blackness of Baker Street, perhaps musing on the blackness of the human heart.

"Ah, you have returned to consciousness, Watson. Good. Well, let us hope we can finish with this sorry case soon enough."

"You think you have solved it already, then?"

"Hardly that, my dear fellow. There are too many unknowns as yet. Tomorrow, the hotel, and then the porters."

The following morning found Holmes and I entering the lobby of the Midland Grand Hotel. Although I had visited this renowned establishment before – once, as I recall, to meet an Edinburgh surgeon come to the Middlesex Hospital to conduct a particularly complex operation – I was as always taken aback at the sight that greeted me.

The place caters to a wealthy clientele, as reflected in the lavishness of the architecture and interior ornamentation. Indeed, the design is more reminiscent of some medieval cathedral than a London railway hotel, with its a vaulted ceiling, high pointed arches, and pillars surmounted by carvings of flowers, fruits and fleurs-de-lis. But it is as far as it could be from the gloomy Gothic piles with which we are familiar these days. Instead, it is as a cathedral would have been in the Middle Ages, all visible surfaces brightly coloured to dazzle the eye, reds, blues and greens predominating, with more gold leaf than I have ever seen in one place before. Rather too ornate for my taste, but undoubtedly impressive.

On this occasion, after we had made ourselves known to the receptionist, we were shown, not up the swooping staircase to the splendours of the coffee room where I had previously met my colleague, but to the altogether plainer office of the day manager. Holmes had interviewed the man, a shrunken elderly party by the name of Horrocks, on the previous day, and, following the discovery of the theft, the manager had requested him return to investigate it.

"I trust you will be able to get to the bottom of this matter quickly, Mr Holmes, and recover the stolen property," he enunciated gravely. "I assured Mr van de Groot that he could ask for no better than yourself in solving this heinous crime. He awaits your visit." Holmes nodded, but the man continued. "So far only a few people know of it, and my hope is that we can recover the diamonds before the story leaks out. That is why both Mr van de Groot and I have agreed not to involve the police. You understand, how badly such a thing reflects on the reputation of the hotel, Mr Holmes. We here at the Midland Grand pride ourselves on maintaining the very highest of standards. If our guests cannot trust the security of…"

"Quite," said Holmes, at which interruption, the man raised thin grey eyebrows. He was not, I think, used to being stopped in mid-flow.

"I should like, if possible," Holmes went on, "to speak first to the maids who serviced the Dutchman's room and that of Mr Chance."

Mr Horrocks, tight-lipped now, consulted a list.

"It is the one girl," he said finally. "Molly Bliss."

He rang a bell on his desk and a liveried page with a cheeky face, who, from the speed of his arrival, must have been standing right outside the door awaiting the call, hopped in smartly. Mr Horrocks gave the lad instructions to fetch this same Molly.

"She should be about her work on the third floor," he told him.

The page saluted and hopped out again.

"I wonder, Mr Horrocks, is there," Holmes asked, "a quiet room where we can speak to the girl?"

"You can stay here," he replied. "I have no objection."

"Thank you, but I should prefer somewhere private."

That is to say, as we all understood his words, without your presence, sir. The manager was clearly again put out, so I decided to intervene.

"You must understand, Mr Horrocks," I said, "the girl is more likely to be frank and relaxed with us if her superiors are absent."

"But what can she possibly tell you?" he asked. "Unless…" He bristled, "unless you think Molly herself is part of this gang. Girls, these days…"

"No, no. Not at all," Holmes interrupted quickly, before Mr Horrocks got started on another hobby horse. "It is just that she may have seen or heard something that can help us. Something she may not even know is important."

"Very well," the man grudgingly acquiesced. "You may still use this room, I suppose. I shall make myself scarce. I have, after all, many important duties to attend to."

"Thank you, sir. Most obliging of you," I said. Holmes shot me a look.

While we waited for Molly to arrive, Mr Horrocks sat frowning and silent, drumming bony fingers on a desk rather too large for such an undersized person.

"You have a magnificent establishment here," I said at last, to try and sweeten the atmosphere.

"Yes, indeed. I have a great responsibility in making sure everything runs like clockwork… This business has quite upset me, you understand."

"Of course. Rest assured Mr Holmes will do his utmost to catch the thieves and recover the diamonds."

"I pray so," Mr Horrocks replied, at the same time casting a doubtful eye on the detective, who, his back to us, was studying a crudely executed portrait, affixed to the wall, of the manager himself.

After what seemed an unconscionably long time, the page returned with an undernourished girl, hardly more than a child, whose big eyes, moving from Horrocks to myself and finally to Holmes's back, were filled with terror. It seemed as if she had recently been crying for her face was flushed and tear-stained.

"Now Molly," the manager said, fixing her with a significant stare, "these men are going to ask you some questions. I hope you will be a good girl when you answer them, and tell them what they need to know."

She nodded, wide-eyed, hovering.

"Sit down, do," he went on impatiently, indicating an empty chair on which she gingerly perched herself. "Now, I am going to leave you for a little while. Don't be afraid."

"We don't bite," I added, smiling at her.

"Of course, you don't," the manager said tartly, and left the room, followed by the page who gave Molly a big wink.

Holmes spun around, making the girl jump.

"Be yous the po-lees, sirs?" the girl asked, looking from one of us to the other.

"No, Molly. Not the police. I am Sherlock Holmes, a private detective, and this is my colleague and friend, Dr Watson."

"A doctor," the girl looked even more confused.

"Nothing to do with the matter in hand," I reassured her.

"Now, Molly," Holmes said briskly, "I believe you are responsible for cleaning the rooms belonging to both the Dutchman and the elderly gentleman, Mr Chance."

The girl stared at him for a moment or two and then burst into an avalanche of tears.

"Now, now, Molly. What is it?" Holmes asked, put out, his voice become gentle for once.

"I din mean it. I din mean anything. And now 'e's dead," she burst out.

"Do you mean Constable Walters, my dear?"

"Yessur. Jim... Oh, lawd forgive me."

Holmes sat down beside her.

"Just tell us everything. How you got to know Walters."

"It'll make you feel better to get it off your chest," I added, and she gave me a grateful look.

"It will, sir. I 'ope so. I bin that fussed..."

She poured it all out.

" 'E come 'ere after all the robberies, d'you see."

"What robberies?"

"From the strongroom, the safes."

"Are you telling us there has been more than one?"

"Oh yes, sir... There's been a few." She grinned then, exposing teeth in dire need of attention. "I weren't supposed to know about it, but you can't help finding out, can you?"

"No, quite right."

"You won't say nothing to the old 'Orror, will yer, please? 'E'd kill me."

"Mr Horrocks?"

The girl nodded.

Holmes shook his head, smiling. "Your secret is safe with us."

"Anyhow, since the robberies, Jim always called in to see me. Good to me, 'e was." She gave a wan little smile. "Ever so kind to me, Jim was. Give me this, 'e did."

She fished a locket out from under the blouse of her uniform.

"Can I see?"

She took it off and passed it to Holmes, who raised his eyebrows and then gave it to me. Gold or base metal, I was not sure.

"So then 'e tells me 'ow 'e's on the trail of a crimbinal mastermind." Her eyes glowed with excitement at the memory.

"And 'e asks for my 'elp. Asked me to tell 'im if any of my guests had partic'lar valubles. So 'e could lay a trap for the villain, like."

"So what did you tell him, Molly? About Mr van de Groot."

" 'Oo?"

"The Dutchman."

"Oh yes, 'im. I told Jim all about the diamonds. 'E asked me what number safe they were in, and all."

"I suppose you hardly knew that."

"Yes, I did, sir. I did, cos Groot left 'is key one time on the bedside table when I bought 'im clean towels. Snatched it up, 'e did, but not afore I saw the number. Unlucky 13."

"And you passed that information to Constable Walters."

"Yes, I did, sir… I reckoned it was all right cos 'e was the po-lees, like… D'you think…would Jim be alive today if I didn't of?"

Holmes shrugged his shoulders.

"Oh, lawd." She looked to be on the verge of tears again.

"We don't know, Molly," I said. "But I doubt that you telling him made any difference." I did not necessarily believe that, but the poor child was already upset enough. No need to make it worse.

With regard to her other gentleman, Mr Chance, Molly could tell us nothing that we did not already know. She had never seen him.

After we sent her away with further reassurances, Holmes stretched out in Mr Horrocks's chair.

"Now Watson, whyever do you suppose our esteemed manager failed to inform us of the previous thefts?"

"I don't know. To preserve the reputation of the hotel, perhaps."

"Hmm. Well, we can but ask him."

"What about the reputation of little Molly Bliss? He'll know that it is she who has told us."

"You are right. We'll try and keep Molly out of it. But, first of all, we should have a word with this Dutchman. Let us go to his room."

Joop van de Groot was a large fellow in all respects, over six foot tall with muscles running to fat, causing the silver buttons on his dark blue jacket to stretch almost to bursting point. I put his age in the mid-thirties. A thatch of straw-coloured hair surmounted a ruddy complexion, deep lines marking a weather-coarsened face. After standing to receive us, he sat himself back at a paper-strewn desk, a small aquarium containing several small tropical fish providing an exotic touch.

"Harlequin rasbora and cherry barb! A charming combination," Holmes exclaimed, peering at the little creatures.

"If you say so," the Dutchman replied. "I know nothing of such things. They are pretty enough, I suppose. But I think we are hardly here to discuss fishes." His English was impeccable but his tone was decidedly gruff and unfriendly.

"I apologise," Holmes said. "Ichthyology is a particular interest of mine and these are fine specimens."

The Dutchman shrugged. "They come with the room," he said, turning away from the desk. "So, have you found my diamonds?"

"Alas, not yet. But I hope to have good news soon."

The other looked as if he very much doubted it.

"So when are you planning to return to South Africa?" Holmes continued.

"What? How did you...? Oh, famous detective, you have been asking about me." He gave a sharp laugh.

"Not at all. I knew nothing about you before entering this room. It is you who have told me."

The man almost leapt from his seat, "What the devil!"

"Nothing devilish about it," Holmes replied genially. "Your bleached hair, your ruddy complexion, the freckles on your hands, all speak of one who has worked under a hot sun. South Africa is known for its diamond mines, so that would be the obvious place for you to have visited. Moreover, there is a letter on your desk with the banner heading of one such mine."

"Ha!" the man smacked a big, red, and decidedly freckled hand, on the desk. "Yes, sir. You are correct. I spent fifteen years at Jagersfontein, near Bloemfontein. But now I am back."

"In Amsterdam?"

"Where else? The centre of the diamond industry in Europe, mynheer."

"So what brings you to London?"

"There's a man in Hatton Garden I deal with. I prefer to do it face-to-face."

Holmes regarded him for a moment. The fellow stared back, unperturbed.

"The theft of the diamonds must be a great loss to you."

The man shrugged. "Of course."

"But I suppose they are insured."

"Naturally. I am not a fool, sir."

"Hmm."

I could not understand it. A hostility simmered between the two men. But why? Was not Mr van de Groot the injured party here?

"Well," Holmes said after a while, with a smile. "I hope to be in a position to restore your losses, and avoid the necessity of involving your insurance company."

"Ah!" The Dutchman smiled back. A gold-capped tooth, a canine, twinkled at us. "But you see, I have already informed them."

"Of course, because you return to Amsterdam imminently."

"Yes, I do. There is no reason to stay here now."

"Or are you going back to Bloemfontein, perhaps?"

"Maybe. Not yet…" He smiled again, and then provided Holmes with a detailed description of the gems. I almost whistled at the value placed upon them.

"You see, they include one of the biggest diamonds ever found, uncut of course," van de Groot explained. "Big as a woman's fist." He clenched his own. "Such a beauty, mynheeren, with that characteristic pink tinge of the stones of the Jagerfontein mine…"

He sighed. "It would be truly *wonderful* if you could track it down. In that event, I would reward you handsomely, of course. However, I fear the thieves are already far far away."

"Perhaps," Holmes replied, regarding him steadily.

"If I had known then that the strongroom was not safe, I should have kept them hidden here in my room. Alas, it is easy to be wise after the event, is it not?"

Taking our leave of him, we rejoined Mr Horrocks, back in his office.

"Why did you not inform us, sir," Holmes asked, "that there had been other thefts."

"Did *he* tell you? Ha! Never trust a foreigner to keep his mouth shut."

Neither Holmes nor I contradicted him. Better to blame the Dutchman than poor Molly.

"Anyway," the manager continued, "the previous thefts were all insignificant ones, mere trifles, nothing of great value. And we of course reimbursed our guests for their losses."

"I see. But surely that should have put you on high alert."

Instead of looking discomforted, Mr Horrocks, surprisingly, looked smug.

"As to that, we had good reason to suspect one of the caretakers here, an odd job man – though nothing could be proved and he denied everything. We sent him packing anyway, with a flea in his ear," he said.

"Together with the stolen items, assuming he was the guilty party"

"Well… yes… Unfortunately, it proved impossible to recover the "loot" as I think such blackguards call it."

"What! You didn't think to involve the police?" I could not help exclaiming.

The manager gave me a disdainful glance.

"In point of fact, the police *were* involved, in the person of the sadly late Constable James Walters. However, he agreed with me when I insisted that the reputation of the hotel must remain paramount. It was certainly worth more than a few baubles, a few shillings."

"Presumably," Holmes said, "you rewarded Walters for his discretion."

Mr Horrocks waved a hand in the air. "A trivial sum... In any case, the good Constable was able to advise us on increased security, after Garrick had been dismissed. Alas, of course, as it turned out, not well enough."

"Garrick?"

"That wasn't the wretch's real name, but it was the one we all called him, as a joke, d'you see."

We didn't see, and gave him a puzzled stare.

Mr Horrocks sighed. "After David Garrick, don't you know. The great actor. This fellow was some sort of a failed thespian. Had to take up a menial job here since he couldn't keep body and soul together on what he earned treading the boards, as I believe the expression goes. Quite a dab hand at the picture-framing, as well, in fact." He indicated the painting on the wall. "Garrick's work. The frame that is," adding with a false modesty, "The art work is mine. A self-portrait."

"Ah..." Holmes sniffed, regarding the thing.

"Yes, Inspector Merivale was very interested," the manager continued, "when I informed him about Garrick."

"I see," Holmes said. "And do you know where is Garrick now?"

"I have no idea." It was as if a lamp was suddenly lit in the manager's limited brain. "By God, do you think Garrick was behind this business?"

Holmes made a non-committal gesture, while I tried to remember where I had heard the name before, beyond the famous actor, of course.

"At last," Holmes remarked, with satisfaction, as we quitted the manager and made our way out through the hotel. "The matter is coming together rather well, don't you agree, Watson?"

How could I? I was as puzzled as ever.

"Please explain," I said.

"You mean you really have no idea as yet?"

I knitted my brow with the effort of trying to make sense of the business.

"If Walters," I reasoned at last, "was, as he told Molly, in pursuit of a master criminal, discovered who he was and confronted him, then the villain must have killed him to prevent exposure. But..." I shook my head, "would Walters not have summoned 'the troops' as the station officer affirmed would be his way, rather than face him alone? Unless..."

"Yes?" Holmes's eager eyes flashed with amusement.

"You know all the answers, so why not spare me," I said crossly.

"No, no. Go on. Unless what?"

"Well, unless Walters knew about the robbery and wanted a pay-off. Maybe he was in on it from the start and provided the thief with the necessary information as gleaned from Molly. Or maybe..." I gasped at the thought. "Maybe, he was Chance himself."

Holmes burst out laughing and clapped his hands together, sorely alarming a passing dowager, whose little dog started yapping at us. "Capital reasoning, Watson. And so nearly right. However, you have gone rather too far down the road of speculation. Think about it. It is hardly likely that the constable, well-known in the hotel, would have had the skill or nerve to pass himself off as an elderly guest. No, it is high time for you to ask Inspector Merivale to summon the main actors in this drama, in order at last to get at the truth."

"*I* am to ask him?"

"Yes, Watson, if you would be so kind. I am afraid he is about to charge the wrong person with the murder. In fact, it took all my powers of persuasion to have him hold off already. Meanwhile, there is just one last thing I have to do first. To make absolutely sure, do you see."

Thus it was that an hour or so later found a motley band of people – most of whom were puzzled to find themselves in such a place – assembled at St Pancras station in the rather fine, cigar-scented office of Mr Nehemiah Wright. Present were Inspector Merivale and one of his sergeants, Mr Horrocks, Mynheer Joop van de Groot, the three porters and myself, awaiting the arrival of Holmes, who entered shortly after, accompanied by little Molly Bliss.

"In the interests of discretion," Holmes said, "I thought it more appropriate to meet here than in the hotel, to inform you of the results of my investigation."

"I hope it will be worth it," the director exclaimed. "It is all most inconvenient, you know."

"Apologies, Mr Wright, but I assumed you would wish to hear an explanation of the sad event that took place on your premises," Holmes replied.

Wright nodded, though with something of a bad grace.

"It is a tale of insatiable greed," Holmes continued. "Constable Walters was killed because, as my colleague Dr Watson so rightly surmised, he had discovered the identity," here he winked at Molly, "of the criminal mastermind. However, instead of having him arrested, Walters craved a share of the loot. Whereupon he let himself be lured to the empty and remote platform where he met his end."

"That's quite an accusation against a member of Her Majesty's police force," Merivale interrupted. "I hope you can prove what you say."

"Patience, my dear Inspector, all will very soon be revealed." Holmes made a steeple with the fingers of both hands, and pressed them to his lips. Then he continued. "As you will recall, there were some strange but telling elements to the scene. The missing helmet and truncheon, the out-of-place nightcap. Now, we know from Molly here," Holmes smiling at her reassuringly, "that Walters was well aware of the existence of Mynheer van de Groot's diamonds and even knew into which box they had been deposited."

"What!" exclaimed the hotel manager, glaring at the girl. "You told him! You were part of..."

"Now, now, Mr Horrocks," Holmes said soothingly. "Molly believed she was helping the police, not conniving at a robbery. Anyway, keep that fact of Walters's knowledge in mind for the moment, if you please... First, I wish to consider the mysterious Mr Chance."

"Oh yes, Chance. Well, I'm afraid we haven't been able to find hide nor hair of the man." Merivale shook his head. "He has completely disappeared, as if he were never there."

"On the contrary, Inspector, he is here with us now," Holmes said, his words inspiring not a little consternation as we looked about ourselves. Where the devil was the man?

"Mr L. Chance," Holmes continued. "The L standing for Lucky I suppose. A joke name, just like your own, Garrick."

The porter jumped at being so addressed. "What!

"Though in this case, as it turned out, not so lucky?"

I started at the name. Garrick! Of course. The third porter, who had lurked behind the others and said little. I studied him now: an insignificant-looking individual, medium build, fairish colouring, a perfect tabula rasa on which to write any number of characters.

"By God, it's him!" said Mr Horrocks, like me staring at the man. "I didn't recognise the blackguard in that uniform."

"Interesting you should mention his uniform," Holmes said, "because that is also part of the story, which we shall come to in due course. First, what do you have to say for yourself, Garrick?"

"It's all bull. You can't lay this on me, just because... because Horrocks took against me."

"Do you deny that you entered the hotel in the guise of an elderly man, pretended to stow valuables in the strongroom in order to gain legitimate access to that place, and, on the night before last, entered that same strongroom and broke into box number 13, containing the diamonds belonging to Mynheer van de Groot here?"

"Bull," repeated Garrick (or Jessop, as his real name was). "I'd like to see you prove it."

"You will," Holmes replied calmly.

Inspector Merivale stepped forward. "Thank you, Mr Holmes. You have proved me right after all... Frank Jessop," he continued, "I arrest you..."

"Not so fast, Inspector. Do you not think that if Jessop had stolen the diamonds, he'd be long gone? Not still working as a railway porter."

"But you just said..." Inspector Merivale scratched his head in confusion.

"He's here," Holmes said, "because the box he was trying to rob was as empty as his own. Or rather, he found a heap of glass beads which at the time he took to be the real thing."

"What!" the Dutchman cried out. "Glass beads? What are you talking about? Those diamonds were priceless."

"For the theft of which you are about to receive a huge sum in insurance money, while all the time the genuine gems haven't left your hotel room. As you said to me earlier, they are safer there than in the strongroom."

"*Nee*...What I said was, I wished I had kept them in my room, where they would have been safe."

"So Inspector Merivale's man will find nothing during the search he is conducting at this very moment?"

"Of course not." Van de Groot looked furious, a deep flush creeping over his already ruddy complexion.

"We shall see." Holmes tapped those steepled fingers together. "This is what I think happened. Constable Walters passes information to his partner in crime, Garrick, or Jessop here. Remember, Walters investigated those earlier minor robberies, so would have got to know the suspect. Was it he or you, Garrick, who saw the possibilities for something much more ambitious?"

The porter scowled and shook his head.

"Those baubles you found in his drawer, Watson," Holmes said, "quite possibly they indeed form part of the stash Garrick stole, a pay-off to the policeman for turning a blind eye." He turned to Mr Horrocks, who shifted uncomfortably. "It was Walters who persuaded you against having your employee arrested, didn't he, sir? Not the other way round." The day manager nodded, subdued, and Holmes continued. "So Garrick, disguised as Chance, robs the supposed diamonds, which he stows in the nightcap he is wearing during his nocturnal foray. The glue I found on the cap, by the way, Merivale, was nothing to do with Garrick's picture-framing hobby as you surmised, but everything to do with affixing false whiskers." He glanced at the porter, whose head was bowed, and resumed his account. "Garrick thereupon quits the hotel – as a previous employee, he knows how to leave unseen, avoiding the front lobby – and goes to meet with Walters. However, the pair of them soon discover that the gems are worthless bits of glass. They figure out that van de Groot himself is perpetrating a gigantic fraud, and Walters contacts him with a view to blackmail, so that they will at least get something out of the business."

The Dutchman laughed.

"Such fantasies," he said.

Paying him no attention, Holmes continued, "An arrangement was made to meet away from prying eyes on a remote platform at St Pancras at such and such a time to sort out the pay-off. Correct me if I am wrong, Mynheer, but I imagine you arrived early and positioned yourself behind the pillar." Van de Groot glowered and shook his head, muttering under his breath. "Walters comes to meet you while Garrick stands guard in the body of the station to stop anyone else venturing on to the platform. What happened next? Did Walters produce the fake diamonds hidden in the nightcap? I imagine you had a weapon with you already, a gun perhaps or a knife, but instead, took advantage of what was offered, swung the loaded nightcap at Walters, knocking his helmet off, and then used his own truncheon to bludgeon him to death. Tipping out the lumps of glass afterwards, that lay unnoticed until I found them there amid the general filth of the platform," (Nehemiah Wright bristling at the imputation), "though shards remained in the nightcap as myself and Dr Watson here noticed when we examined it. Cool as a cucumber, you then donned the constable's helmet and wiped the truncheon on the nightcap, thereafter strolling out into the station as if a policeman on the beat."

"What the Dickens!" Merivale exclaimed.

"Note his garb, if you please, Inspector. For all the world the blue jacket and silver buttons of the London bobby. No one would have given him a second glance. Except Garrick, of course. But he, only too aware of the attack and frightened near to death, took cover in the anonymity of his own uniform. After all, van de Groot did not know who he was."

Holmes paused. No one said a word now, agog to hear more, while the Dutchman continued to stare at Holmes, a smirk twisting his lips.

"I imagine," Holmes continued, "from the nonchalance with which you took a life, it is not the first murder you have committed, mynheer."

That smirk broadened into a grin that chilled my heart. Then van de Groot started to applaud slowly.

"What a wonderful fairytale, Mr Holmes. You have a great imagination. Only, there is a big flaw in your reasoning." His wolfish grin revealed that twinkling, gold-capped canine. "My supposed fraud depended on me knowing a theft was about to take place. But how could I know?

"He's right there, Holmes," Merivale said. "He's got you."

"Of course," Holmes remarked calmly, "he couldn't have known."

"He showed me the diamonds," Mr Horrocks put in. "They looked real enough to me."

"Yes, indeed," Holmes continued. "I am sure van de Groot made a great point of displaying the diamonds, the real ones, I mean, before substituting them. He also left the key to his strongbox where anyone entering his room could see it. And elsewhere too, I imagine. Beside his dinner plate, perhaps. On the bar?" Van de Groot shook his great head. Holmes addressed him. "Learning of the previous petty thefts, you were quite ready to use that intelligence to stage the disappearance of your diamonds. How surprised and delighted you must have been when Garrick and Walters made that unnecessary."

"I have never in my life," the Dutchman said, rising to his feet, "heard anything so preposterous. So this man is London's great detective is he? Ha! He is a joke. It is all a fancy. He has no proof whatsoever."

"The proof. Ah! I forgot." Holmes reached into his pocket and drew out a large stone, the size of a woman's fist. He held it up to the light while we all gazed upon it as if mesmerised. "Observe the characteristic pink tinge of the stones of the Jagerfontein mine."

Van de Groot let out an angry yelp and tried to grab the stone.

"I should have thought you would be pleased to have it back," Holmes said. "But oh, I forgot, it never left you, did it?"

"*Godverdomme jij!*"

Van de Groot started to reach into his pocket.

"Stop him. He's armed," Holmes shouted.

Inspector Merivale and his constable jumped forward and, as they grabbed the Dutchman, a pistol clattered to the floor.

We stared at it, frozen with shock. Only Holmes remained unruffled.

"But how did you know where to find the diamonds?" Merivale asked. I was wondering the same thing myself.

"Oh, I knew all along," Holmes elongated himself in his chair with that arrogance of his that so often borders on the insufferable. "Well, at least from the moment I spied the harlequin rasbora and cherry barb in their habitat."

"What!"

"The fish tank," I told him.

"What a strange thing to find in a hotel bedroom. Van de Groot told me it came with the room but that was of course rubbish. He requested it and so the hotel provided it."

"We at the Midland Grand are pleased to indulge our guests," Mr Horrocks remarked. "You would not believe what some of them require. Why, on one occasion…"

"Quite," said Holmes. "On viewing it up close, I noticed the floor of the aquarium was covered with gleaming stones and rocks. What a place to hide diamonds, in plain sight. But I must thank Molly for this."

He held up the huge diamond again.

The girl's pale little face lit up.

"I did good, did I, sir?"

"You did indeed. You see," he told the rest of us, "I asked Molly, while cleaning the room, to pick the biggest stone out of the Dutchman's fish tank and bring it to me. And here it is. I imagine by now your constable will have recovered the rest, Inspector."

"He did it all right. He killed Jim. I saw him beat him to death, the animal." Garrick, realising the game was up and, perhaps reckoning after all that his crimes were not very big ones – stealing non-existent gems and attempting to blackmail a murderer – now decided to tell all he knew.

"He didn't need to do it," he went on. "We'd have settled for a pay-off."

"Would you? Would you really?" the Dutchman spat him. "How could I trust you? You miserable little man! Unlucky Chance! Although…" He had the grin of a crocodile, "On the other hand, I suppose you are lucky, in that I didn't find you, too."

Soon enough, an unrepentant van de Groot, still grinning, was led off in chains, to face the justice that would eventually see him go to the gallows for the murder of Walters and, as it emerged, for many other vicious crimes. Garrick, for his part, spent a mere few months in Wormwood Scrubs, a salutary experience which must have caused him to mend his ways, for subsequently, as we learned with amusement, he at last managed to find employment with a provincial theatre company that specialised in knockabout farce. Ironically, he particularly excelled in the role of a foolish policeman.

Young Molly was rewarded for her enterprise. No longer a lowly chambermaid in the Midland Grand Hotel, but nowadays, in a spruce black dress with a white cap and apron, she serves guests in that splendid coffee room. Indeed, I sometimes go there for the pleasure of seeing her so happy and rosy-cheeked. Moreover, van de Groot's insurance company provided a reward in recognition of the exposure of a serious fraud, and from that not inconsiderable sum, Holmes gave a portion to Molly, some of which she used to fix her teeth.

All in all, then, a happy outcome, although the next time I hear the cry, "Doctor, doctor. Is there a doctor here?" I think I may just slip quietly away.

The Other Woman

It was the middle of November, a bright clear morning. Frost flowers overlaid the windows of our first-floor sitting-room, so that the incessant bustle of Baker Street was, for once, hidden from us. I sat happily enough reading a journal, but my companion was sulking, buried in his armchair, and puffing clouds of smoke into the room from his noxious pipe. Holmes was ever thus when he had no case to solve, and experience had taught me it was better to avoid conversation when he was in this mood. Whatever I said would be met either with a disparaging contradiction or with a dismissive silence.

Suddenly Holmes rose from his seat and hastened to the window.

"I thought I heard something," he said.

Not feeling the need to respond, I merely turned the page of my journal.

"Watson!"

"I heard nothing," I replied reluctantly.

"You never do," he remarked with unnecessary asperity. Then, "Damnation upon this frost. One cannot see a thing."

To my astonishment, he took a coin from the pocket of his smoking jacket, blew upon it for some moments, rubbed it between his hands, and then pressed it against the window. After a minute, he removed it. A clear circle had been made on the glass. Holmes peered through it, then withdrew in disgust.

"Nothing!" he said, sinking back into his chair.

I tried not to appear too self-righteous.

However, almost immediately a sharp knock sounded on the front door.

"Aha!" Holmes exclaimed. "I knew it."

He was suddenly energised. Leaning forward, he grasped the arms of his chair. His eyes sparkled, his nostrils trembled. The greyhound I knew so well, ready to burst from the slips.

In no time, heavy steps were heard pounding up the stairs and then, without ceremony, our door burst open. Behind the very large personage intruding on us in this uncustomary manner, Mrs Hudson stood on her tiptoes, peering over his shoulder, and gesturing apologetically, as if to say, I could not stop him.

Attempting to emulate Holmes's deductive powers of observation, I studied the newcomer carefully. Despite his disregard for the conventions of polite society, he looked to be no uncouth denizen of the street, but, by his dress and bearing, a gentleman. Aged about fifty years, with a trimmed grey beard, he was clad in a suit of high quality that, despite being well-cut, only managed partially to conceal the fact that he was overweight to obesity. Just now, in addition, there was a somewhat dishevelled aspect to him, indicative of one who has been so eager to hasten to his destination that he has omitted to check his appearance. His hair, under the homburg he threw off, was unkempt, his coat ill-buttoned. Perspiration coated his face like a layer of grease and an unhealthy flush coloured his complexion. I judged him to be choleric in all senses of the word.

"Mr Holmes," he boomed, striding towards me. "I am at my wit's end. You are my last hope. You must help me."

"I am sorry..." I started to correct his misapprehension as to my identity.

"Do not refuse me, sir," he interrupted, even seizing hold of my hands. "You must hear me out. If it is a question of money, do not doubt that I am prepared..."

Holmes coughed. The man looked round, taken aback. Apparently, he had not noticed my friend, ensconced as he was in his armchair. Holmes now stood up.

"My dear sir, please calm yourself," he said. "Take a chair, will you… It is I who am Sherlock Holmes. This gentleman is my colleague, Dr Watson."

"Oh God help me! I am so bewildered, I must be going mad. Or else everyone else is." The man fell into an upright chair that rather groaned under his corpulence. "Believe me, I don"t know what to do, who else to turn to. You must help me. The world is gone upside down."

He grasped his head in his hands as if to still his fevered brain.

"You have several advantages over us, sir." Holmes's tones were calm, although I sensed the excitement beneath at the prospect of a challenging new case. "In the first place, you now know our names, but we remain ignorant of yours. And secondly, we will not be able to help you unless you tell us exactly what is the matter that has brought you here so precipitously."

"Of course. Of course. I am Montgomery Beresford." Spoken with some pride, and indeed I had heard of him. Head of a merchant bank in the City of London, a man reputedly of astronomical wealth and a ruthless iron will. Something serious indeed must have happened to reduce him to his present state.

The banker paused, as if to let the eminence of his name sink in.

Holmes was unimpressed. After all, he had assisted more illustrious clients than this man in the past.

"I must again request that you explain why you are here, Mr Beresford?" he said. "What problem is exercising you to such an alarming extent?" Holmes regarded the man fixedly, no doubt hoping to hear of some intriguing mystery.

"It is my wife, Veronica. She has disappeared."

Holmes gave a great sigh. A banal enough case, after all.

"Can I suppose," he said languidly, "that your wife is somewhat younger than you?"

"Yes, she is twenty-two."

"And no doubt pretty."

"Very. I should never have chosen to wed a frump."

Holmes sighed again. I could guess what he was thinking: an attractive young woman married to a much older and, to be frank, somewhat unprepossessing man. Wealth or no wealth, she had no doubt had enough of him.

"No, she has not just run off, Mr Holmes," the banker insisted, reading our thoughts, "What happened is much stranger than that. Fantastic, even."

"Go on."

"Veronica is a child in many ways." Mr Beresford shook his head. "Innocent and trusting. At least, so I thought. A girl of simple interests, easily diverted. To be honest, I picked her off the street... Well, not exactly. She was working in the florist shop where I buy my daily buttonhole."

He wore no buttonhole today. Another sign that he had hurried to us without delay.

"A simple soul, do you see. A flower in her own right, ready to be plucked... By me."

It was a strange and not altogether pleasant way to be talking about his wife. I could not help myself from frowning, as did Holmes. The banker pressed on regardless.

"It was a pleasure and challenge for me to lift her out of the gutter, so to speak, and make a lady of her." He sighed. "I judged that I was making headway in that respect, albeit more slowly than I had hoped. However, I liked to relax the strict regime imposed on her from time to time and indulge her little whims."

He paused, shaking his head again.

"The point, please, Mr Beresford."

The banker did not care to be interrupted and continued in a sharper tone. "The point here, Mr Holmes, is that when a circular arrived at the house announcing a forthcoming performance of some kind of a magic show, she pleaded for permission to go to see it, saying it was her favourite entertainment in all the world."

He cast brooding eyes upon us.

"Of course, such a spectacle would not be to my taste at all, and I tried to argue her out of it, but you know the pretty wiles women use." He looked to us for concurrence. "Soft words, tears, promises, accusations…" He mimicked a foolish girlish voice: " 'Oh, I get so lonely, Monty, without you.' " Adding somewhat dismissively, "Monty being her pet name for me, do you see… Of course, it is true gentlemen," he continued, "that I am a very busy man, and that she has to spend much time sequestered in the house."

We nodded to express understanding, although I could not but recall that my dear Mary had been well able to find plenty to occupy herself in my absence. Oh, how I missed her, dead far too young.

"And so," the banker was saying, "Last eve I finally agreed to take her to the show… Damnation take it!" he exclaimed, clenching a fat fist and hitting it off the arm of his chair. "If only I had refused."

The theatre in question turned out to be a seedy enough establishment in a less than salubrious part of town.

"I was in favour of turning back, but Veronica begged me. "Now we are here, Monty, dear," she said, "we might as well go in." So we did. An unforgiveable weakness I shall regret for the rest of my life." To our consternation, he began hitting himself repeatedly on the forehead with that same clenched fist.

"My dear sir…" Holmes began. Beresford took a deep breath to recover himself, and continued his account.

"The show was as tawdry as I had expected and attended by a very low class of patron. All sorts of vulgar acts of the music hall variety. The worst was the magician, a sleazy individual, by his name and execrable accent some sort of an Italian, whose tricks were crude and obvious." He shook his head. "An out-and-out scapegrace, gentleman, who would be abhorred in polite circles."

Veronica, however, according to her husband, was enchanted, applauding every silly sleight of hand and illusion.

Then, at a certain point, the magician invited a member of the audience to come up and assist him.

"The fellow was requesting *"una bella donna"* and had the cheek to look quite pointedly at Veronica. Well, Mr Holmes, before I could stop her, she had jumped to her feet, rushed forward and climbed on to the stage. I was both flabbergasted and shocked. The ruffians in the audience laughing and pointing at my wife in the most indecorous way. *My* wife!"

He spluttered angrily at the memory.

"What happened next?" Holmes asked.

"The fellow got her to go into some sort of upright box. A vanishing cabinet, as I understand it is called."

"And she vanished."

"Indeed, she did." Mr Beresford paused, looking at us significantly.

"Yet," Holmes rejoined, "as I recall from visits to such spectacles myself – and Watson will confirm this, for he has been present as well – after the oohs and aahs of amazement have died down, the magician will close the door of the cabinet again, before reopening it, whereupon the disappeared person will return. Did this not happen in your case, Mr Beresford?"

"Oh, the fellow closed the door all right, waved his wand and babbled some incomprehensible nonsense before finally reopening the door with a flourish. And there she stood."

Holmes frowned. "I don't quite understand," he said.

"A woman stood there, dressed as my wife and very like. But it was not Veronica."

For once Holmes, no less than I, was rendered speechless.

"Not her?" he said at last.

"I can assure you of that, Mr Holmes. I know my own wife."

A broad smile lit up Holmes's face.

"How wonderful!" he said.

Mr Beresford was less than impressed with this response.

"I can assure you, Mr Holmes," he replied coldly, "that it was not wonderful at all. It was frightful, particularly since no one else seemed to notice the difference. Not the audience, not the magician, even when I seized the fellow by the scruff of his neck and gave him a good shaking."

"Apologies, Mr Beresford. I meant no belittlement of the seriousness of the matter," Holmes said ruefully. "I used the word in its original sense of inspiring wonder. You have presented us here with a most intriguing conundrum."

The other nodded, somewhat appeased.

"Of course, I have to ask again," Holmes continued, "if you are absolutely sure that the person who emerged from the box was not Veronica."

"How many times must I say it? She bore a close resemblance to my wife, though without Veronica's bloom, if I might say so, or the refinement I have been so assiduous in cultivating. This person wore identical clothes and jewellery, dressed her hair in the same way, and yet without a scintilla of a doubt, it was not she."

Holmes rubbed his hands together. This was exactly the sort of mystery he had been hoping for. There was a long, thoughtful pause.

"We can rule out magic, I suppose?" I asked to break the silence. Not because I believed it myself, but because heretofore I had felt somewhat excluded from the interchange. The other two looked at me with disdain, and I smiled shamefacedly.

"Of course, it could not be," I mumbled.

Another explanation, which I had not been inclined to voice, was that Mr Beresford was indeed mad, or at least mistaken for some deeper personal reason. Could it be that subconsciously he wanted rid of the wife to whom he professed such attachment? A wife who had turned out to be a disappointment to him? I had recently become aware, through my reading, of the most interesting notions of Herr Sigmund Freud regarding displacement. Perhaps Mr Beresford had projected the image of a stranger on to his wife because he quite literally felt estranged from her. I wondered what Holmes would make of my theory.

He, meanwhile, was avidly questioning our visitor.

"How many minutes passed between Mrs Beresford entering the box and the emergence of this other woman?"

"Long enough, I suppose…"

"Long enough for someone to change clothes with your wife?"

The man looked exasperated.

"I cannot say exactly how long it was. I was beside myself, Mr Holmes. Thinking of how strongly I would chide her on her return for making a fool out of me."

He clenched his fist again, a gesture not wasted on Holmes.

"I have to ask, Mr Beresford," Holmes asked, "is there any reason why your wife might wish to disappear?"

Again the man looked as if he might explode.

"None! After all I have done for her. She has been abducted. That's the only possible explanation."

"Yet you have not received a ransom demand,"

"Not yet."

"Hmm," Holmes said. "Well, who do you think this woman is, if not your wife?"

The man sighed deeply.

"I have no idea except that she has the audacity to claim to be Veronica. As I said, none of the audience believed me. Nor did the policeman who came on the scene while I was… I was questioning the magician."

Apparently, it was only after Mr Beresford had revealed his identity to the constable that he avoided being arrested for affray.

"The Italian chappie was making an enormous fuss about nothing. I had hardly touched him. In fact, I am sure that, given a little while longer, I could have got him to tell me exactly what had happened. Only the woman who was pretending to be my wife whispered something to the constable, presumably spinning some yarn about my state of mind, for they all started looking at me with pity as if I was stark staring mad… The very way you are looking at me now, Doctor."

He stared balefully at me. Holmes often tells me that my face is an open book.

He now murmured in soothing tones, "Not at all, my dear fellow. What you say might seem fantastic now, but I can think of at least three rational explanations for what has happened here. Abduction is certainly one possibility. But," he admonished before the man could interrupt him, "before I elaborate, I should like to visit the theatre to talk to the magician, and also to confront the woman in question. Where is she now?"

"In order to avoid a scandal, I took her home with me last night. But the situation is intolerable. It cannot be allowed to continue, Mr Holmes."

"Clearly not…"

"Thank you so much for believing me. It is a great relief."

Holmes gave an enigmatic smile. I knew that he would not fully believe this extraordinary tale, until he had examined all the evidence for himself.

"I imagine you have many servants, Mr Beresford," he said. "How did they react when you arrived home?"

"The woman would only have been seen by the butler who opened the door for us. Baines is old and short-sighted, so would hardly have noticed anything was amiss. In any case, she hurried up to her room, her face half concealed by a scarf, claiming a throbbing headache."

Holmes held up a forefinger. "She knew the way, then."

For the first time, Mr Beresford was silenced.

"My God!" he said at last, clutching his head. "Am I mad after all?"

"Do not distress yourself, sir. I am sure you are as sane as Watson here." Holmes's lips curled in a not completely pleasant smile. "Again, I can think of good reasons why the woman in question might be aware of the layout of the house."

"Was she not at least attended by her maid?" I asked.

Holmes looked at me for once with appreciation.

"A good point, Watson."

"No," Mr Beresford replied. "She said that she was far too upset to see anyone."

"Interesting and telling. Clearly, she wished for no one to regard her too closely."

Or, on the other hand, I thought to myself, she was utterly distraught at the unreasonable behaviour of her husband.

"I am inclined," Holmes stated, making a steeple of his fingers, "first to visit the theatre and interview this magician…. What is his name?"

Mr Beresford pulled a paper from his pocket.

"This was the circular that was delivered to the house," he said.

"Maggiorino the Magnificent!" Holmes read aloud, chuckling. "Clearly the fellow doesn't suffer from false modesty."

"He hardly lives up to the title. A seedy little man in grubby velvet," the banker remarked scornfully, adding, "Do you wish for me to accompany you to the theatre? I have to say, I should rather not after last night."

"No," Holmes replied. "Watson and I will go. You will be better off staying at home, keeping a watchful eye on this supposed imposter."

Once more, Mr Beresford reared up. He really had a very short fuse.

"There is nothing supposed about it, Holmes," he said.

"Well, well. Let us trust we can get to the bottom of things, and quickly."

The establishment in question, Jabot's Music Hall, was situated in Shoreditch, a squalid and overcrowded area of the city, though also home to many theatres and other places of entertainment, catering to the largely working-class inhabitants of the locality as well as to members of the upper classes wishing to "slum" it, as the saying goes. I fully comprehended Montgomery Beresford's distaste at having to visit such a place.

Jabot's presented a run-down exterior, its peeling plasterwork resembling some chronic skin condition, a lantern with a broken glass pane hanging over the entranceway. The dilapidation persisted to the inside, although I could imagine that, by night, the faded and tattered red velvet of the upholstery, the dust on the curtains, the filth on the floor, would be tempered by the soft effect of the gaslights.

We were soon accosted by a stout red-headed, red-faced individual, pulling a jacket over his less than scrupulously clean shirt even as he hurried towards us. This, as it turned out, was Jabot himself. He muttered cryptically something about "'avin' to see to the dogs" (it turned out later that he had been referring to one of the regular acts, Miss Dimples and her performing poodles. The said Miss Dimples having been laid low by an attack of the vapours, Jabot had to feed the dogs and look after their animal needs), before asking us our business.

"Maggiorino, is it. "E's gorn."

"Already?" Holmes asked.

"Up and left first thing. After that unpleasantness last night, see. "E got on 'is 'igh 'orse and legged it."

"Do you know where he's gone?"

Jabot spat on the floor.

"Don't know and don't care. Bringin' a mutton shunter to the premises, gives it a bad name."

"The constable, you mean." Holmes was all sympathy. "Yes, I heard. What exactly happened here?"

"'Oo wants ter know?"

The man was suddenly suspicious.

"This is Dr Watson," my companion replied amiably, "and I am Sherlock Holmes, acting on behalf of the gentleman present here last evening, who, as I understand it, had some sort of altercation with Signor Maggiorino."

Whether it was this explanation that had the desired effect or perhaps it was the production of a golden guinea, but Jabot suddenly became quite overly loquacious.

"Sherlock 'Olmes, is it. I 'eard o' you, guvnor. Often wondered if you'd be up to doin' a turn "ere."

Holmes burst out laughing.

"Doing what, exactly?"

"Oh, I 'eard 'ow you can read people like a book from appearances alone... Go on, then, tell me about me."

"I hardly think..."

"Go on. For a larf. Then I'll tell you what you want to know."

Holmes sighed, and studied the man from head to toe, turning him about in a theatrical way that I had never seen him employ in the past.

"Well," he said finally, "I hope you enjoyed your breakfast of ham and fried eggs, washed down with a goodly glass of..." he sniffed... "small beer." Judged perhaps from certain fresh stains on the man's jacket. "You don't live here on the premises, for your boots and trousers display recent signs of the sticky yellow mud found on the banks of the Thames, so I imagine that your abode, though not far, is situated somewhere between Tower Bridge and Limehouse. From your distinctive gait, I deduce that you have spent time at sea, and from your complexion – the skin of persons of red-hair suffering unduly from exposure to the sun – that you have in the past travelled to southern climes. The tattoo on your arm, that I noticed before you put on your jacket, looked to be the work of a Pacific islander, perhaps someone from Tahiti?"

Jabot's mouth hung open, displaying an unfortunate absence of healthy teeth. "Astonishin'!" he exclaimed. "Correct in every pertikular, Mr 'Olmes. If you ever wanted a turn in Jabot's, just say the word. I can see the poster now…" He looked dreamily into the distance.

"Thank you," Holmes interrupted the revery. "I am most honoured by your offer, Mr Jabot, although I am far too busy to consider it at present… But speaking of the poster, how is it that my client received a circular regarding your theatre at his house in Hampstead, so far distant from here?"

The man looked puzzled.

"Can't answer that one. We don't post out nothink like that, guvnor. Only stick a few notices up in the locality. People 'ere abouts knows we give a good show."

"Hmm. Most enlightening." Holmes nodded thoughtfully. "Well, perhaps you will be so good as to describe what happened last eve, as you recollect it."

The man scrunched up his face in an attempt to remember.

"Maggi's act was goin' on as usual," he said finally. "Then "e called for some person in the audience to join 'im on stage…"

" *Una bella donna,* as I understand it. A beautiful woman. This, I take it, was his usual practice?"

"Not at all, Mr 'Olmes. But see, the assistant what usually done it, she took poorly of a sudden so 'e 'ad to hextemporise."

"I see."

" 'E asked for the *bella donna* coz the audience likes to see a pretty girl on stage. And this one what come up last eve, a right basket of oranges, she were."

He grinned appreciatively at the memory.

"And when she reemerged, did she look anyway different to you?"

Jabot scratched his head.

"See, that's what the gent claimed. To me, at first anyway, she looked hexactly the same."

"At first?"

" 'Onestly, guvnor, I couldn't say she looked different in any way, but then I and't 'ad a good dekko before... But ask yourself, "ow could she not be the same one what went in?"

"Magic?"

I looked sharply at Holmes, for stealing my line.

Jabot wheezed a laugh. "Yeah, right on, guvnor."

"But now you say you have doubts it was indeed the same woman?"

"Only coz the gent was so very sure of 'isself."

"Tell me, where exactly were you standing during the performance?"

Jabot pointed to the side of the stage. "Just there, behind the curtain, like what I always do."

"So if some exchange had taken place at the back of the stage, you wouldn't have seen it."

"It wouldn't 'ave 'appened like that anyway. The lady would 'ave gone down under the stage on a lift, and then be brought up again minutes later."

"I see. Can you show us?"

Jabot led the way up on to the stage and indicated the position of a trapdoor, about three feet square. He explained how the cabinet would have been neatly positioned over this and a lad below the stage would, at a given moment, set in motion the lift mechanism to lower the volunteer out of sight of the audience, raising her again when required.

"So if any exchange were effected, this lad would have known about it."

"You'd think so, wouldn't you, but, see, Tommy's not the sharpest knife in the box. Just shook "is 'ead when I asked. Said 'e didn't see nothink."

"May I speak to him anyway?"

" 'E ain't 'ere just now. See, 'e only comes in for the show."

Holmes frowned.

"Curiouser and curiouser," I ventured.

"Not curious at all, Watson," Holmes retorted, though not unkindly. "We are not in Wonderland now. If indeed there has been a switch, then the whole thing must have been carefully planned. Let us go and speak to the person claiming to be Mr Beresford's wife."

"We all thought the gent 'ad gone off 'is rocker," Jabot put in. "Then, when 'e started with the fisticuffs it stopped being a joke. No wonder poor Dimples took bad. See, she was due on after."

"Was she, indeed? Might I have a word. Perhaps she saw something useful."

Jabot shook his head. "Can't see 'er agreein' to that, but I'll ask."

Miss Dimples, as it turned out, did not only agree, but proved utterly thrilled to meet the great detective, Sherlock Holmes, and could not stop giggling girlishly and fluttering her eyelashes at him. Indeed, the very sight of him brought about a miraculous recovery from her purported attack of the vapours, a condition, incidentally, absent from any of my medical textbooks.

We had found her reclining backstage on a dingy ottoman, surrounded by her performing poodles – six absurdly clipped white canines – one tiny white-gloved hand pressed over her eyes.

No, she uttered in a faint voice, she could not possibly face visitors. However, after I identified myself as a doctor, the same little hand beckoned me over. A perilous enterprise, for the dogs, small as they were, stood guard over their mistress, and started yapping so aggressively that I quite feared for my ankles. However, in a more commanding voice than before, she told them to sit and stay, which they obediently did, all in a row, though continuing to eye me with suspicion and malice.

She made room for me on the edge of the ottoman. I rather reluctantly perched there and asked what was the matter.

From a distance I had taken Miss Dimples, in her frilly and beribboned white dress, ivory complexion, rosy cheeks and golden curls, for a very young woman. But now I discovered her, on the contrary, to be well advanced in years, heavily powdered and rouged, and the curls, quite obviously, a wig. Speaking in the false accents of one attempting to show herself better bred than she was, she explained the source of her malaise, a weakness caused by shock at the sight of a huge gorilla of a man attacking poor little Maggi.

"With may overly sensitive nature, doctor, Ay 'ave not been able to exercise the image from may mind. Good 'eavens, would the creature turn on me next? Ay was quate terrified."

I assured her in soothing tones that we had come to find out exactly what had happened, and were hoping that she, as an invaluable witness, might be able to help us.

"Ay fear not, doctor," she replied. "Ay was quate blinded by terror."

"Now, now, Dimples," Jabot said. " 'Ere"s Mr Sherlock 'Olmes come all the way from Baker Street to talk to you…"

"Sherlock 'Olmes," Miss Dimples sat up abruptly, the poodles cocking their heads expectantly, pompom tails hitting the floor in counterpoint. "Never Mr Sherlock 'Olmes, the famous detective?"

"None other, madam," Holmes replied, stepping forward and holding out his hand.

The dame seized it and covered it with kisses, much to my amusement and my friend's discomfiture.

"Oh, Mr 'Olmes," she said, smiling broadly – and one of her cheeks indeed dimpled, "what a honour."

He somewhat warily took my vacated seat beside her.

"Now Miss…er… Dimples, I am sure, if you put your mind to it, a clever and observant lady like yourself will be able to recollect something useful."

She gazed up at him soulfully, one of her gloved claws still clutching his hand.

"Well…" she said. "That's as maybe."

"Good. Now, why don't you lie back down, close your eyes and imagine that you are standing behind the curtains," he urged, talking as if to a child.

Dutifully, she did as she was told.

"The magician has just invited someone from the audience to join him on the stage," Holmes continued.

"Yes, that were different. Usually 'e'd use 'is assistant. She weren't on that night for some reason."

"So I understand… In your opinion, did he single out one particular lady?"

Miss Dimples frowned in an effort at remembering. She shook her head.

""E said something in "is own lingo, but…"

"*Una bella donna…*" Holmes prompted.

"That's it…Yes… But Ay don't think 'e looked nowhere speshal. In any case, with them footlights, you know, it's 'ard to see into the audience."

"Of course… So Mrs Beresford…"

" 'Oo?"

"The lady in question. She comes on to the stage."

"Gawd bless 'er. She were that excited. Laughin' and smilin', she were."

"Good. Well done. So then she entered the box."

"Maggi told 'er not to be afraid when she disappeared."

"I see."

"Ay 'eard 'im add that 'e would make sure she were safe."

"Not that she got back safely?"

"No, Mr 'Olmes, but, being a foreign gent, poor little Maggi's command of the English language leaves much to be desired."

She clearly assumed her own command of it was flawless.

"Hmm," Holmes said. "What next?"

"Well, she disappeared, didn't she." Miss Dimples opened her eyes and looked at Jabot. "Can ay say 'ow, Alf?"

He nodded.

"I showed the gents already," he replied.

"Right you are... So she went down as always and, as far as Ay knew, she come up again. Like what always 'appens."

"Can I stop you there for a moment, madam?" Holmes said. "How long was she under the stage?"

"Oh, quate some time. You see, Maggi likes to draw things out. So 'e opens the door and if she ain't there, 'e pretends surprise, closes it and waves 'is wand some more. 'E's a real showman is Maggi. Anyway, after she come back for real, next thing, that 'orrid man comes rushing on the stage and starts knocking poor Maggi about while the lady tries to calm 'im. You stepped up then and pulled him orf, Alf, didn't you. So very brave."

Holmes smiled at her. "Vividly described, madam... Now, I can tell by looking at you that you are a lady of fashion." She giggled. "Think hard. Was there anything at all different about the lady's appearance when she returned?"

Miss Dimples closed her eyes again and kept them closed for so long that I started wondering if she had fallen asleep.

" 'Er bonnet," she said at last.

"Yes?" Holmes leaned forward.

"It was tilted to one side when she went down. When she come up again, it was tilted to the other." She opened her eyes, making them big. "Is that what you want to 'ear, Mr 'Olmes?"

"If that is what you saw," he replied dryly.

"Ay think so..." She gave a little frown. "Oh, Ay don't know. Ay can't be sure... She looked just the same to me." Miss Dimples lowered her voice. "If you ask me, Ay think 'er hubby was jealous that Maggi 'ad laid 'is 'ands upon 'er."

Holmes raised his eyebrows.

"Laid hands how?"

"Oh, just took 'er "and to 'elp her down from the box. Though 'e 'eld on, ay thought a little too long. But then, Maggi likes all the pretty ladies." She smirked and fluffed up her fake curls. "The naughty man. Eyetalian, don't you know. Didn't Ay 'ave to tell 'im over and over, Alf, Miss Dimples ain't that sort of a girl?"

She gave Holmes a nudge, and while he recoiled and hastily stood up, Jabot remained expressionless.

"Thank you, madam," my friend said. "You have been most helpful."

" 'Ave Ay?" The dimple twinkled in her faded cheek. " 'Ave Ay, Mr 'Olmes? Oh, come and see the show, do. And visit me in may dressing room after. May un-dressing room, I should say." She winked suggestively.

"What an absolute horror!" I exclaimed as we made our way out of the theatre. "I think she would have gobbled you up if she could."

"I rather feared the same thing myself," Holmes replied ruefully. "At least she told us something useful."

"Did she?"

"Seeing nothing amiss is good negative information."

"The bonnet business…"

"Made up, probably. She wanted to tell me something and it was all she could think of. However, maybe it was true. If so…" He knitted his brows in thought.

"There's the hand-holding," I continued, adding with a grin. "The magician's I mean. Not Miss Dimples's."

Holmes glared at me. "Please don't remind me, Watson. This is not an occasion for frivolity."

"I was just wondering, could Mrs Beresford have run off with Maggiorino?"

"It seems most unlikely from what we have heard of the man. And how would they have had a prior occasion to meet? It sounds as if Mr Beresford keeps his wife well tucked away."

I then proceeded to describe my own theory as to what might have happened.

"Displacement..?"

"Herr Freud is most convincing on the subject."

"I know that, Watson. I have, of course, read his paper for myself... Well, it's a theory. Let us see what happens when we meet the lady, whoever she is."

A cab carried us all the way across town to the wealthy suburb of Hampstead, where Mr Beresford's elegantly white plastered house stood in a street of similar dwellings. An aged and bent individual, attired in the neat black attire of a butler, opened the door to us. This must be Baines. He was clearly expecting us, for he admitted us readily, showing us into an empty salon, and requesting us to wait there.

Holmes prowled the room which was decorated, to my eyes, in an impeccable, if somewhat impersonal style, as if a professional decorator, rather than the residents, had been responsible for the furnishings. A piano stood in one corner, its lid open and a set of exercises by Herr Czerny on the music shelf. I imagined the bored wife sitting before it, reluctantly picking out notes for a husband who wished his flower girl wife to become accomplished. On a wall nearby, hung a large portrait of a very pretty young woman, presumably the self-same Mrs Beresford. Holmes stood in front of this image for a good while, as if imprinting it on his mind.

We were left waiting at least fifteen minutes by the ormolu clock on the mantelpiece. I supposed the lady was unwilling to descend and submit to scrutiny, perhaps from fear of being revealed as an imposter, perhaps bitterly offended that her husband should even suggest such a thing.

At last, the door opened and a slight young woman entered, the banker at her heels. It proved impossible to see her face, however, hidden as it was by a heavy veil. In a low and melodious voice, she explained, that she was suffering from a bad headache and could not tolerate bright lights.

"But madam," Holmes replied, "your husband has boasted so much of your beauty that we should be sorely disappointed not to witness it for ourselves, even for a brief moment. Do not be cruel, I implore you. Lift the veil, so that we can gaze upon you."

I should add here that the lady was so far not aware of our true identities. Mr Beresford had introduced us as colleagues, visiting on business, who had expressed a burning wish to meet his wife.

She reflected on Holmes's words for a few moments. Then she raised her veil. Because she was standing in front of the portrait of Mr Beresford's wife, it was a simple matter to make the comparison. The resemblance was striking, even if the image in the painting showed a young woman happy and relaxed, her cheeks rosy, her eyes bright, while the person before us looked strained and pale, a difference explained easily enough by her headache, not to mention her husband's rejection of her. I had not the slightest doubt that this was Veronica, the true wife of Montgomery Beresford, Herr Freud's theory becoming ever more likely as an explanation of what had transpired.

I looked across at Holmes, who also, frowning, was evidently comparing the woman in front of us with the portrait. Surely he would come to the same conclusions as myself.

He spoke at last.

"Tell me, madam," he asked in a soft voice, "where is your sister?"

The woman gasped and let the veil fall over her face once more.

"What sister?" Mr Beresford exclaimed. "My wife doesn't have a sister."

"So you agree, then, that this woman is your wife."

117

"Not at all." An angry flush mounted to the man's cheeks. "I don't know what rubbish you are talking. You say Veronica has a sister. Why? To what end?"

Holmes smiled.

"You claim, sir, that this is not your wife. However, you cannot deny that an extraordinary resemblance exists between her and the portrait of Mrs Beresford. If she isn't your wife, then she must be a very close relative, a sister in fact."

The banker was beside himself with fury.

"How many times must I repeat that my wife has no sister. I would know of it, were it true..." He banged a fist on the top of the piano, forcing out a groan of protest from the instrument. "The devil take you, Holmes! You are like all the others, after all, trying to make me out a liar or a madman."

"Holmes, Montgomery!" the young woman exclaimed, clearly shocked. "You have brought Sherlock Holmes here to question me?"

The man, ignoring her outburst, was pacing about the room liked a caged animal, all but foaming at the mouth. The high colour had risen to his cheeks again, rendering them more purple than red. I quite feared he might explode.

Suddenly he picked up a vase and threw it at the portrait. It smashed against the canvas and, falling to the ground, shattered into pieces. The young woman flinched as if she herself had been hit, while even Holmes was shocked into silence, I reflecting that if Beresford were not a madman, then he was doing a very good job of imitating one.

The banker spun around, strode over to my friend and would, I reckon, have seized him by the lapels of his jacket, had not Holmes, an expert in the art of baritsu, raised his fists. Beresford then collected himself to some extent, and continued in quieter tones, "I invited you here, Holmes," he said, "because I expected you to clear up the mystery. Instead, you have started prattling on about a non-existent sister. I don't claim to know who this woman is..."

"Precisely," Holmes interrupted him. "So instead of "prattling" your own denials, please let me do my work and interview this person, whoever she is, to get at last to the truth."

Mr Beresford shrank back, as much as a man of his height and girth could manage.

"Go on then," he said begrudgingly.

Holmes turned back to the young woman.

"I repeat, madam," he said softly, "where is your sister?"

"I assure you, sir…" she started to reply in a trembling voice.

"No," Holmes interrupted. "No more lies, if you please."

The woman stood silent for a while.

"Very well," she said at last, her voice almost inaudible. "It will make no difference now, anyway. Veronica is long gone from this vile marriage, from this cruel man. By now, she is far from here in a place where he will never find her."

"Aha! The truth at last." Mr Beresford swung around. "I knew it! So Veronica's run off with one of her many lovers, has she? Fool that I was, I should have known better than to try and force a rose out of a ditchweed." The man's face having become deformed into a mask of hate, far from that of the respectable banker the world knew. With a sudden rush, he launched himself upon the young woman. "You will tell me, miss, where she is right now, or it will be the worse for you."

Holmes and I managed to pull him away with some difficulty, the man displaying almost superhuman strength.

"This will not do, Mr Beresford," Holmes told him. "If you wife had a good reason to disappear, I need to hear it. Violence has no place here."

"Thank you, Mr Holmes," the woman said with dignity. "Yes, indeed. I am, as you have guessed, the sister of poor Veronica, her twin in fact. My name is Madeleine Swann. She, having all too soon discovered the truly monstrous nature of her husband, kept my existence from him, for my own safety. Not that he showed any interest in her family."

"Why should I bother with low-lifes?" the man muttered. "Anyway, Veronica said she was an orphan."

"That is true, "Miss Swann continued sadly. "Both our parents are dead."

"You have accused this man of cruelty towards your sister. With justification, I trust," Holmes remarked. I wondered how he could doubt it, having just witnessed the man"s intemperate behaviour.

"If you had not come here today, Mr Holmes," she replied, "there is no doubt that he would have beaten me black and blue as he did my sister so very often."

"Is it true?" Holmes turned to the banker. "You beat your wife."

The man shrugged his shoulders. "Fuss and bother over nothing. I laid no hand upon her unless she was asking for it. The girl is obstinate, you know. She does not seem to comprehend that a wife's duty is to obey her husband in all things, at all times. The result, I suppose of ill-breeding and bad example."

Holmes looked at me gravely.

"You who have been married, Watson, what do you say to that? Do you agree with Mr Beresford?"

My beloved Mary had been dead for over a year, but my heart was still utterly broken.

"Not at all. I respected my wife as an independent individual. We were best friends, partners in life."

The banker sneered.

"Words of someone who is not a real man. A foolish weakling."

"If you like," I replied amiably. "But you know, I prefer to be considered that. I would never have raised a hand against Mary."

The banker shook his head, a mocking expression on his face.

"But why, Miss Swann," Holmes continued, "did you take your sister's place in such a dramatic fashion? Why did she not just escape when out of sight under the stage?"

"He would have gone after her immediately. She would not even have had time to leave the theatre. You should know that her husband is absurdly jealous and guards her like a prisoner, with the connivance of all but one of his servants, who agreed to carry notes between us."

"Who? Which one?" Mr Beresford struggled to free himself from our grip. "It's Nancy, isn't it, the little traitress. I shall dismiss her instantly without a reference."

Of course, he would.

"You will find that she is already gone," Miss Swann continued with dignity. "Nancy too is better off out of this place." She turned to Holmes, "My poor sister was never permitted to leave the house without an escort, so it was lucky for us if it was Nancy's turn, because then we could grab a brief meeting. It was on one of these expeditions, that we devised the plan for Veronica's escape."

"What if Beresford had refused to take her to the theatre?" I asked.

"It was only with the greatest difficulty that my sister managed to persuade him," she replied. "How she debased herself in the attempt to win him over!" She glanced at the simmering banker in distaste. "What he made her do, I'd be ashamed to relate…" Verily the man was a monster. "We were hoping," she continued, "that he would fail to notice the switch at once, since we are almost identical. Alas…"

"As if I cannot recognise my own wife," the banker growled. "As for my practice of keeping your errant sister under my thumb, miss, it has been shown to be clearly justified by what has happened."

"But the theatre, the magic show?" Holmes asked. "Why that?"

"Oh, didn't I say. Apologies. I am Maggiorino's assistant. Usually, I am on stage with him, but to effect the switch, I had to tell Jabot I was taken poorly."

"Did no one, Jabot himself for instance, notice your extraordinary likeness to your sister?" I asked.

"Stage make-up and a wig change my appearance considerably. And I do not usually present myself as a lady."

"I suppose you persuaded Maggiorino to go along with the substitution," Holmes said.

"Yes, but he didn't know why. I told him that it was a practical joke."

"A practical joke!" The enraged banker once more tried to free himself from our grasp, but we held him firm. "I wish I had killed the snivelling little trickster while I had the chance. And when I get my hands on the ungrateful slut I took into my house for a wife, it will be all the worse for her..." He reared up. "I hereby charge you, Sherlock Holmes, to bring my wife back to her lawful place."

Holmes shook his head, which exasperated the man even more.

"If it is a question of money, man, the sky is the limit," Beresford bellowed.

"It may well be," Holmes replied, "but no amount of money would persuade me to force any woman to live in a state of fear and violence. I wish Veronica a long and happy life far from you, sir. Come Miss Swann. Your work here is finished. Ours also."

Leaving the wretched banker grinding his teeth, he offered the lady his arm, which she took gratefully, and together we left that splendid, heartless house.

Looking back at it, I remarked, "It is so true that money doesn't buy happiness."

"Thank you, Watson," Holmes replied drily. "Ever ready with an original thought..." He addressed his companion, "So what will you do now, Miss Swann? Continue to work with Maggiorino the Magnificent?"

"Maybe," she replied smiling. "Or maybe I will join my sister and Nancy, our faithful friend, wherever they are..."

We were walking down the high street and soon reached a little tea shop.

"Before we go our separate ways," Holmes remarked, as if the notion had suddenly taken him. "Let us go in here and share a refreshing pot of Darjeeling. Perhaps I can press a cake upon you, Miss Swann."

I could not say which one of us was the more surprised, the lady or myself, but we followed Holmes into the shop. With all appearance of satisfaction, he helped her into a seat at a small round table before settling himself into another, I did likewise.

"Well," my friend said. "This is all very charming. Do you not agree?"

A white linen tablecloth and napkins, chintz curtains and cream cakes were hardly objects I had deemed close to Holmes's heart. He was up to something.

It was while we were sipping the tea and Miss Swann and I were preparing to consume our Victoria buns (Holmes eating nothing), that he sat back.

"You are a very clever young woman indeed, Miss Swann."

She looked up at him innocently. "Am I?"

"You thought you could fool everyone, even Sherlock Holmes."

"What do you mean?"

"Spin a yarn, no matter how far-fetched, with sufficient confidence, and people will believe it?"

She neatly cut her bun in quarters.

"I still do not know to what you are referring."

"Who is this person, Watson?"

"Why, she is Madeleine Swann, twin sister to Veronica Beresford." I was bemused at the question. Had he himself not got her to admit her identity.

He smiled and shook his head.

"She isn't?" I asked.

"This chit of a girl has skilfully performed what I think might be termed "a double bluff". While insisting she was Veronica, by using various tricks and devices she managed to convince her husband,

and then even you that she was an imposter. The real Veronica was long gone. But, in fact, she sits before us now. Am I not right, Mrs Beresford?"

She stared at him in silence.

"Oh, do not worry," Holmes continued. "I have no intention, as I already informed your husband, of forcing you to return to him. Once I realised what kind of a man he really was, I was content to connive at your deception of him."

"How did you know?" she asked. "And when?"

"Apart from the sheer preposterousness of the tale, do you mean? Apart from the unlikelihood that, had Veronica a sister, her husband would not have known it, despite what you tried to suggest? I knew it when I viewed you before the portrait."

"But Holmes," I said, "they were supposedly identical twins."

"There is no such thing," he replied. "There will always be little differences. However, in this case there were none at all. It would be beyond belief that the little mole above Veronica's eyebrow, as depicted in the portrait, would be exactly replicated in her twin, and yet that is what she would have us believe."

Miss Swann's, or rather Mrs Beresford's hand strayed to the spot.

"You must be applauded, as I have said, at managing to change your appearance and bearing so subtly between going into the box and emerging from it."

"I did not know if it would work," she said finally. "But I was desperate to escape before he killed me. I was sure he would eventually, you know, in one of his rages. My accusations against him would never be believed. He is powerful, with influential connections, while I am friendless and alone, apart from dear Nancy, of course."

"No doubt he chose you for that very reason, hoping to mould you into the willing little slave he wanted."

She nodded. "But I proved stubborn and unamenable, which he loathed."

"But how," I asked, "did you happen to visit the theatre on the very night when Maggiorino's assistant was unable to perform? Surely you could not have foreseen that?"

"Oh, that was the easy part, Doctor. You see, it is Nancy's sister, Madeleine, who is the magician's assistant. That is what gave us the idea in the first place… And Madeleine proved only too happy to accommodate us."

She laughed.

"So now, gentlemen, I am free of that monster, for ever. With the money from the pawning of the jewellery I have managed to bring out with me, my faithful Nancy and I shall emigrate to America and start a new life there."

Upon which final note, she popped a small piece of bun into her mouth. "Delicious," she said.

The Adventure of the Old Russian Woman

"Whatever do you ladies think you're doing?"

It was past twelve noon of a crisp winter's day. I had just returned to Baker Street from an extended constitutional stroll around the Regent's Park to work up an appetite for luncheon, only to find Mrs Hudson and her two maidservants, Clara and Phoebe, far from the kitchen where I had assumed they would be busy preparing a delicious meal, sitting instead on the stairs leading up to Holmes's and my rooms. This astonishing sight was followed by Mrs Hudson placing a finger on her lips, to hush further conversation. She gave a little jerk of her head, calling my attention to what could be heard from above. It was the most glorious violin music imaginable.

Holmes must have been practising secretly, was my first thought, since never in my experience had he played so melodically. Far from it, indeed. I could understand why our landlady and her maids were entranced. I paused with them to listen.

Brahms, I thought to myself, or perhaps Schumann. When the piece finally came to an end, I bounded up the stairs to congratulate my friend, only to discover that it was not he who had been playing, but, rather, a small stout individual in his middle years, pale of countenance and with fine light hair that curled down over his collar. Holmes, meanwhile, was seated in his customary chair, his chin resting on his steepled fingers.

"Ah, Watson," he remarked. "Here you are at last. Allow me to introduce Mr Suvorov."

The man, having laid down Holmes's violin, gave a continental bow.

The name was instantly familiar to me.

"Not Ruslan Suvorov?" I exclaimed.

The man nodded assent, with a polite smile.

To say I was astonished to see him there in front of me would be a mighty understatement. The London music world had been agog for days with news of the visit of this world-famous violinist, invited to perform at the Royal Albert Hall over two nights, one of them having already passed to great acclaim, critics even comparing Suvorov favourably to the great Joachim. I myself had tried to buy tickets, to no avail. They were completely sold out. And now he had condescended to give an impromptu recital here in our modest rooms. What was the explanation?

"You have a fine instrument here, Mr Holmes," the man remarked in a soft accent I should have recognised as Russian, even had I not known the nationality of the visitor.

"Thank you," Holmes replied. "It was sold to me cheaply as a fake."

"A fake!" exclaimed Suvorov. "Never! This is undoubtedly the genuine work of Antonio Stradivari! I could not be fooled."

"Indeed," Holmes replied. "The man who sold it to me had no ear for music. In fact, I believe he was deaf."

"I should envy you, did I not possess a fine Stradivarius of my own."

"But I am sure," Holmes continued, "that you did not come here simply to play a tune on my violin."

Play a tune! I winced, but detected in my friend's tone – could it be? – something approaching envy. He always wished to be the best at everything, in this case an impossibility!

"I should not have bothered you with such a trivial matter, Mr Holmes, had my wife not urged me to consult you. Tatiana has long

followed the accounts of your exploits as written up by the Doctor."
Here he bowed again towards me.

"So then how can I assist you?" Holmes asked. "And please be seated."

Mr Suvorov took the armchair facing Holmes – my usual place, which I willingly ceded to the great man – while I sat myself in an upright chair at the table.

"In my youth," our visitor began, "I did some foolish things, as I suppose most of us have."

He paused. Holmes said nothing. I doubted that my friend was guilty of any youthful follies whatsoever, but I certainly was, so gave an assenting murmur, as much to encourage the man to proceed as anything else.

"You must know," he continued, "that in Russia there are groups of mainly young men – idealistic, yes, but sometimes given to extreme acts – who wish to overthrow the existing autocratic order and install a fairer society in its place. I associated myself with such a group for several years, before my musical studies took me away from St Petersburg to Paris, where I was too immersed in work to engage any longer in such activities. In addition, by then, I had a wife and child to consider, my son Vanya, you know, just now studying to be a doctor in Moscow." The indulgent smile of a proud father passed quickly over his face, before he added, "Imagine my astonishment, therefore, when I received, but two days since, this message in the post."

He reached into his breast pocket and took out a missive which he handed to Holmes. Before opening it, the latter studied the envelope itself with great care.

"Postmarked Belgravia," he said. "A salubrious area and one that, as I believe it, hosts the embassy of the Russian Empire."

Mr Suvorov nodded. "Indeed. In fact, I have been invited to play there this week at a private function. However," he added, "I hardly think the message came from that establishment."

Holmes removed a card from inside the envelope and looked at it for a moment. He then passed it to me without a word.

"I am afraid," I said, regarding it, "that my grasp of Cyrillic isn't what it was."

Both men looked at me. Of course, I have never even attempted to get to grips with the Russian alphabet, let alone those languages that use it. My attempt at a joke had fallen flat on its face. Mind you, I don't think Holmes, in this instance, was better placed than I to read the thing. Under what seemed to be a single word, was a bisected rectangle, half black, half red.

"It simply says "Remember"," Mr Suvorov explained. "The symbol beneath it…"

"Represents the anarchist movement," Holmes added. "Yes, I recognise that."

"You were an anarchist?" I asked, shocked. Newspapers frequently report the atrocities committed by such groups.

"As I said, I was young. I was idealistic. Indeed, I stand by those ideals today. However, I cannot condone any violent methods employed to realise them."

"So why, after so long, do you think these people have contacted you again?" Holmes asked.

Mr Suvorov shook his head.

"I have not an idea. It is not as if I have been difficult to find, having been in the public eye for several decades."

"But not perhaps in London."

"No. It's my first visit."

"Hmm…" Holmes drummed his fingers on the arm of his chair. "Whoever sent this will no doubt follow it up with a further message. Until that time I fear there is little I can do for you."

"That is what I expected you to say, what I told Tatiana. But you know what wives are like."

I nodded again, while Holmes, who has never experienced the joys and pains of matrimony, stayed silent.

"The least I can do," Mr Suvorov continued, "is to invite you to my concert tonight."

"I understood all the tickets were sold," I said.

"There are always places kept back for honoured guests. My wife has a box. Please do not offend me by refusing.

Holmes smiled. "We should not dream of it, Mr Suvorov. It would be both an honour and a delight. Thank you so very much."

With that, our visitor took his leave.

"What a charming man," I said.

Holmes was frowning.

"Yes, but I fear that his troubles are only starting. Whoever sent that message will assuredly follow it up."

The Royal Albert Hall was full to bursting with people keen to hear the playing of the famous violinist. An excited buzz filled that vast auditorium as Holmes and I made our way to the box where we found Madame Suvorova already installed, together with a couple she introduced to us as her brother, and his wife.

"Count and Countess Razumov," she told us.

Madame Suvorova was a small plump woman in, as I judged, her early forties. Her jet black hair was pulled back so tightly from her forehead that it made me wince to look upon it, but otherwise she had a sweet, if not pretty face, her Slavic features buried in the flesh of her cheeks, which dimpled when she smiled. Her eyes were the soft grey of an autumn sky.

Her brother, the Count, was a gaunt version of herself, small too, but slight, clean-shaven with cheekbones that stood out cadaverously under grey eyes that on him looked wintry. His sleek black hair lent him something of the look of a predatory animal. But he was all courtesy, apologising, in French, for his lack of English.

For some reason I did not care at all for the appearance of his wife, the Countess, lean as a boy and so long in the body that, without seeing her stand, I felt that she must tower over her husband.

Gingery curls over rouged cheeks did nothing to dispel the impression of a hard and cold woman. Perhaps conscious of her status, she bestowed on us the very slightest of acknowledgements – in French – and then turned her back on us to regard the assembled audience through opera glasses.

Madame Suvorova herself spoke English quite charmingly, although, to my ears, with more of a French accent than a Russian one. She said nothing to Holmes about her fears for her husband following the receipt of that enigmatic note. I suppose it was hardly the place. In any case, the concert was about to start.

Holmes, sitting back on his upholstered armchair, long legs stretched out in front of him, eyes closed, listened intently, and entirely without moving. For my part, while I enjoy listening to music, my thoughts tend to wander all over the place. I am afraid, moreover, that I am very much the dilettante, and can seldom put a composer's name to the piece being played. I know that the first half of the programme featured Peter Tchaikovsky and another Russian, whose name I had never heard before and the which, being barely pronounceable, I have already forgotten. Ruslan Suvorov was accompanied both times by an accomplished pianist, a man whose splendid whiskers made up for the baldness of his pate.

During the interval, a steward appeared with a tray holding little squares of bread covered with black caviar, as well as four glasses and a bottle of champagne on ice. Rapid words in Russian were exchanged, Madame Suvorova looking displeased, apparently embarrassed that there were not enough glasses to go round. I protested that I did not care for champagne, it being nothing less than the truth, but this would not do, and the Count sent the poor steward off with a flea in his ear – as if it were his fault – to bring another glass. Meanwhile a little smile played over the thin lips of the Countess, for the which I liked her even less than before.

"My husband and I hope, gentlemen," Madame Suvorova was saying, "that you will be able to join us after the concert for dinner at Romanos."

Despite the Italian-sounding name, I knew that this fabled restaurant, which I had never previously had occasion to visit, was renowned for the excellence of its French cuisine. I looked across at Holmes, who, I was pleased to see, graciously nodded his acceptance of the invitation.

"Whatever has happened to the man?" The waiter having failed as yet to return with another glass, Madame Suvorova rapped her fan impatiently on the velvet edge of the balcony.

It was again impossible to insist that I did not wish for a drink, so, since I knew – or thought I knew – my way around the concert hall, I offered to go in search of the fellow, or at least to collect another glass myself. The way was not quite as I remembered, however, and, thinking it might be a short cut to the bar, I soon found myself on an unfrequented staircase. Descending it, I was most taken aback to observe below me none other than the maestro Ruslan Suvorov himself in intense conversation with a young lady of astonishing beauty, garbed in the very height of fashion... I should amend that. Despite my not being up-to-date on ladies" dress, I could tell that her style was not that generally seen in London but rather continental, French or Italian. The pair did not notice me and, reluctant to disturb them in what seemed a most impassioned colloquy, I returned the way I had come, somewhat puzzled.

By happy chance, I met the same steward, now heading back to our box with the extra glass, and full of apologies.

"I understood four from the lady," he said, "though her English was not of the best."

The Countess then, I thought, wondering if it was a genuine mistake on her part, and if not, whyever should she wish to stir up mischief?

She gave me what I thought was an ironic glance on my return. No, I did not care for her.

The company had kindly left me several little squares of the caviar on bread, and I was vouchsafed another ironic glance, this time from Holmes, whose conservative taste in the matter of food, I reckoned, would not extend to sturgeons" eggs. I, however, am quite partial to the delicacy, especially when the quality was as good as this. Not so much, all the same, that I would pay good money for it, a juicy steak being more in my line. However, I complimented Madame Suvorova on the flavour.

"Beluga," she replied "Pearls of delight exploding on the tongue, do you not agree, Doctor?"

Before I could reply, the Count exclaimed looking down into the auditorium. *"Tiens! C'est Katya Maslinka! Qu'est-ce que cette salope fait ici?"*

I followed his gaze and saw that he was indicating the same beauty I had observed so recently on the stairs with Ruslan Suvorov. Whyever, I wondered, would the Count refer to her so very disparagingly? The girl was now accompanied by an old woman whose dress would suggest rather the steppes of Central Asia than a fashionable concert hall in a metropolis, being all homespun weaves with a scarf, if you please, tied around her head. A strange companion, indeed, for a lovely young lady. As we watched, the old woman, as if sensing our interest, turned to look up at us with one of the most evil and vindictive stares I have ever seen. She then addressed the other with a crocodile smile. I could not see the young woman's responding expression for she had her back to us.

"And that witch, old Kuragina!" exclaimed Madam Suvorova. "What are they doing here in London?"

"No good, you can be sure," the Count replied in English.

Just then, the lights went down for the second half of the concert. It was Beethoven, the Kreutzer sonata, as my programme indicated, but I was so distracted by the previous incident that I could not pay proper attention to that intricate and challenging piece. Only that it was met with uproarious applause at the end.

"And yet," Holmes whispered to me, "I feel that the maestro did not respond to the music as whole-heartedly as I should have expected. And see, those mysterious ladies did not even await the ending of it."

I again looked down into the auditorium. Two seats were empty. Those of the Russian women.

Ruslan Suvorov had left the stage, but the applause continued unabated. His accompanist stood by his piano still, as we awaited the return of the maestro to acknowledge the plaudits of the audience, and perhaps even grace us with an encore.

We waited and waited but there was no sign of him. Soon the audience took up a chant of "Suvorov! Suvorov!" but still nothing. His accompanist looked off into the wings but evidently there was no one there. Eventually, the curtain came down and people started shuffling, somewhat discontentedly, to the exits. Not before Holmes had rushed from the box, myself following after.

"I fear something bad has happened," he told me as we hurried down to the lobby, where he asked a doorman if he had seen Ruslan Suvorov leaving.

"Not him," came the reply, "only two ladies who got into a coach that was waiting for them... Mind you, sir, the maestro would not come out this way, but would use the stage door."

"Of course," Holmes said. "Where is it?"

On being informed that it was several doors along, around that circular building, we made haste thither, only to find it already blocked by enthusiasts hoping to catch a glimpse of their hero.

"Some 'ope," an old chestnut vendor remarked, standing by with his barrow of hot roasted nuts to tempt the passers-by. " 'E's long gawn."

"What did you see?" Holmes asked.

"Well now," the old man replied with a crafty look. "If only I could remember…"

"Give him something, Watson, and quick," Holmes said.

I fished a half-crown, all the change I had, out of my pocket, and gave it to the man, who took it without even a thank-you.

"Let me guess," Holmes went on. "A coach drove up, and he got into it."

The old man laughed, revealing toothless gums.

"If you knowed it, why d'you ask?"

"Two ladies within, I suppose."

"No, not a bit…" The old man paused for effect. "One loverly lady and one 'orrible old crone. They went that way," he offered, without being asked, pointing to the road that led to the city centre, "and that were the last I seed of 'em. Good riddance, too."

"Did you notice anything distinguishing the coach from all the others, a coat of arms, for instance?"

The old man shook his head.

"The look that old one give me were enough to freeze me blood. Like a curse, it were. I looked away after that."

"Well," Holmes said to me, as we made our way back to the front of the concert hall. "At least it seems that the maestro left of his own accord and was not forced."

"So do you think Mr Suvorov and the young lady have an understanding? It seems surprising under the circumstances."

Holmes shrugged, "At this stage, who knows."

It was then I told him of my previous sighting of the maestro with the lady on the stairs.

"Their conversation did not strike me as that of lovers. However, I am no expert on Russians, whom I understand to be a passionate race."

"Good heavens, Watson!" Holmes threw up his hands in exasperation. "You did not think of mentioning this before?"

"I hardly had a chance," I replied, somewhat peeved. "In any case, it is only in retrospect that the encounter has taken on any significance."

"Tsk," was Holmes's response to that.

By now we had arrived back at the concert hall lobby where Madame Suvorova and the Countess were standing waiting.

"*Bozhe moi*, Mr Holmes, wherever did you rush off to?" Madame asked.

"Where is the Count?" Holmes countered, presumably not wishing to alarm the ladies too much.

"He has gone to fetch Ruslan… Though I am most surprised… I hope he is well. It is most unlike my husband not to do an encore."

The Countess, meanwhile was smiling at her feet, though I could not imagine what she found amusing there.

Soon enough, the Count returned, unsurprisingly to us, without the violinist but with a bearded man I recognised as the accompanist.

The Count spoke rapidly to Madame Suvorova, who seemed to me to turn pale at his words.

"Mr Benson says that he was most astonished when Ruslan failed to return for his encore," he explained to us.

"We had rehearsed it," the pianist said. "Fauré's *Berceuse*, you know."

Holmes nodded. "A crowd pleaser."

"I felt most ridiculous standing there on stage waiting for him to come back, I can tell you. He might have let me know what his intentions were."

The man was clearly more concerned for his own dignity than for any fate that might have befallen Mr Suvorov.

"So where is he?" Madame asked.

Mr Benson shook his head. "Apparently he just rushed off."

It was then that Holmes told of what we knew, of Mr Suvorov mounting a coach whose passengers already comprised the two women we had seen in the concert hall. Madame Suvorova turned away abruptly, and might have fallen but for her brother's supporting arm. The Countess continued to grin at her feet.

"It may be nothing," the Count said in English. "I suggest we go to Romano's as planned in the hope that Ruslan will join us there."

"I should like to know," Holmes interpolated, "who these women are and what might be their relationship with Mr Suvorov."

The Count shot him a dark look, as if to say not in front of his sister, who assuredly was already worried enough.

"Katya was a student of his in Paris, and the old woman is, I believe, her aunt," Madame Suvorova said in shaky tones.

The Countess suddenly chuckled, as if she had heard something extremely amusing.

"If you are thinking," the Count said, again in English (his command of the language seeming to increase with every speech he gave), "that there was more between them, an attachment, my dear, you are quite wrong, Ruslan is devoted to you."

"So you say," Madame replied bleakly. "But you have seen her. How lovely she is."

"*Et jeune aussi*," added the Countess, eyes glinting spitefully. "*Comme les hommes d''un certain âge aiment les jolies jeunes filles ! Tu le sais bien, mon chéri.*"

I could not but wonder if the Countess's reference to the predilection of older men for fresh young women, was of a more personal nature. Certainly, if I were her husband, I think my eye might rove as well.

"Her youth is neither here nor there," the Count put in, giving his wife a sharp look. He added something further in French but so fast that I could make nothing of it.

It was agreed, then, that we should proceed to the restaurant, in the hope that Mr Suvorov might turn up there as planned. Though Holmes, while insisting I go, said that, with Madame's permission, he would make some inquiries of his own, to try and establish the whereabouts of the maestro. Depending on what he found out, if anything, he might, or might not, join us later.

I am not sure if he was invited as well, but the pianist, Mr Benson, showed every intention of accompanying us to Romano's. Finding myself travelling in a cab with him, it turned out that he was an inveterate gossip and, I am sorry to say, ready to imagine the worst of his musical partner.

"These continentals, Dr Watson," he confided gleefully, "are not like us Britishers. I should know. I've accompanied the best, and worst of them. They have the morals of rabbits. I'm not one whit surprised that old Suvorov's lower instincts, if I might put it that way, got the better of him."

Distasteful though it was to hear this man speak so crudely – this same man, whose sensitive rendition of the classics he had so recently been playing would lead one to imagine that his view of humanity was equally uplifting – I felt it incumbent on me, in the interests of the case, to lead him on to speak even more freely.

"So had you observed anything untoward between Mr Suvorov and the young person in question?"

Benson shook his head, regretfully, as it seemed to me.

"No, never set eyes on her, but he's a sly one, Dr Watson. Great artiste, of course but very sly. Not one for confidences. Butter, you'd think, wouldn't melt in his mouth… That's what you'd think, if you didn't know any better."

By now we had reached the restaurant, possessed of a handsome creamy yellow entrance fronting on to the Strand. Our companions had arrived just before us and were now making their way inside, the Count waving at us to follow. We were greeted effusively by the owner's second-in-command, one Signor Antonelli, who showed us to our table. The place, known for the Bohemian set who frequented it, actors, writers, musicians and so forth, possessed a suitably exotic décor, suggestive of a Moorish interior, arches leading into booths enhanced with a series of seascapes that, to me, recalled the

Bosphorus, its deep blue waters set with islands, castles and mosques. I found it a little strange, seeing that the place was owned, as its name suggested, by an Italian, the "Roman", and that the menu featured French cuisine of a high order.

Sadly, most of our party, myself included, had little appetite, the exceptions being the Countess and Mr Benson, whose little eyes veritably glinted at the variety of comestibles before him. I ordered the famous shellfish soup, "crème Pink'un" but found it too rich for that time of night and merely took a few spoonfuls before pushing the dish away.

Madame's eyes strayed constantly to the door. Each time it opened, she sat forward, clearly hoping that it would be her husband who appeared on the threshold. Each time she was disappointed. For my part, I was hoping for Holmes, also in vain.

Conversation hardly existed. And when the "Roman" himself, a dapper little man, with a neat black moustache, appeared at our table, clearly distressed that his food was not producing the usual delightful effect (our two exceptions notwithstanding), we could only try to assure him that it was not the food that was at fault.

We stayed there for a miserable two hours until the waiters started making all the signs of wishing to clear and close up. But just as we were gathering ourselves together, retrieving our coats and cloaks, Ruslan Suvorov himself burst into the place. To me, he looked as if he had aged by ten years. It was surely hardly an amorous encounter that had detained him.

"I'm so sorry," he said. "Let me explain." And then spoke in Russian.

Whatever he said, it failed to satisfy his wife, who spoke back angrily to him, seized her wrap and stormed out, followed by the Countess, who paused at the door to look back at us, a smirk on her face.

"Look after the ladies, Sergei," Mr Suvorov urged his brother-in-law, and then sank down at the table, his head in his hands.

The Count hurried off, leaving only Benson and myself standing staring at each other and at the man before us.

"Wherever did you disappear to?" the pianist asked at last. "I felt most ridiculous, standing there like a fool."

Mr Suvorov shook his head.

"Of course, she didn't believe me," he said. "Why did I even think my stupid excuses would satisfy her?"

I sat down beside him.

"We are at a disadvantage here," I remarked gently. "Would you care to explain, maestro?"

He raised his head to me.

"Dr Watson, believe me. I am not in love with that Katya girl. Everything I do, I do for the sake of my wife and son. Their well-being is all to me. Let no one touch a hair of their heads..." He sighed, evidently deeply troubled.

"Is it?" I asked carefully, "anything to do with... the matter we discussed before?"

He stared up at me again, a wild look in his eyes. Then, to the astonishment of Benson and myself, he leapt up and raced out of the door.

"Well now..." the pianist said at last, absently picking up a petit four, and popping it into his mouth. "What in heaven's name was all that about?"

He looked at me as if expecting some explanation of my last words, the which I of course was not about to divulge. I just shook my head.

Leaving the restaurant – Signor Antonelli assuring us that the bill was settled, though I left a few coins on the table for the patiently waiting staff – I looked for a cab to take me back to Baker Street. It seemed that Mr Benson was determined to accompany me.

"Yes," he said. "That's my direction too."

I should much have preferred to travel without the gentleman and his probing questions, and was relieved when he alighted at Baker

Street station, without, I might add, offering to pay his share of the fare. I last saw him ambling towards the Underground.

Back home, I was more than relieved to find Holmes, also apparently newly returned, about to light up his infernal pipe. I explained what had happened at the restaurant. He shook his head at the intelligence.

"Something is very amiss here. I fear something bad happened after that concert, Watson."

I asked him if he had discovered anything.

"I went back to the doorman to ask if he had recognised any distinguishing marks on the carriage taken by the two ladies, but without any luck. The man's powers of observation are even worse than yours, Watson. However, I am not entirely disheartened. The pair are very conspicuous and someone must surely have seen them. I have put Wiggins and the Baker Street Irregulars on the case, and am hoping for enlightenment through them. By the way, Watson, do you recall that our friend, Mr Suvorov has been requested to play at a private function at the Russian embassy?"

"Oh yes. He mentioned it when he was here. Is Benson accompanying him, I wonder?"

"I think not, Watson. Why do you ask?"

"Excellent pianist he may be, but I must say, I don't like the man. And not just because he is tight-fisted. I shouldn't be at all surprised to find he is up to something."

I was somewhat miffed at Holmes" reference to my supposed shortcomings, and wished to show that I too was capable of useful insights.

"Hmm," Holmes said, dismissively. "Meanwhile, another chat with our violinist friend might be in order."

It was easier said than done. The next day, when we visited the hotel where the couple were staying, it transpired that the row between Mr Suvorov and his wife had resulted in him being banished.

"I threw him out, Mr Holmes," she remarked coldly, "I have no idea where he is now. No doubt with his mistress, Katya Maslinka."

"He assured me that his relations with that person were not of that nature," I said.

"Ha!"

"I believed him," I continued.

"What other explanation can there be?"

"That, Madame," Holmes said, "is what we hope to find out."

"I pray to God you do."

We bowed and left her, trembling, tears in her eyes, looking out the window.

"Poor woman," I said.

In the hotel foyer, we found Count Razumov, stretched out in a chair, reading a paper and smoking a cigar, a cup of black coffee beside him. He jumped up at the sight of us.

"You have seed Tatiana," he said, in his broken English. "How she is?"

"Upset," Holmes replied abruptly. "We are wondering where her husband might be. Do you have any idea, Count?"

"No." He shrugged his shoulders. "I regret it."

"I understand he is to play for the Russian ambassador."

"Yes, tonight. Great honour."

"And will you be there as well."

"Alas, it is very private concert." He paused. "Someone so important will be visiting."

"From Russia?"

"I suppose. Some brother or cousin of the Tsar, I believe. Some Grand Duke." He waved a beautifully manicured hand in the air dismissively.

"I wonder," Holmes said, sitting down beside the man and lowering his voice, "if you can tell us more about this woman Katya…."

"Yekaterina Fyodorovna Maslinka! Claims to be daughter of rich Moscow merchant." He shook his sleek head. "I doubt. To me, she is creature of streets."

Surely not, I thought. From my admittedly brief glimpse of her, she seemed elegant, so refined.

"You are surprised, Doctor," Count Razumov remarked, smiling. "I assure you, it is truth. But forget her. It is old woman you must ask for, Mr Holmes. That witch Kuragina. Girl is just puppet, in my opinion. Sent to trap." He paused, and leaned forward. "You must know it. I trust my brother-in-law. He loves my sister true. But if the child says he did this and this to her, well…" That hand in the air again. "Who do people believe?"

"They do this to extort money?"

"Perhaps." He shrugged. "Who knows it?" He rustled the sheets of the newspaper as if to indicate that the interview was over.

"You don't, I suppose, happen to know where they are staying, this witch and her creature?"

"Sergei!" The Countess, silent as a cat, had come up behind us. Her voice was sharp enough, however.

"Ah, *voilà, ma cherie*! At last you are ready… My regrets, gentlemen."

We were dismissed, and left, bowing to the lady who barely acknowledged us.

"Did you notice," Holmes said as we exited on to Park Lane, "the man was reading The Times? Perhaps our friend's English is rather better than he makes out."

"Or perhaps he is just trying to improve his command of the language," I replied.

Holmes chuckled. "Watson, you are wonderful. Your practical common sense sweeps away my dark suspicions."

Back at Baker Street, Mrs Hudson, with a shudder, told us "that boy" was waiting for us. Wiggins had returned and was in our landlady's kitchen, "eating my biscuits like they're going out of fashion, Mr Holmes", and generally getting in the way.

"Send him up to us, if you please, Mrs Hudson," he told her.

The same Wiggins, biscuit crumbs adorning the front of his grubby jacket, was soon standing before us, very pleased with himself. One of his Irregulars had tracked the Russian women to a shabby hotel in Pimlico.

"The 'otel Waldon, it is, Mr 'Olmes. Not the sort o' place a fine lady usually stays in, 'er with all 'er furs and pearls. As for t'other old 'un… that figures, awl right."

"Is your man there now?" Holmes asked.

By "man" he meant some raggedy little shrimp, of course, but Wiggins accepted the designation as a right.

" 'E is, Tommy is. And 'e won't leave off watchin' til you tells 'im to."

"There's no time to be lost," Holmes said, frowning. "I'll go there now. Wiggins, wait for me to change. And Watson, you stay here to see if there are any further messages from the Suvorovs."

I was a little put out to be assigned such a passive task, but I supposed Holmes had his reasons, and, indeed, after he re-emerged from his bedroom, he was no longer recognisable as the eminent detective, but garbed much like an adult version of Wiggins, a labouring man, and somehow even suddenly grizzled. His ability to disappear completely into some guise or other, never fails to astonish me: it is a skill I shall never fathom.

He was holding a piece of paper with scribbled writing on it.

"I'll get Mrs Hudson to send Clara to the telegraph office with this, so watch out for any reply, Watson. It's of primary importance."

The two of them, then, having bade me farewell, made their way out into the street. From my upstairs window, I watched them walk away, marvelling how Holmes" gait had even changed to a kind of stumbling limp. Assuredly the stage had missed an opportunity with him, consummate actor that he was.

Now all I had to do was wait, and fruitlessly at that because there was neither sight nor sound from the Suvorovs, nor from anyone else involved in the case. Three copies of the Lancet, hitherto unread, helped me pass the hours fairly well – particularly an article on a new painkiller, acetylsalicyclic acid, that avoids the irritant qualities of previous such remedies, an exciting breakthrough for the medical profession and those they tend. I admit, however, that my eyes frequently strayed to the window again, to see if Holmes or anyone else was heading my way. The only person to arrive was the telegraph boy with a missive that Clara brought up to me. I was tempted to open it, I admit, but of course did not. In fact, I must have finally dozed off, for I opened my eyes to find my friend standing over me, still in those rags, a quizzical expression on his face.

"I am sorry to disturb your nap," he said.

"Holmes!" I exclaimed. "Any news?"

He sat down and rubbed his dirt-encrusted hands together.

"I believe so, Watson." He grinned. "You are looking at the latest member of an anarchist cell operating out of the Hotel Waldon."

I nearly leaped out of my skin.

"Good Lord!"

"Well, maybe I am getting ahead of myself... Knowing in advance the reputation of the place, I approached the reception desk, in the person of an angry labourer recently made jobless on account of my radical politics, the sort these people like to recruit, along with disaffected intellectuals. At first, I was fobbed off by the oaf at the desk, but persisted, and was finally allowed through to a back office, where a heavily bearded individual stared at me for a long time, unnerving me somewhat, I must confess.

"Heavily bearded!" I exclaimed. "Not Benson!"

Holmes sighed. "No, not Benson, however much you want it to be. This man was, I believe, Polish, and I must have convinced him to some extent... Oh, Watson," he smiled at the recollection, "You should have heard me rage against the evils of capitalism! My interlocutor, who omitted to introduce himself for obvious reasons, asked a load of questions and said I should call back in a day's time, after which I suppose he will have made full inquiries. No matter that they will lead nowhere. It has been enough to prove to me I am on the right track." He smiled at the memory. "Once outside I approached Wiggins's boy, as if to give him a coin (which in fact I did – he well-deserved it) to ask if the Russian women were still within. He told me they were, unless there was a way out the back. I am sure there is, but could see no good reason for them to use it. The women could not know, surely, that we are on to them."

"So what does it all mean?" I asked. "And how does it relate to Ruslan Suvorov?"

"I think I know the answer to that, but confirmation is needed… Ah!" He spotted the telegram. "There's a reply. Excellent! But now I must rid myself of this fancy-dress." And, without another word, he disappeared into his bedroom, clutching the message.

How aggravating he is! He must have known how much I was dying to be enlightened. When he eventually emerged, clean, and in his usual "at home" garb of a mouse-coloured dressing-gown over an old pair of trousers, and sat down and reached for his pipe, I hoped at last to hear of his suspicions, as well as the contents of the mysterious telegram. All he told me, however, was that I was to go to the Hotel Waldron that evening, where I should hope to find the old Russian woman and perhaps her young protégée.

"If they are not there, then one of Wiggins's boys can, I trust, take you to them."

It was hardly a role I relished.

"What then, Holmes?"

"Stay with them, or at least with her, the witch. Never let her out of your sight. Oh, and take your revolver. Just in case."

"That serious?" I gaped at him.

"Who knows. Perhaps. Anyway, in that sort of a den, it's as well to be armed."

"Where will you be?"

"I," he replied, "will be attending a recital at the Russian Embassy… Close your mouth, Watson. You look quite foolish with it hanging open."

"Madame Kuragina, if you please!"

In response, the disreputable-looking individual seated behind what passed for a reception desk at the Hotel Waldron, scratched his chin and shook his head.

"Never 'eard of 'er, guv."

"Come now. That's not true, is it?" I hoped I knew the sort he was, and slid a shining guinea across the counter to him. If he were part of the anarchist cell, he would surely not rise to the bait. Luckily for me, he was simply the venal creature he appeared to be.

"Oh, you mean the Russky," he said, slapping his forehead with one dirty hand and sliding the coin off the desk with the other. "Room seven. First floor up them stairs, guv. Or you can use the lift."

That structure looked decidedly unreliable, so I took the stairs, and, without waiting for a reply to my knock on the door of number seven, walked inside.

The room was permeated with an evil-smelling bluish fog emanating, as I soon realised, from the pipe the old woman was smoking. She didn't seem surprised or frightened to see me, but fixed me with a basilisk glare that would have turned me to stone if it could. She was not alone, though her companion wasn't young Katya but, to my enormous astonishment, none other than the Countess Razumova. For her part, that lady was considerably put out at the sight of me.

"Dr Watson," she mumbled. "You here? Why?"

"I might ask the same of you, Countess."

She looked up at me, recovering her sang froid quickly enough, taking on her usual arrogant mien.

"Kuragina... how you say it?... she reads my fortune. Has gift."

She then said something in Russian to the old woman, who removed the pipe from her mouth, gave me another freezing look, and spat on the floor.

"What future did she see for you, then?" I asked, ignoring the disgusting gesture. "A good one, I trust."

The Countess shrugged. "But you... you want fortune read too, perhaps?"

She curled her lip, mocking me.

"No," I replied, laughing (trying to appear more at ease than I really was). "Just a friendly visit, you know."

I sat myself down in a chair between the women and the door.

Kuragina spoke again, quickly.

"But you are not with friends here," the Countess said, as if translating. "Kuragina says please to go."

"Where is the charming Katya?" I asked.

"Oh, I see now..." The Countess laughed nastily. "You want to be good friends with pretty young miss. Like all men."

I sat back. If that's what they thought, so be it.

"Well, as you see. She is not here... She is at Russian embassy. At concert,"

Was she indeed! How ever had she managed that?

"Ruslan insisted she be present!"

I should have liked to wipe that grin off her face, but instead we just stared at each other in silence for a while. Then a timepiece on the wall chimed the hour. Ten o'clock.

The old woman barked a laugh, and muttered something.

"How sad," the Countess translated. "You understand, Dr Watson, I know not what Kuragina means when she says it is too late now."

"Too late for what?"

The Countess spoke Russian to the old woman and, listening to the reply, raised a gloved hand to her throat. I could tell she was suddenly frightened by what she heard.

"Tell me," I said.

"I cannot… I have not words in English."

"Say it in French then."

She gabbled out something in that tongue.

"More slowly, if you please."

"She says," (I translate) "the pig is dead now."

"Who? Suvorov?"

"Perhaps, too. But she means Grand-duke."

The Countess stood up, as the old woman babbled some more.

"I think she is mad. She says Ruslan will have stabbed the Grand-duke by now."

Kuragina started nodding and laughing a mocking, gloating laugh. Suddenly, the Countess made a dash for the door. I caught hold of her arm and pushed her back down on to her chair, then drew my revolver.

"You are going nowhere, either of you," I said.

At the sight of my weapon, Kuragina laughed all the more. The Countess, however, started shivering with terror.

"I know nothing of this, Doctor," she bleated, all dignity and arrogance gone from her. "I swear it on lifes of children."

"We'll have to wait and see," I said, wondering at the same time what I would do if the other denizens of the hotel decided to call upon the old woman. I felt myself to be in a horrible predicament, but, for Holmes's sake and following his instructions, resolved to remain at my post, come what may.

It seemed an age, but eventually steps were heard on the stairs. I cocked my gun.

Kuragina smiled at me.

"Katya," she whispered. "Katyushka."

But it was not she. I confess, I was never more relieved in my life to see Inspector Lestrade and his constable than at that moment. Even now, the old woman was unmoved. She let herself be led from the room and down the stairs, quite docile, I following behind, closely guarding the still trembling Countess. In the lobby, we were confronted by a man wearing what I subsequently discovered to be Tsarist uniform. He addressed a few words to Kuragina, who on the instant fell back, emitting a terrible scream.

What happened next was frightful to witness. The old woman thrust something into her mouth, and immediately started writhing in agony, foam boiling from her lips, eyes starting from her head, only to collapse at last in a heap of rags on the floor. I rushed forward to examine her. With her last strength, she bit my finger to the bone, then fell back, quite dead.

Now it was the Countess's turn to start screaming, until, someone – and I think it was Holmes, who had suddenly materialised – slapped her hard on the cheek, and she went silent.

A democratic group, we were all present in the seldom used front parlour of Baker Street, Holmes, myself, Mrs Hudson, Clara and Phoebe, Maestro Suvorov, Madame Suvorova, even Benson, who had somehow managed to tag along, and whom Mrs Hudson subsequently complained of being as bad as Wiggins, eating all her scones.

It was just one day after the events described above. Holmes had returned from Scotland Yard only an hour since, bringing the visitors with him. I was of course most anxious to learn the details of the case, but meanwhile had to be patient and sit quietly with the others, listening entranced to the virtuosic tones of Paganini's *Caprices*, as interpreted by the maestro, now proudly wearing a medal on his coat.

After the improvised concert, tea, biscuits and scones, together with a glass of neat vodka for the gentlemen, brought by our guests to be tossed back, Russian style, in a toast; after the emotional thanks and farewells of the Russians, all bear hugs, kisses and tears – even Mrs Hudson, to that lady"s great embarrassment, was subjected to such continental manners – I could at last retire to our upstairs room with Holmes to learn all.

It seemed that the Hotel Walden had been under scrutiny by the Powers That Be for some time. When the old woman and Katya moved in, interest was heightened, especially because of the forthcoming visit of the Grand-Duke, a man distantly related to Queen Victoria, and especially hated by the anarchists. An attempt on his life was likely, but where and how was not evident: the man was always surrounded by guards. It was a lucky chance that we happened to observe a connection between Kuragina and Ruslan Suvorov, and, knowing that the latter was to play in front of the Grand-Duke at the Embassy, Holmes concluded this was likely to be where the attack was to take place.

True fanatics, of course, hold their own lives to be dispensable for the good of the cause, but, from what we knew of him, Mr Suvorov would not willingly agree to complicity in such an action, and not simply because it would prove fatal for him too. Holmes concluded that blackmail must be involved, and, in view of Mr Suvorov's anguished words at the restaurant – "Everything I do, I do for the sake of my wife and son. Their well-being is all to me. Let no one touch a hair of their heads…" as recounted back to him by myself ("and I thank you for that, Watson. Well noted") – he suspected they had got at Mr Suvorov by threatening his family. He thereupon consulted (by that telegram) his brother Mycroft, who was already well informed about the whole sorry business and whose connections ranged to the Russian Empire and, indeed, far beyond. The elder Holmes was able at once to pull certain strings. As a result, Ivan, Suvorov's son, was quickly removed from the hospital in Moscow where he was studying, to a place of safety, and was even able to send a message to his parents, confirming this.

However, since no one knew where Mr Suvorov had gone, the reassuring note could not be delivered immediately. It being too late to cancel the recital, Holmes was thus given a special dispensation to attend the Embassy recital, to convey in person the good news to the violinist. Suvorov fell upon his neck with relief.

"That vile creature, Kuragina, told me my son, darling Vanya, was already in their hands," he told Holmes. "How was I to know this was untrue? She said that he would be tortured and killed if I did not fulfil their wishes. She also threatened my beloved Tatiana, telling me no matter how I tried to protect her, she would never be safe."

The violinist then grasped Holmes's hand in his.

"Please understand that my own life would be as nothing if my beloved family was taken from me. Better I should die, even in disgrace, than that they should suffer."

He had then showed Holmes the stiletto, which had been secreted in his violin case. It was with this weapon, provided by the old woman, that he was to stab the Grand-Duke, at the very moment when the latter was presenting him with the high Order of Alexander Nevsky, for his services to music.

"I was most relieved, Watson," Holmes told me, "to take charge of the deadly thing."

However, the plot was even then only partly thwarted. When Mr Suvorov failed to execute the deed, Katya Maslinka, poor pawn that she was, jumped up shouting "*Trus! Trus!*" (the word apparently meaning "Coward"), and pulled out a pistol which she aimed at the Grand-Duke, Luckily the gun misfired, but, in the ensuing fracas, the girl was fatally injured by one of the Grand-Duke's entourage. It was that news – the death of her darling, rather than the failure of the plot – that had so overwhelmed Kuragina, driving her to swallow the poisoned pellet she kept hidden about her person.

"Really, Holmes," I said, nursing my throbbing finger. "What a position you put me in! I might have shot the old woman myself. Or the Countess. How was I to know the place was already crawling with Lestrade's men?"

Holmes leaned back, an amused smile playing on his lips.

"I could see how much you wanted to be involved, Watson," he replied. "You did well, my friend. She might still have slipped through our fingers, but for you."

I was only somewhat appeased.

"So what of the Razumovs?" I asked.

"The Count is innocent of all involvement. He would hardly hurt his sister, whom he loves dearly. Moreover, his relations with his wife have been strained for a long time. That lady, however, is a different kettle of stinking fish. Entirely without morals or ideals, and in it for the money they gave her. I suspect she would have no qualms about poisoning her sister-in-law, if paid to do so. A quantity of arsenic was found in her boudoir."

"Good gracious." I remarked, "How very Grand Guignol. The whole business, indeed, is like the plot of some preposterous melodrama."

"Russians," Holmes agreed. "Such a passionate people!"

He seized his Stradivarius and started to attempt the Paganini, whereupon I made my excuses and set off for another calming stroll round the Regent's Park.

A Matter of ABC

"I have to say, Watson, this really isn't good enough. Wherever has the dratted woman got to, now?"

Holmes drummed impatient fingers on the breakfast table, the cause of his irritation being our landlady, Mrs Hudson. She, who was usually so prompt, was late, on this dismal February morning, in bringing us our boiled eggs and toast. I should add that there was often a diverting element to this daily ritual: while I happily settled for whatever was placed in front of me, Holmes was most particular regarding his eggs. Five minutes and fifteen seconds for a just set white and a soft yolk. Any less, he claimed, and the albumen would be disgustingly runny; any longer and the yolk would be too set for the soldiers of toast. If he complained, which he did frequently, Mrs Hudson would reply sharply, "Mr Holmes, I have better things to do than stand over a hot stove counting seconds. If you don't like the way I make your egg, why don't you cook it yourself, over that Bunsen burner of yours?"

"Do you not think that *I* might have better things to do?" was Holmes's customary riposte.

At which, Mrs Hudson would sniff and swish off out of the room with our cleared plates, only pretending to be offended. The pair of them relished their verbal duals.

On this particular morning, however, the ordinarily punctual lady was nowhere to be seen. We waited a little longer, Holmes becoming ever more testy, until he flung down the morning paper, leapt to his feet and expressed the startling notion that he was going to find out exactly what was going on "down there".

To venture into the kingdom below stairs where Mrs Hudson reigned supreme! I had to be part of this epic confrontation and followed him to the kitchen.

An astonishing sight met our eyes as we burst through the door. Even Holmes was taken aback. An unknown woman, in the throes of a violent hysterical fit, was clinging desperately to our landlady, who, in turn, was trying without success to calm her, while Phoebe, the little scullery maid, stood awkwardly in the corner, looking on with big eyes.

"Oh, Dr Watson," exclaimed Mrs Hudson. "Thank goodness you're here. Please try and pacify Nelly, will you, for I cannot."

Holmes, never at ease in the presence of powerful female emotions, rather shrank into the shadows with Phoebe, while I tended to the distressed woman.

"Now Nelly," I said, for I did not know what else to call her, "take some deep breaths."

I tested the pulse in her wrist and then laid firm fingers upon her burning forehead, encouraging her in her breathing. Gradually she calmed down.

"Now, please tell us what is troubling you,"

The fit looked about to start up again.

"It's her son, Ralph," Mrs Hudson explained quickly. "My nephew."

Suddenly everything fell into place. This Nelly had to be Mrs Hudson's widowed sister, with whom she had journeyed to Paris a year or so earlier, as I remembered, in order to extract the same young blade from a pickle[3]. Now, it seemed, he was causing trouble again.

"I'm sorry about your breakfasts, gentlemen," Mrs Hudson remarked, "but Nelly was in such a state. I couldn't leave her."

---

[3] See *Mrs Hudson Goes to Paris*, by Susan Knight (MX publishing, 2022)

I assumed that she would not trust Phoebe, ever accident-prone, to negotiate the stairs safely with a laden tray.

"Are these our eggs?" Holmes asked grimly, indicating a pot bubbling on the stove.

"Oh dear!" Mrs Hudson exclaimed. "They must be well and truly done by now... Never mind," she continued, "I can add them to a kedgeree for supper, and boil up two fresh ones for you now."

"Make a good strong pot of tea as well, Mrs Hudson, if you please," I said. "I think we could all do with a cup. And then, perhaps, your sister... Mrs... er..."

"Morris."

"Yes, thank you. Perhaps Mrs Morris can then explain exactly what is troubling her."

I ignored the dark look shot my way by Holmes. My concern had to be with the lady. Her colour was unnaturally high, and her pulse was racing. I quite feared for her heart: sharing her problem might help to ease her mind.

So, while Mrs Hudson busied herself making tea, and Holmes, refusing to sit with me at the kitchen table, leaned against the Welsh dresser tapping an impatient foot, Mrs Morris relayed her tale. It seemed that, after returning home from Paris with his mother to the northern city of Liverpool, the young man could not settle.

"You see, Doctor, Ralph had so wanted to succeed as an artist in Paris, that the thought of getting an ordinary job in an office or bank, as his late father had done, appealed not at all... And Ralph could have been an artist, Martha, couldn't he? He possesses a natural talent."

"Mm." Mrs Hudson's back was non-committal.

"I suggested he take up his brushes again but he refused. Or only, he said, as a house painter. Of course, he was joking."

Being on the estuary of a large river that emptied into the Irish Sea, Liverpool bustled with ocean-going vessels as well as smaller craft. Ralph soon found employment as a clerk in a shipping office, the which, according to his mother, engendered in the restless young man a yearning to travel, to seek his fortune, as he told her, in the colonies.

Was this then, the source of her anguish, that her only son might leave her for distant parts? No, not at all. *That* she would not have minded (a muffled snort from Mrs Hudson). The problem was that, all too soon, Ralph had found himself in bad company, with fellows who led him astray.

"Of course, he's not paid nearly enough by the company for all the work that he does. He is so very very conscientious, you see." (Mrs Hudson's back twitched). "So poor Ralph is always short of money. Running up debts all over the place, Doctor, which I've often had to settle for him."

"Money you can ill afford." Mrs Hudson, turning at last, placed a big teapot on the table.

"Yes, but Martha," her sister continued. "Ralph has assured me there would be severe reprisals if the debts were to remain unpaid. Nasty people might come looking for him. He might even be shipped abroad against his will at Her Majesty's pleasure." She stared at us through wide open and slightly foolish eyes. "That means as a prisoner, doesn't it?.. Oh, I've been so afraid for him."

Mrs Hudson's pursed lips, as she poured tea into cups for us all – stirring a heaped spoonful of sugar into Nelly's – seemed to say that such a fate might not be a bad thing, and might even put manners on the boy. Ralph was clearly no favourite of hers.

"So then, as I said," her sister continued, "he met these fellows, Ken and Bill. They came to the house one time, and one time only. Two bad lots and no mistake. I told Ralph to have nothing more to do with them. But did he listen to his mother?" Her look challenged us. "Of course not." She wrung her hands. "Oh, if only dear George were still around to tell him what"s what."

"Nelly's late husband," Mrs Hudson explained.

"He was my rock…" She gave a little sob. A tear ran down her cheek.

"What about Ken and Bill?" I asked, to stem any further sentimental reminiscences.

"They told him," she continued, pulling herself together somewhat, "that there was good money to be made elsewhere by an enterprising fellow like himself."

"Good money, is it!" Mrs Hudson exclaimed. "Bad money more like."

She took a judgemental sip of tea.

"Make money how?" I asked.

"He wouldn't say. When I asked if it was dishonestly to be got, he laughed and said "Of course not". But could I believe him, gentlemen? Dear Ralph is so easily led, you see."

"All no doubt very distressing for you, Madam," Holmes interrupted. "But I am afraid Dr Watson and I have pressing business to attend to."

I could not imagine what he meant, unless it was to feast on our delayed breakfast, and assumed he simply wished to hear no more of what seemed to him a banal enough domestic saga. He beckoned to me.

"I trust properly cooked eggs will follow us shortly," he added.

"Oh no, Mr Holmes. Please stay a while longer," Mrs Hudson begged. "I was hoping you could give some assistance to my poor sister."

Holmes raised eyebrows that nearly disappeared into his hairline. "Did you, indeed?"

"There is an element to her story which may intrigue you."

Holmes's expression clearly implied, if that was the case, tell Nelly to get on with it. With a resigned sigh, he slumped into a chair.

"Ralph has disappeared," Nelly said. "And I am afraid something terrible has happened to him."

She started to shake again. I took hold of her hand, and held it firmly, until the tremor ceased. She then removed a letter from her reticule and held it out to us. Holmes took it, scanned the contents and passed it over to me. Written in a wobbly, uneducated hand, it read as follows:

Dear Madam. Your son is in grave danger. If you wish to know where he is at and what he been doing, consult ABC. But take care. One false step and all is over. Signed, *A Well-wisher.*

"What the devil does that signify?" I asked. "Consult the ABC rail guide, perhaps."

Mrs Morris shook her head.

"I have no idea what it means, Doctor. But it terrifies me. How will I know if I have made a false step or not?"

She looked from Holmes to me and back again, a pleading expression on her face.

"Tell your tale from the beginning, Mrs Morris." Holmes said, kindly enough. I think the letter had indeed piqued his interest. "When did you last see Ralph?"

"Well," she replied, "he failed to return home from work on Friday, although…" becoming a little embarrassed, "that is not altogether out of the ordinary, Mr Holmes. He's young, do you see, and likes to go on the town with friends, sometimes forgetting to tell me first."

"Out all night?" Holmes asked.

Nelly nodded.

"Tsk," from Mrs Hudson.

Holmes held up a finger to forestall interruptions.

"The first time he didn't come home, I got so very anxious. But Ralph hates it if I make a fuss, so, on this occasion, I tried not to be too much concerned. But when he didn't come home all weekend, then I really started to worry. And yesterday evening I received this frightful missive. I could not think what else to do, so I took the first train down this morning to see if Martha could help."

"You mean, if Martha's lodger could help," Holmes replied. "Well, perhaps he can."

He studied the envelope in which the letter had come. Now, while you and I might see nothing out of the ordinary, what Holmes can glean from a seemingly plain piece of stationery frequently amazes me.

"Posted in London," he said. "Which is presumably why you travelled down."

The lady looked flustered.

"No, no, it was to see Martha... and yourself... Was it really posted here, then?"

Holmes sighed.

"You can clearly observe the mark over the stamp. It was applied at a post office in Bow at 3.30 pm on the day before yesterday, the letter subsequently transferred by night train to your home city – as evidenced by that countermark here – thus enabling it to be delivered to you the following day."

Mrs Hudson smiled. She was used, as I was, to witnessing Holmes's powers at work. Her sister, however, looked at Holmes as if he had just performed a magic trick.

"Furthermore," he continued, taking up the letter from the table where I had placed it, "we can see from the handwriting that a woman has penned it. Do you have any well-wishers in London, Mrs Morris?"

She shook her head.

"Only Martha."

"Well, I didn't write it," exclaimed that lady.

"Of course not, my dear," her sister said. "But there is no one else I can think of."

"I guessed not," Holmes continued. "In any case, such anonymous persons, in my experience, are usually far from wishing anyone well. Quite the opposite, in fact. The script suggesting a person of limited education."

He held the paper up to the light.

"Cheap stuff, no watermark, purchased in any stationer's shop."

He sniffed it. "No perfume... Yet a faint whiff of... what is that, Watson?"

He passed it to me. I could smell nothing, and gave it back.

"Almost imperceptible, and yet... Bow!" he exclaimed loudly, smacking the table, making the rest of us jump, and the china cups rattle on their saucers. "What does that say to you, Watson?"

I gave him a blank look.

"Bow bells. Oranges and lemons. Dick Whittington," Mrs Hudson suggested.

Holmes shook his head.

"Nothing so harmless," he said. "The proximity to Limehouse, plus the faint whiff of ammonia from this letter, give rise to certain conclusions. Watson, you are familiar with such, I think."

I nodded, knowing now what he meant and yet was reluctant to speak the word aloud to the ladies. Opium. The opium dens of Limehouse. If Ralph had fallen victim to the people who prey on human misery in those establishments, then God help him.

"Mrs Morris," Holmes said. "I shall do my best to find your son and restore him to you."

Her gratitude was overwhelming. If he had not dodged out of the way in time, I think she would have embraced him.

"Of course, you can stay here, Nelly," Mrs Hudson said, "while the gentlemen look into the matter."

Her sister smiled gratefully, and hugged her instead.

"Ken and Bill..." Holmes asked, "I don't suppose you know their last names?"

Mrs Morris shook her head.

"Perhaps they work in the same office as your son."

"I didn't get that impression. His office is a most respectable establishment."

"Nevertheless, perhaps someone there knows them. Please to write down the address for us and we will check it out."

He had quite forgotten breakfast in his eagerness to get started on the search. I, however, had no intention of embarking on a new adventure on an empty stomach, and said as much. Whereupon Mrs Hudson sprang into action, and soon Holmes was dipping a soldier of toast into a perfectly boiled egg.

It proved gratifyingly simple to discover the full names of the two men implicated by Mrs Morris in the disappearance of her son. Holmes, off on another mission, had delegated to me the task of contacting by telephonic means the office where Ralph was working. The helpful clerk was only too happy to give me the information required.

"Ken Bourne and Bill Ward, the laziest pair of good-for-nothings we've ever had working for us, Dr Watson. Good riddance to them if they've gone for good."

So, despite Mrs Morris's protestations, the two men had indeed worked in that most respectable of establishments. Not in the office, however, but as casual labourers in the docks.

The clerk was further able to provide their last address, a boarding house in what he described in supercilious tones as "a most unsavoury part of the city." Interestingly, however, the men had not been seen since the previous Friday, the day Ralph failed to return home.

"I hope young Morris will recover soon," he added. "His mother told us he is ill."

Cunning Nelly, covering her son's absence from work with a little fib.

"Nothing too serious I hope, doctor," he added.

I mumbled something non-committal, thanked him and bade him goodbye.

It would be too much to hope that the boarding house indicated would also be contactable by telephone, and such proved to be the case. Instead, I sent a telegram enquiring if Bourne and Ward were still in residence, hardly expecting a response. However, a reply came back almost immediately. It seemed the two had left on the previous Friday without paying their bill, the aggrieved landlady, a Mrs Bridget O" Faherty, broadly hinting that I might pay off what was owed!

I did not need Holmes to tell me that the disappearances of both Ralph and his cronies at precisely the same time was hardly a coincidence. But where were they? Had they come to London, from where the anonymous letter had been posted? For what reason? What, indeed, was the purpose of that mysterious letter and who had written it?

I returned to Baker Street to find Holmes already back from his own expedition.

"Well," said he, lighting his pipe, "you've had better luck than me, at least."

He had travelled to the East End of the city to enquire among his various, mostly disreputable, connections there regarding ABC, but no one was able or willing to enlighten him. He agreed with me, however, that Bourne and Ward were key to the search.

Once more we descended into that part of the house occupied by Mrs Hudson to get a description of the two men from Mrs Morris.

"Oh dear," she said, all flustered, "I can hardly tell you. I only saw them briefly, not wanting to linger in their company…" Her voice dropped to a whisper. "They had been drinking, you know."

"Well now, Mrs Morris," Holmes said, "I am sure you can do better than that. What ages were they for instance."

"Oh, young, I suppose. Well, not that young. Not as young as Ralph."

"In their twenties, thirties…?"

"Yes."

He tried to suppress a sigh.

"Were they dark or fair?"

"Neither particularly."

"Hmm."

"One was quite fat. I noticed that, because his jacket was too small to button across… across his stomach. Bourne, I think, that was. Or Ward."

"Probably," Holmes replied drily.

"Now Nelly," Mrs Hudson broke in. "Think. Didn't you tell me they had Cockney accents?"

"Oh yes," her sister replied, "they sounded most rough."

"That's a help," I said, encouragingly. I think Holmes rather intimidated her.

"The fair-haired one was quite tall," she continued, "compared to the other one."

Holmes threw up his hands in exasperation. "Mrs Morris, you just said neither was particularly fair or dark."

"Sorry," she said timidly, "but now I come to think of it, one was fairer than the other. Not white-haired, you understand, just… fairer."

"How were they dressed?" I asked.

"Oh… Yes, I can tell you that. Flashy. That's how I'd describe it. Cheap and flashy. Big checks on the fat one's jacket. A striped waistcoat on the other."

"Blood out of a stone," I said, a while later, back in our room, shaking my head.

"Not quite," Holmes replied. "While blood cannot under any circumstances be extracted from a stone, squeeze Mrs Morris hard enough and at last something emerges. Not much, admittedly. However, I think that if I put the Baker Street Irregulars on the case, we might be able to track down the fellows."

"You think they are in London, then?"

"Most probably. In or around Limehouse."

No sooner said than done. But once Wiggins and the other band of street urchins who made up the Baker Street Irregulars were on the hunt in the East End, there was little we could do in the meantime. Holmes was inclined to pack Mrs Morris off back to Liverpool, although the lady was most disinclined to go, until he suggested that perhaps Ralph had returned in the meantime and was as worried by her absence, as she had been by his.

"If that, sadly, is not the case," he said, "perhaps further letters have arrived from your well-wisher regarding his whereabouts."

She was persuaded, at last, after our assurances that we would most certainly inform her of any developments this end. Mrs Hudson, having seen her safely on her way, confessed to me subsequently, that, much as she loved her sister, it had been something of a trial to have her under her feet all day and night.

"So difficult to get anything done," she said, looking around herself as if critically, whereas to me everything seemed as neat and tidy as ever. "Phoebe, of course, is no use at all."

She often complained about her maid, who, truly, seemed more of a hindrance than a help, forever breaking things, burning things, and generally creating more work for her employer. However, when I once asked why she did not dismiss her, Mrs Hudson's face softened.

"I wouldn't have the heart, and anyway, she's better than she used to be." (The which I rather doubted from my own observations.) "Her poor mother has it hard, you know, Doctor, with so many children, another on the way, and the husband a useless piece of work if ever there was one. No, I could never dismiss little Phoebe."

Mrs Hudson was able to give us a more objective view of young Ralph than we had received from his mother. Or perhaps "objective" is the wrong word, since I had been correct in my surmise that she had a pre-existing low opinion of him. Selfish, lazy and self-indulgent, with a deep-seated sense of grievance against a world that would not properly recognise his merits, summed him up in her eyes.

"Merits, by the way, that exist only in the minds of himself and his doting mother. None of it being entirely his fault," she conceded. "Ralph has always been his mother's pet, spoilt rotten by her, especially after George died and she had no one else at home to cosset."

"What age is the young man now?" I asked.

She thought for a moment. "Twenty-three in years but adolescent in behaviour."

No, Ralph was certainly not a favourite.

"Of course," she went on, "I pray nothing bad has happened to him. Perhaps he has just decided to escape his mother's clutches for a while."

"To sow his wild oats," I suggested.

She pursed her lips. "He did quite enough of that in Paris," she said.

While awaiting developments in the case, Holmes and I pursued our separate interests, my friend employing a lean time in the detection world to throw himself into a study of cuneiform script, myself attending to my medical practice, sadly neglected of late.

Three days passed before we heard again from Wiggins, shown up to our rooms by Mrs Hudson with more enthusiasm than she usually displayed at the advent of the little ragamuffin. He entered with a broad grin that revealed a missing incisor.

"You have good news for me," Holmes surmised.

"I 'ave that, guvnor," Wiggins replied, expanding a meagre chest proudly. "Bobs found 'em." He grinned further. "Bobs yer uncle, so ter speak."

This mysterious discourse was elucidated by Holmes.

"Bobs being one of Wiggins's trusted lieutenants," he said.

"Yus," Wiggins confirmed. "And a bloody good leftynent, "e is, too."

"Tsk," from Mrs Hudson, who had remained to hear what the boy had to say.

"Pardnin' my French, Mrs H," Wiggins said apologetically. "I forgot you wuz there."

"Get on with it, will you," Holmes urged.

"Yeah, well, Mr H, they be 'oled up in Bow, like what you said. Mornin"side Road. Number 23. Big 'ouse belongin' to a dame name of Ada Clyde. And what goes on in that there 'ouse, I'd blush to repeat in front of a lady."

He nodded respectfully towards Mrs Hudson.

"You are sure it's Bourne and Ward."

"Oh, yus. Them all right. Well, one all the time. The other visitin', like."

"Is Ralph there, too?" Mrs Hudson broke in.

Wiggins shook his head, "That fact, Mrs H, I am unable to confirm nor deny." The pompous phrase sounded most comical coming from a street urchin. "But," he continued, "no sign of 'im. O" course, that there Clyde woman has sevral 'ouses… and when I say 'ouses, I means…"

He gave a knowing wink.

"Yes, yes," Holmes said. "We understand. Can you tell us where they are all located?"

"All in doo course, Mr H. Be assured my leftynents are on the job. Day and night." Wiggins fell silent, and stood looking expectant.

Holmes fished a sovereign out of his pocket and tossed it to the boy, who caught it expertly.

"Excellent work, Wiggins. I hope to hear from you again very soon."

"Perhaps," I said to Mrs Hudson, "you can find some buns or biscuits for this most deserving young man."

"I'm sure I can," she replied, at which point the two of them left the room, Wiggins grinning broadly.

"What now?" I asked Holmes.

"Simple as ABC," he replied, "assuming Ada Clyde's middle name is Betsy or Bernardine or some such."

I clapped my hands together. "Of course. ABC, how slow I am... I presume, from Wiggins's broad hints, the woman in question runs a bawdy house or two."

"That is the inevitable conclusion," he replied, and frowned. "But how Ralph would fit into her scheme is unclear."

"Heaven forbid," I said, shaking my head at the thought, "he has become a procurer..."

"Let us not speculate yet," he interrupted me. "However, I shall have to visit the house at Morningside Road."

"Alone?"

"Unless you wish to enjoy the pleasures on offer there yourself."

"Good Lord, Holmes! Surely you do not intend going there as a client!"

"The easiest way, my friend. If Bourne and Ward are on the premises, their function is to discourage unwelcome visitors." He laughed. "Fear not. I shall maintain my virtue despite any temptations to the contrary."

I had no fears on that score. Nevertheless, I spent some uneasy hours awaiting his return that night, and must confess I had recourse to the brandy bottle on several occasions to keep up my spirits, the latest issue of The Lancet failing to enthral. I eventually sat, light dimmed, at the window, looking out over Baker Street in the hope of discerning the familiar tall and lanky returning figure of my friend.

I must have glanced away for a moment, for, without having observed anyone approach, I heard the front door open and close, followed by steps on the stair. Seconds later, Holmes had joined me in the room.

"In darkness, Watson!" he remarked,

"I was dozing," I lied.

"Hmm." He stood over the lamp and lit it, heavy shadows emphasising the gauntness of his face. He had donned one of his many disguises for the enterprise, and it was a sea-faring man I saw before me, reeking of strong spirits, he having splashed abundant quantities of rum over his pea-jacket.

"This coat will need cleaning," he remarked, casting the thing from himself.

"Well?" I asked. "How did you get on?"

He slumped into his chair and gratefully accepted the glass of brandy I offered him.

"I sometimes despair of the human race, Watson. How certain people use the power they have to inflict suffering on the weaker and more helpless. Those poor unfortunate girls…"

Having entered the house at Morningside Road, and, after paying the required amount to a person who had to be Bourne or Ward – a fat and greasy individual in a checked jacket that did not button up properly – he was shown into a seedy enough salon, where a number of half-clad girls lounged, looking tired and bored.

"Cheer up, trollops," Ward (or Bourne) had urged in sharp tones. "'Ere's Midshipman Smiff come to sail away with one 'o youse to Paradise."

"Smith?"

"It is the usual appellation, is it not, Watson, for someone wishing to maintain their anonymity?" Holmes explained. "I took my time choosing a girl, rejecting anyone pert or brazen, or else cowed and broken. Sarah, a little older than the others, seemed the best of a bad lot, and we duly ascended the stairs to a musty-smelling bedroom, stained sheets on the bed. Even if I were as drunk as I pretended to be, I doubt I could have brought myself to lie down upon them."

He went on to explain how he had, with difficulty, stopped the girl from disrobing completely.

"I had to gain her trust, and give a convincing reason why I did not wish to avail of her services. I told her that I had been away at sea for longer than expected and was now looking for my daughter, whom I feared had fallen on hard times in my absence, adding that I suspected she might have entered such a place as this to earn her keep."

"Did she believe you?"

"I don't know, but she became more friendly when I produced a sovereign. No, there was no Antoinette in this house, she said, but might be in one of the many others."

"The last letter I received from her, I said, posted to me in Bilbao, (I might as well have mentioned Timbuctoo, Watson, for all the girl knew of such places) she mentioned having met a woman called Mrs Clyde... Well, no sooner had I uttered that name, than Sarah shuddered. "If she's met Ada," she said, "God 'elp 'er, mister." I urged her to tell me more. She was reluctant at first, but when I produced another sovereign, her greed or need overcame her fears."

Ada Clyde, it seemed, owned a string of "houses" across East London. When asked how she managed to stay out of public notice, Sarah gave Holmes a "queer look". But, at last, she revealed that the woman had protection.

" 'Igh-ups look after 'er, mister. 'Igh-ups with strange tastes, cruel tastes." Holmes related her words as he remembered them. "This 'ere 'ouse ain't much, mister, but it suits me. Ken ain't bad, treats us fair most times. 'E don't expect us to do nothing except the usual. There's another 'ouse I've heard tell of...Well, all I know, mister, is that some girls go in and don't come out again. Boys, too. That's what I meant, mister, God 'elp your daughter if she's in there."

I looked at Holmes in horror. "Boys! Could Ralph be in such a place?"

"I hope not, Watson, but that's as much as Sarah was able or dared to tell me. I left her there, reluctantly, because she seemed a nice enough girl, not utterly corrupted, and in other circumstances might have led a respectable and happy life."

It was very late, the sky beginning to pale into dawn. We agreed to sleep for a few hours and then plan our next move. Perhaps Wiggins would come up with more useful information in the meantime.

I found it difficult to settle, the probable effect of too much brandy, which set my heart and mind racing. Could Ralph really have entered one of those terrible houses? Yet, the young man was surely able to extricate himself if he so wished. He was no wretched indigent, but had a loving family to support him.

The following morning had Holmes and I sitting glumly in our room, the mood not lightened by the lowering skies hanging over Baker Street. My head was throbbing so badly, despite the nostrum of feverfew I had taken, that I could not settle even to read the newspaper, while Holmes, smoking an evil pipe over pages of cuneiform script, annoyed me greatly by exclaiming "Fascinating!" or "Most interesting", from time to time. All the same, I felt that his absorption in those strange wedge shapes was feigned, and that his ears, as much as mine, were pricked to listen out for a visitor.

At last, the doorbell rang, and we both perked up. It was not Wiggins, however, who appeared, but Mrs Hudson, bearing a telegram in her trembling hand.

"From Nelly," she said. "I am sure of it."

Holmes ripped it open. He scowled.

"Nothing," he said. "No sign of the boy. No new letter from the well-wisher."

He screwed up the yellow paper and tossed it on the floor.

"Your sister might have spared herself sixpence."

Mrs Hudson picked up the scrap and hurried out, before Holmes could see her tears.

"That was harsh," I said.

"It's this accursed inactivity," he replied. "Damn the Sumerians." He swept the cuneiform scripts off the table.

"Well," I said, rising to my feet and stepping carefully over the scattered sheets. "I am going for a walk in the Regent's Park, to clear my head. Will you join me?"

Holmes looked out of the window. "It is raining," he said, "and in any case, Watson, one of us has to stay here in case Wiggins turns up."

I did not mind the rain, for it was only a light drizzle, after all. Moreover, I was anxious to escape the oppressive effects of Holmes's bad temper, as well as the thick plumes emitting from his pipe. Once outside the house, I immediately felt a lightening in my spirits, despite the cloud still hanging over young Ralph. There is something reassuring about crowds of people all busy with their own concerns. A matter of perspective, I suppose.

Briskly directing myself towards the park, I nearly collided with a girl hurrying, head down, in the other direction. Something about her, caused me to turn and look after her. It was not at all that she was pretty, and her plain dress hardly revealed an enticing figure – she dragged a leg behind her and had the suggestion of a humped back – and yet something about her intensity of purpose compelled my curiosity. This turned to surprise, when I saw her pause outside 221b Baker Street before limping away, turning, lingering and finally knocking on the door. I hastily retraced my steps, hoping that her business was with Holmes, and not some domestic trifle to do with our landlady.

It seemed that the latter was, after all, the case. Holmes was alone when I re-entered. He looked up, a smug smirk on his face.

"That was quick," he observed. "I knew the rain would discourage you."

"Not at all," I said. "It is most refreshing out, but I thought I saw a visitor arrive."

He leaned back and sighed. "As you can see, you were mistaken."

At that moment, however, the sound of footsteps on the stairs gave the lie to his remark. Mrs Hudson entered, followed by the same young person I had observed in the street, painfully thin, bent under the hump on her back, her wizened face prematurely aged.

"This is Delia," our landlady informed us, veritably sparkling with excitement. And when the newcomer shrank into a timid silence, added, "Go on, dear. Tell the gentlemen what you told me."

"Oh, m'm," the girl said at last, in a rush. "Can't you say what I said?"

"It would be better coming from you," Mrs Hudson replied.

"Why don't you sit down," I said in gentle tones, since the girl looked terrified. "Mrs Hudson can bring us up some tea.

"Oh no," Delia replied. "Don't go, m'm, if you please."

Was it we who frightened her so much? Why? Because we were men? I had a horrible suspicion that this young person had good reason for her fears. And yet, as her story emerged – in fits and starts, it must be said – it seemed that she had suffered at the hands of both sexes.

"If *she* finds out what I done, she'll kill me. Bill, too. I shouldn't never 'ave come."

She looked around wildly at the door, as if about to bolt out of it.

"What is it that you have done, Delia?" Holmes asked.

She stared at him.

"Come 'ere, o'course," she replied at last. "If *she* finds out... Oh, Lord."

She covered her face with her hands as if that would make her disappear.

Holmes looked helplessly at Mrs Hudson.

"Delia knows where Ralph is," she said.

Apparently, this astounding statement broke the ice as far as the girl was concerned. All of a sudden, she started talking in a rush.

"See, 'e don't know yet what she's really like. But I do. I know."

It took time and patience to follow her thread but, to summarise, Ralph had arrived the previous week at the house where Delia was working, in the company of Bill – her brother, as it turned out.

"Such a nice-looking young man," she said. "Nice and polite to me. Not like the others… I could see "e was different from them. Not cut out for… for… the life."

She hesitated, and glanced at Mrs Hudson.

"What is this "house"?" Holmes asked. "Somewhere for men to come?"

Delia almost laughed, then.

"Oh no, mister. Not in that 'ouse. No men visitors there."

"Not women, surely?"

"Ladies, more like. 'Oity-toity ladies…" She looked at Mrs Hudson again, as to apologise for her words. "You should see 'em with their stays off, m'm. Not quite so uppity then."

Holmes was as aghast as I was. Of course, there were, sadly, plenty of brothels in London where men went to have relations with women. Places too, I am afraid, where men went to meet with boys. But a house for rich women to pleasure themselves with young men, that was new to us both.

She, Delia, as she told us, was the slavey, the cleaner and cook, the butt, too, of any discontent on the part of the visitors or, indeed, of the lady of the house, herself.

"Ada Clyde?" Holmes asked.

Delia shrank at the name.

"She's a devil," she whispered, as if the woman herself were within earshot. "If she finds I've come "ere…""

"You are the "well-wisher" who wrote to Ralph's mother, aren't you?" Holmes suddenly exclaimed.

Oh, that all-too familiar expression of disbelief at the detective's seemingly supernatural sagacity! Finally, the girl nodded.

So there was no malicious intent there, after all.

"It was well-written, Delia," I said.

Too well-written for the likes of her, perhaps.

"I copied some of it from a book, sir." That explained it.

"How did you know where to send it?" This from Holmes.

"I asked the young man about where "e come from. Liverpool. "E also told me "e "ad an aunt "ere in Lunnon. Living along a famous 'tective."

So Ralph boasted of the connection. Holmes smiled. "Why should you concern yourself with Ralph in particular?" he asked.

""E don't know what she's like." Delia shivered. "Oh, Lord."

"What danger is Ralph in, exactly?"

Delia, glancing again at Mrs Hudson, coughed and then resumed her account.

"There's another 'ouse… That's where she sends 'em when she gets tired of 'em."

"Another house?"

"An 'orrid place, as I've 'eard tell. Ada wanted to send me there… See, some of 'em visitors would like freaks like me. That's what she said." The girl gave us a timid look. "But Bill said, "Not my sister, Bea. Not Dee!" I can thank him for that, at least."

Holmes shook his head. "You must try to be clearer, Delia. Who is Bea?"

"Oh sorry, sir. That's what Bill call Ada. Beatrice being "er middle name, see. I wouldn't dare. She's Madam to me."

"Ah." Holmes sat back, making a steeple of his fingers. "Now I understand. ABC."

The girl smiled properly for the first time, and almost became pretty.

"Yes, sir. ABC. That's what the girls call "er behind "er back. Code, like."

"So what about this other house, then?"

"Awful, the things that go on there, sir, Bill says. Won't tell me what... Yer hair would stand on end, Dee, 'e says... And see, I'd be afraid Ada plans to send the young man there."

"But surely he can leave whenever he wants," I said.

She looked at me sorrowfully.

"Not now she's got 'im 'ooked. Poor chap don't know which way is up no more."

Mrs Hudson gasped in horror.

Delia explained further how Ada Clyde sent Bill and Ken around the country from time to time, to find pretty boys and girls, and lure them to London with promises of wealth. This appalling woman would then choose a few favourites, and feed them drugs to make helpless addicts of them.

"Then send them to that there 'ouse. Or sell 'em."

"What!"

"There's people, Bill says, what likes to buy slaves."

In England! In the eighteen-nineties! Surely not.

The girl gave us the address of the house Ralph was in. Mrs Hudson urged her not to go back, most kindly offering for her to stay in Baker Street until a suitable new position could be found for her. Delia demurred, however.

"Oh, I have to go back, m'm. For 'is sake, God bless 'im."

Had she fallen in love with Ralph simply because he had said a few kind words to her? My heart went out to the poor creature.

"Anyways, if I don't go back, they'll surely find me, and it'll be all the worse for me then."

Mrs Hudson insisting on feeding her some nourishing soup before she went back, Delia left our room with our kindly landlady. Holmes and I then discussed our best means of proceeding.

"We should alert Inspector Lestrade," I said.

Holmes shook his head. "Not yet, Watson. We have no proof that any criminal activities have actually taken place."

"Running brothels isn't criminal?"

"Well, of course, we could urge Lestrade and his men to go in and clear the swamp. But I suspect this Ada Clyde, from what Delia has told us, is protected by influential friends. High-ups, she said." He shook his head. "When I say "criminal", I mean regarding Ralph."

"Then perhaps we could simply buy Ralph back," I said. "Supposing that money talks to this Ada Clyde."

"He might not wish to be rescued, Watson. After all, he's become dependent on the Clyde woman for his drugs. He may even like the life. Remember what happened at Aldershot."

I did indeed. When the National Vigilance Association planned to close the brothels there, offering the women the chance to reform, they were met with a protest march of 90 prostitutes, and had to give up.

"All the same," Holmes continued. "I think an interview with ABC should definitely be our next move. I am most curious to meet the devil who inspires so much fear."

Easier said than done. We had no notion in which of her many houses Ada Clyde could be found at any particular time, having omitted to enquire this of Delia. Luckily, later that day Wiggins finally turned up with a scrawny cross-eyed little fellow in tow. This was Bobs. Something about the lad caused me to make sure to keep a firm grip on my wallet and fob watch.

"Well, Bobs," Holmes said. "What have you to tell us?"

Bobs looked sideways at Wiggins. At least, I think he did. It was hard to tell where his eyes were directed.

"That's all right, Bobs," Wiggins said. "I'll do it… Bobs can't talk," he explained.

I regarded the lad with more compassion then, though I still would not have trusted him near my valuables.

What followed was an astonishing mute conversation of flapping hands. Holmes watched intently, for I knew he had studied this mode of communication. However, it seemed the boys had developed their own version, which was as foreign to him as cuneiform script to me.

Much of what Wiggins translated confirmed what Delia had told us regarding the various houses, their addresses, the sort of clients catered for in each. Bobs had no knowledge of the house of horrors, but was able to inform us, through Wiggins, that, every morning, Ada Clyde attended the one serving ladies.

"That's when they go. See, it's s'posed to be a dress shop," Wiggins said. "Though no one ever buys nothing. Well, not dresses, anyways." He scowled disapprovingly.

"Is Ralph there?" I asked.

Bobs shrugged his shoulders, and twisted his hands into a maybe/maybe not shape.

"Bobs wouldn't know Ralph from Adam, Watson." Holmes regarded me reprovingly, as if I should have known better than to ask. "But young men are there, aren't they, Bobs?"

The boy nodded vigorously. He swept grubby fingers across his face in a curl and preened himself, as if to express handsome. Something he most definitely was not.

"We will hope to accost Madam Clyde tomorrow morning," Holmes said, reaching for his money pouch. "Good work, boys."

Bobs grinned broadly, while Wiggins said coolly, "Fanks, guvnor. Anytime," adding hopefully, "Will Mrs H 'ave any spare biscuits today, d'you fink?"

"I'm sure she has," Holmes replied and the two lads scampered off down the stairs, the front door slamming after them fifteen minutes later. Not just biscuits, then, but tea or maybe table beer, and some of our landlady's most excellent scones.

The next morning, we duly set out for Bow, where Ada Clyde's "dress shop" was situated. Hardly the most salubrious part of the city for ladies to visit, though the house looked to have pretensions above its neighbourhood, a brass sign on the wall reading *Exclusive*

Paris Fashions, stones steps leading up to a front door painted white and surmounted by a stained glass panel featuring swirling pink flora. Headless mannequins stood in the bay windows, clad in gowns of silk, a little faded and dusty, when one looked closely.

Following our knock, the door was opened by a maid clearly expecting someone quite different, for she became quite flustered. Before we could introduce ourselves, a man pushed past her, presumably Bill or Ken, a tow-headed individual with the flushed and coarse complexion of a heavy-drinker. The man was sporting the red silk waistcoat with yellow stripes described by Mrs Morris, that distinguished his otherwise unexceptional slovenly dress. Challenging us to know our business, he looked ready to slam the door in our faces. However, Holmes politely enquired if Madam Clyde was within, and presented his card. Without a word, the fellow stalked off, presumably to search out his employer, leaving us standing on the threshold by the open door, the little maid trembling uncertainly, not knowing whether to go or stay. We might as well enter, so we did and stood in a hallway decorated to reflect feminine taste of an extreme variety. Dimly lit, it was all very pink, not to say rosy. Frills and flounces adorned every part of the furniture, coyly covering even the legs of the side table and chairs. A pair of large gilt mirrors, considerably foxed, faced each other across the hallway, our reflections within them disappearing off into infinity. A crudely executed painting of a reclining nymph hung over the side table, her ample breasts bared, a wispy scrap of diaphanous material covering her lower regions. Over this simpering maiden, a lustful satyr crouched, as if about to pounce.

"Intriguing, is it not?" A low voice tinged with amusement caused me to spin around.

The woman had approached quite soundlessly, and now stood regarding us with a quizzical expression, Bill or Ken at her shoulder.

I cannot speak for Holmes, but Ada Clyde was not at all as I had imagined her to be. Not some sly old crone, immensely fat, like a spider at the centre of a web, but a slim and elegant woman, of uncertain age. Indeed, she looked quite the part of the couturiere she pretended to be, in her neatly tailored dark grey suit, a pink silk scarf at her neck. With skin of an extraordinary whiteness and hair to match, eyes so pale as to be colourless, I wondered could she be an albino.

I muttered an embarrassed reply, but she had no further interest in me. All her focus was on Holmes.

"Follow me," she told him. I stumbled on behind, as she led the way into a small parlour, rather less frivolously accoutred than the hall. To maintain the pretence, a tailor's dummy, pigeon-breasted, stood in one corner.

"So," she said, after dismissing her bodyguard and seating herself in an armchair, gesturing for us to do likewise, "to what do I owe the honour of a visit from Mr Sherlock Holmes. I rather suspect you do not wish to purchase a gown."

"We represent the concerned parent of a young man," Holmes replied. "I believe he is living here."

"Living here! In a dress shop. Whatever gave you that notion?" She smiled. Against her pale lips, her teeth showed yellow, with little gaps between them. It was unaccountably horrible and I shivered.

"Let us not play games, Ada," Holmes said. "Ralph Morris. Brought here from Liverpool by Ken Bourne and Bill Ward, the foolish lad thinking to make his fortune. I doubt he knew what was awaiting him."

The woman stretched back, crossing one slim leg over the other, and studying the detective. Then she leaned forward.

"Oh, but he did. It was all made quite clear to him." She laughed, a gurgling chuckle. "Since you seem to know so much, I won't beat about the bush... You see, what we do here, gentlemen, could almost be called charitable work, bringing pleasure to ladies whose husbands, if they have any, have failed abysmally in that regard... You are not married yourselves?" Neither of us deigned to respond.

She laughed again, then pulled a bell rope. After a while, Delia entered, clearly aghast to see us. Holmes discreetly pressed a warning finger to his lips, having already instructed me, quite unnecessarily – I am not that foolish – to express no recognition, should we encounter the girl.

"See if dear Ralph is free at the moment, Delia, and if so, ask him to join us."

The girl bobbed awkwardly and limped out, casting a last terrified look back at us.

"Another charity case," Ada Clyde remarked. "I am all heart, as you see." She slowly tapped slim fingers on that swelling part of her anatomy. "But I am remiss," she added, starting to rise "a glass of champagne for my esteemed visitors."

We both demurred.

"A pity," she said, subsiding again into her chair. "I find it so much more amicable, under trying circumstances, to share a drink."

A light tap on the door was followed by the entry of Delia with Ralph. I suppose some might call the boy good-looking. He was almost as tall as Holmes, gingery curls forming a halo on his head. Indeed, in the loose white shift he was wearing, he could have served as a model for one of those rather too pretty boys seen in the paintings of Signor Caravaggio. However, unfocussed eyes rather spoilt the overall impression.

"Thank you, Delia," her mistress said, dismissing the girl, who scurried out. "Now, come over to me, darling," she addressed Ralph. "I see we have disturbed your nap. So sorry."

He approached her, a foolish smile on his face, and stood by her chair. She took his hand.

"These gentlemen have come from your mama."

Ralph regarded us blankly.

"They want to take you home."

I could see how she caressed his hand.

"Home?" he said peevishly. "No, I don't wish to leave. This is my home now. Please tell my mother that."

Ada Clyde smiled, that same fearsome smile.

"You see. His mother has no need to worry. Her little boy is happy here with us."

"But this life, Ralph…" I started to say.

Holmes cut me short.

"No, Watson. Ralph has answered. He has made his bed here and must sleep in it. Come." He stood to leave.

I was astounded. Why would Holmes give up so easily? However, there was nothing for it but to follow him out. As we went down the steps in front of the establishment, a veiled woman was ascending them. She gave an involuntary squeak of shock at the sight of us, and hurried past, into the house.

Holmes emitted a low chuckle.

"The Duchess of X, if I'm not very much mistaken," he said.

I had no interest in Duchesses.

"What was that about, Holmes?" I asked. "Are you really planning to leave Ralph to his fate? You know what Delia told us. He will end up in the House of Horrors."

"My friend, there was no point in continuing the discussion with that woman present and Ralph in the state he was in. Anyone could tell he had been smoking opium."

"Yes, but what are we to do now?" I paused. "I suppose you are going to tell me we must kidnap him." My laugh was cut short by the expression on Holmes's grim face.

"If it comes to that," he said.

He strode ahead of me, veritably trembling with rage. It seemed he intended to walk back to Baker Street, all of six miles, to work off his suppressed energy. As for me, I had no such impulse, especially given the dank chill of that wintry morning, so I called to Holmes that I would take a cab. Without turning, he raised his arm and made a dismissive gesture.

Once home, I warmed myself with a glass of Mrs Hudson's Smoking Bishop, and awaited the arrival of my companion. The drink, the heat from a blazing fire and the excitement of the morning caused me to doze off, and I was only awakened by someone bursting into the room. It was not Holmes, however, but the boy Bobs, in a highly agitated state, Mrs Hudson behind him.

"I couldn't stop him, Doctor," she said, apologetically.

"That's all right," I answered, rising up. "What's the matter, Bobs?"

I could make no sense of his waving hands, only their urgency and the fact that he wished for me to follow him. Disregarding my previous suspicions of the lad, I threw on my coat and followed him out. It seemed walking would not do it. We must take the cab awaiting us.

Back we journeyed all the way to the East End of London, Bobs hopping up and down on his seat with impatience. I could not imagine what we might find when we arrived, though was filled with a sense of foreboding. The driver seemed to know where to stop, the entrance to a dark alleyway. Bobs jumped out and ran into it, I following more circumspectly. Was it a trap after all? However, I soon discerned a figure slumped against the slimy wall of the place. It was Holmes!

I rushed up to see what had happened, and was shocked at his appearance, an ugly gash on the side of his head. Blood all over his coat. He looked up at me, a despairing expression on his face.

"They killed her, Watson!" he said. "They killed her."

My eyes followed his gaze. What I had taken for a heap of rags beside him was in fact the broken body of poor little Delia, beaten to death.

"I tried to stop them," he continued, "but I was too late. They would have killed me too, but I got the better of them."

"Ward and Bourne?"

"The same. That she-devil must have guessed it was Delia who had alerted us."

While he spoke, I examined his head. The cut was much less severe than I had at first thought. In fact, the blood on his coat did not come from any wound that I could see, and I surmised it belonged to one or both of his would-be assailants.

"I don't understand," I said, "how you came upon the scene in the first place."

"It was Bobs," Holmes replied. "He has been keeping an eye on the place and must have seen them drag little Delia out. He came chasing after me, and brought me back here, where the two thuggees were setting about the girl... I was too late to save her, Watson."

He held his head in his hands.

"But one of them was her brother," I exclaimed.

"I know. Can you imagine the evil there? But, Watson, I am responsible."

"No, you are not." I spoke in a firm voice, although inwardly I was much less certain. We should have insisted the girl stay with Mrs Hudson.

"You sent for me," I continued, "but this is surely a matter for Scotland Yard?"

"Bobs has alerted a constable. They should be on their way... However, I doubt they will find anyone at the House. Ada Clyde and her gang will be long gone by now. Although they might have to carry Ward. I think I broke his back."

I shall not linger over the details of the arrival of Scotland Yard, in the formidable person of Inspector Lestrade. And Holmes was almost right. A search of Ada Clyde's known houses proved fruitless as far as tracking down the woman and her two officers. However, the houses were by no means empty: ABC had abandoned her boys and girls and their visitors without a warning. I can only the imagine the consternation of the Duchess of X and others, when burly constables burst in upon them.

One other person was missing. Ralph.

"There is apparently another house, the whereabouts of which we are ignorant," Holmes informed Lestrade. "I have heard it called the House of Horrors. Perhaps you know of it."

Lestrade shook his head. "I'll ask the local men, but I think word of such a place would have reached the Yard before now. We knew of this particular house, of course, and the one in Morningside Road, as well as a couple of other, but were instructed to turn a blind eye." He sniffed. "Went against the grain, of course. But the order came from high up… The very top, in fact, if you get my meaning."

Surely not a royal edict! However, I could not help but recall how whispers had gone around about the involvement of Prince Albert Victor, Duke of Clarence, in the Cleveland Street scandal, with some people even claiming that the Duke was Jack the Ripper himself. I myself had never believed a word of it but now started to wonder.

Lestrade refused to say more on the subject. Just now, in any case, our priority was to track down Delia's murderers, and find Ralph, if it was not already too late.

"There is no alternative," Holmes said. "I shall have to consult with Mycroft. At least I always know where to find *him*."

Holmes's older brother seldom went anywhere except to walk from his rooms in Pall Mall across the road to the Diogenes Club, or else to his office in Whitehall. Even so, he seemed to know everything that was going on everywhere in the kingdom and beyond.

Holmes consulted his fob watch. "Just now he should be at his desk. We will go there instantly, Watson."

I was taken aback. "Surely you wish to change and clean yourself first," I said, regarding his filthy, blood-stained coat, the cut on his head crusting over now into an ugly scab.

"There is no time to be lost in trivialities," he replied. "Anyway, Mycroft will think it is one of my disguises."

But will the doorman even let us in, I wondered?

There was no need for me to worry. The man in question never raised an eyebrow, clearly recognising Holmes. He even gave a little bow on admitting us.

I had met Mycroft on several previous occasions, and was always struck by the absence of any physical resemblance between the brothers, Holmes so long and lean and lithe, the older man, obese from inactivity and too much rich food. With a head buried in his fat neck, Mycroft always reminded me of some huge toad. No, they were totally dissimilar, until, that is, one caught their eyes, the same steely grey, the same penetrating stare.

Mycroft greeted us with a fat smile.

"Good heavens, Sherlock, whom have you killed now?"

Holmes was in no mood for levity, and set out in brief harsh terms what had transpired. His brother's wide face contracted into a deep frown.

"Ada Clyde!" he said. "Our hands have been tied regarding that virago. Someone," he raised his eyes to the ceiling or to heaven, "wants her left alone. I surmise she must be in possession of some incriminating material which certain people of influence wish to keep hidden."

"Blackmail!" I exclaimed.

Mycroft shrugged enormous shoulders.

"That would fit," Holmes remarked.

"As to the House of Horrors," Mycroft continued, "rumours have come to me, but its location – even if it exists outside the realm of fairy-tales – remains unknown. I am sorry not to be able to help you further."

Could not, or would not? At any rate we were dismissed, and had no alternative but to thank him for his time, and leave, sorely disappointed.

Sometimes, however, lucky chance lends a hand. We were hardly back in Baker Street when word came from Lestrade for us to return immediately to Limehouse. A cab stood waiting to convey us thither. At least Holmes had the chance to put on a clean coat, passing the soiled one to a shocked Mrs Hudson, with instructions to "see to it, please."

We then proceeded on a route across the city that was becoming all too familiar. This time our destination was a local police station, where we found Lestrade, together with a very sorry, bedraggled specimen of sub-humanity lying flat on a trestle table, his check-patterned jacket sodden. This, we finally established, was Bill Ward.

He eyed Holmes venomously. "That's the blighter what broke me back," he spat. (In truth, using a much more offensive word to designate the author of his ills. I have refrained from reproducing it, to avoid offending the susceptibilities of my readers.)

"You killed your sister," Holmes countered.

"I did not," Bill shouted trying to rise up, but subsiding in agony. "That was Ken, that was. Dee weren't meant to die. Just get roughed up a bit. Teach her a lesson, like. But Ken got carried away."

"I didn't see you trying to stop him."

"No... well you didn't see everything, mister. Anyways, Bea was furious after. Yelled at Ken "ow "e spoiled everything, specially after she 'eard you was there and we didn't finish you off, too."

"Tell the gentlemen how you come to be here," Lestrade said. "It'll amuse them."

Bill evidently did not wish to share the joke.

"After all I done for "er, and all," was as much as he would say.

"He was found half-drowned off Limehouse dock," Lestrade said.

"Bea said I weren't no use no more. Told Ken to get rid of me, so he tipped me into the water. Some mate, eh!" He shook his head with difficulty. "After all I done."

"So where are they now?"

"Planning a bunk, I reckon. That was always the idea, if things got too 'ot."

"A bunk how and where to?" Lestrade asked, and, when the man remained stubbornly silent, he added, "It'll go better for you, if you talk, Bill. We mightn't pursue the murder charge."

"I'd be better off dead anyways," came the reply. But then he reconsidered. "Plan was to take the cruise ship from Lime'ouse to Liverpool and then over to Amerikay. Bea reckoned no one would look for us on a pleasure steamer. That's probably what they done."

"Did they take Ralph with them?" Holmes asked.

"Reckon they did. Bea said "e was their insurance."

That sounded ominous, but at least, if Bill was right, Ralph was still alive.

He closed his eyes, wincing in agony. Rotten as he was, I could not but pity him. Lestrade must have read my thoughts, for he said, "We'll be taking you to hospital now, Bill. See what they can do for you there."

The ruffian made a slight nod. Perhaps he knew there was not much to be done.

Holmes, wasting no sympathy, addressed the local constable who was standing by.

"What about this cruise ship, then?"

"Goes around the coast, sir, stopping at Plymouth and Falmouth. Takes four days… I wouldn't fancy it in this high wind, though."

"Plymouth! That's good. We can pick them up there."

"It should arrive tomorrow, sir."

"Excellent!"

Thus it was that we were waiting at the quayside by Plymouth Sound – Holmes and myself, Lestrade and his men, together with an over-excited Mrs Morris, newly arrived from Liverpool – when the cruise ship Pride of Kent docked the following afternoon. Lestrade boarded first, instructing the Captain not to let anyone disembark under any circumstances. He then enquired of the steward about our quarries. Of course, they were not using their real names but a description soon elicited a nod of recognition.

"That there woman. She's an odd one. Only comes out after dark," the steward said.

"Just like a vampire," I mused, thinking of Mr Bram Stoker's recent novel.

Holmes gave me a hard look. This was no time for flippancy. However, the bloodsucking propensities of Dracula seemed to me not so very far distant from the activities of Ada Clyde.

The steward led us to the lady's cabin. Low moans could be heard from within, and, fearing the worst, Holmes, with Lestrade, broke through the door.

An extraordinary sight met our eyes. The moans were coming from a man, bent over in apparent agony, Ada Clyde standing beside him.

"The fool can't get it into his head that we've docked," she said. "No cause to be seasick now."

It was all turning into something of a farce, especially when Mrs Morris pushed past me and exclaimed, "That's Bill or Ken. I'd know him anywhere."

Ada Clyde turned tired eyes upon us. "Who in heaven's name is this person?" she asked.

"I'm Ralph's mother, Mrs Eleanor Morris. Ralph's my son. What have you done with him?"

"Ralph?" Ada looked as if she had no idea what Mrs Morris was talking about. Had she taken drugs too? Or was she simply acting? "Who are you all?" She looked at Holmes. "Oh, I know. The insulting detective… I mean consulting." She gave a little laugh.

Lestrade coughed, then became official, informing Ken Bourne that he stood accused of the wilful murder of Delia Ward, and Ada Clyde, no high-ups able to protect her now, of instigating the said act.

"Rubbish!" she snapped. "I loved that girl like she was my own daughter."

"Bill done it," Ken said, raising his head. "If 'e said 'twas me, "e's lying in 'is teeth."

"Ken!" The warning shot out of her like a bullet.

"Why not say it, Bea? Bill must'a turned nark on us for them to be 'ere."

She slapped his face hard, fury overcoming her prudence. "You told me you dealt with Bill."

The man gave Lestrade a cunning look, and continued in wheedling tones. "Yus, you said to finish 'im orf, Bea, but, see, Bill were my friend. Couldn't do it."

"No, you just pushed him into the dock, and left him to drown," Lestrade said.

"Fool!" She was about to strike him again when Holmes intervened and held her back.

"Where is Ralph?" he hissed in her ear.

"Who?"

"You know very well who."

The steward stepped forward.

"There's another cabin," he said.

"You go Watson," Holmes told me. "I want to keep this slippery snake where I can see her."

The steward led myself and Mrs Morris to the adjoining cabin. It proved to be empty, however.

"Oh, Lord! What has she done with him?" Mrs Morris exclaimed.

I was wondering the same thing. Had he been dumped at sea, too, as an inconvenient appendage?

Just then a crewman joined us.

"Bit of a row on deck, sir" he said, to the steward.

We followed him up, and found a familiar slim young man struggling between two muscular sailors, a few passengers looking on with the usual fascination evinced by witnesses to a fracas.

"They won't let me go?" he shouted. "I demand to be let off the ship."

"Ralph!" Mrs Morris cried.

"Mother!" He stopped fighting, and curled into a ball, a pitiful expression on his face. "Oh, mother dear! You've come."

The sailors released him into her embrace.

"Take me away from this horrible place, mother," Ralph begged her.

"Of course, my darling boy." She made towards the gangplank.

"Not yet, m'm," the steward told her. "Everyone's to stay on board. Captain's orders."

She looked pleadingly at me. I shook my head.

"Nothing I can do. The Inspector will wish to interview Ralph."

The young man burst into tears. I regarded him with disgust.

"Why did you leave like that, without a word?" his mother asked.

"Bill and Ken promised I'd get rich and quickly." He frowned sulkily. "But I didn't. She took the money. Told me it was to pay for my keep. Still, you know, it was quite fun at first. All those old women making a fuss of me." I shuddered. The lad had a strange idea of fun! "Then it got horrible, mother. Bea got horrible. Told me I was becoming a nuisance and that she'd send me to… to a horrible place. And she wouldn't give me any more of the… the…"

"Medicine?" I suggested.

"Yes. Medicine. That's right... Really mean of her. Then she dragged me on to this horrible ship."

"My poor boy." Mrs Morris stroked his hair, while he nestled into her embrace.

To think poor Delia had paid with her life trying to protect this worthless individual.

At that moment, Lestrade arrived on deck, followed by the prisoners.

Ada Clyde looked disdainfully at Ralph.

"The cause of all my troubles," she said. "Your mummy is welcome to you."

It was while they were leaving the ship that it happened. Because the gangplank was so narrow, we all had to descend in a single file. Somehow Ada managed to slip through the guard ropes and plunged into the water. Mrs Morris screamed, while the rest of us looked on in horror. Then an enterprising sailor jumped in after her, but Ada's heavy dress must have caused her to sink straight to the bottom. The sailor emerged some seconds later from the filthy water, shaking his head. Another lad pulled him out.

"Well," Lestrade said, "I suppose that's one way of dealing with the problem."

Ken emitted a harsh laugh. "More fool you lot," he remarked with satisfaction, "if you think she's gorn. Bea can slip out of any sittiation, she can. You can bet ya life she'll be back some day to plague yous all."

It was true that Ada's body was never recovered, but that was explained by the tides, or by the debris at the bottom of the dock. If she had got entangled in that, she would stay there forever. Ken made a less lucky escape and – the jury disbelieving his account – was duly sentenced to be hanged for Delia's murder, as well as implicated in the disappearances of many others. Lestrade kept his promise to save Bill from the gallows. Instead, the rogue received a sentence of life imprisonment, and languishes yet in Wandsworth prison, a pitiful wreck. Mrs Morris took Ralph back to Liverpool by train, eschewing the chance to continue their journey on the cruise ship. Mrs Hudson informed us later that Nelly never lets the boy out of her sight. How long, I wondered, will he put up with that?

As for the House of Horrors, try how he might, Holmes was unable to track it down.

"Perhaps it only existed as a threat," I said.

"Maybe," Holmes replied darkly. "But maybe not."

He neatly cut the top off his boiled egg, and sighed deeply.

"Mrs Hudson," he shouted. "this egg is too hard."

Inspector Gregson at Bay

"Mr Holmes, I am being blackmailed."

These were the stark words that greeted me as I joined Holmes for breakfast. Even more astonishing was the identity of the speaker, for I soon recognised the familiar fair-haired figure of Inspector Gregson of Scotland Yard, one of the most upright of men, and one who surely would have no sufficient blot on his character, to render him vulnerable to such threats.

"Come in, Watson," Holmes said. "I am sure the Inspector will not mind having you privy to his account."

Gregson nodded.

"Of course, Mr Holmes," he replied. "I know that the doctor is your valued assistant. I shall be happy for him to hear of the unfortunate circumstances that have brought me to this pass."

I took my seat at the table laden with all the usual breakfast fare, including some juicy looking kippers. But, although I was hungry, I decided it would hardly be appropriate even to start buttering a slice of toast. Since Holmes and Gregson already held cups of tea, however, I poured one for myself, while the Inspector started to explain.

"Over the past few months, gentlemen, I have noticed a change in my son, Philip. He is no longer the open cheerful young lad my wife and I have heretofore known and loved, but is become secretive and troubled. At first, I put this down to the natural restlessness of youth."

"What age is he?" Holmes asked.

"He is but seventeen years old, apprenticed to a printer, and up until recently doing well. However, it seems now that he has been missing work, and providing all manner of unlikely excuses. Finally, Mr Clarke, the printer, contacted me to ask if I was recovered from my illness, and when he might expect Philip to return to work… Mr Holmes, I was shocked. I have not had a day's sickness since I was a boy with the measles."

"So what did Philip say when you confronted him?"

"He mumbled some excuse about his mistreatment at the hands of his employer and fellow apprentices, and that he feared to go back, something I very much doubted. Mr Clarke is a gentle, kindly man, and, in the past, Philip had nothing but good to say of him. As for the other lads, they all seemed to be friends."

"You mentioned blackmail. Where does that come in?"

Inspector Gregson buried his head in his hands, overcome. At last, he pulled himself together, and continued.

"Where did we go wrong, Mr Holmes? My wife and I consider that we have been neither too strict nor too lax with the boy, yet did not notice that he had fallen into bad company. Only yesterday…"

His voice broke.

"Take your time, my friend." Holmes's tone was unusually gentle.

Again, Gregson got a grip on himself.

"Philip failed to return home last night. Instead, we received this missive."

He pulled an envelope from his inside pocket and gave it to Holmes, who extracted the note within. He read it, frowning, then passed it to me.

Father, it read in a shaky hand, *forgive me. I have fallen prey to some bad men and owe them a considerable sum, gambling losses. They are holding me until the debt is settled and threaten that if it is not, then I shall pay with my life.*

"Good heavens! How abominable!" I exclaimed. "But can you not just pay it, man, however much it is?"

"I suspect that it is not as simple as that," Holmes said. "Am I right, Gregson?"

"Indeed. My first thought on reading this was indeed to pay whatever the villains asked, somehow or other, retrieve my poor son, and then try and hunt them down."

"But the man who brought the letter to you had other ideas."

Gregson looked astonished.

"How did you know that?"

"The envelope bears no stamp, so it was hand-delivered. There is a greasy thumb print on the front of it and similar fingerprints on the back, which suggests it was waved in front of you before you snatched it away, as this torn edge indicates. In addition, your son makes no mention of the sum involved. If money were the object of the plan – or rather, your money – then you would need to know how much to pay. I assume some rascal gained entry to your home and threatened you there."

"Indeed, Mr Holmes and with a pistol. Luckily, my wife and daughter were occupied in the kitchen, for, were they present, I cannot imagine the effect of the news upon them." He shook his head at the memory. "I offered to pay whatever was asked but the villain replied that nothing would be enough. Instead, he told me that I could be of immense assistance to the gang – he didn't call them that, of course, he said "to me and my friends" – in a trivial matter that would cause me no bother. And that thereafter Philip would be returned safe and sound."

"The nature of this trivial matter? Some crime, I suppose."

"You have it, Holmes," he replied. "They plan a robbery. So far, I know no more than that. Once they are convinced that they can trust me, they will provide further details. My role, as outlined by this miscreant, will be to clear the way for the robbers, keeping the Metropolitan police occupied elsewhere on the night in question, and thereafter taking over the subsequent investigation, muddying the waters to the extent that the perpetrators remain undiscovered. I told the fellow that it would not be up to me, that I could not guarantee that I should be called on to investigate."

"What did he say to that?" asked Holmes.

" 'You had better be,' was the grim reply. He told me that if I betrayed them, I might expect to see my son again only as a cold corpse."

"The monsters!" I exclaimed. "But why come here?" I continued. "Why not tell your colleagues at Scotland Yard?"

Gregson raised a despairing face to mine.

"If you had children of your own, Dr Watson, you would not ask such a question. If I consulted Lestrade or Hopkins, do you think those villains would hesitate to carry out their threat and kill my son."

I felt remorseful. He was right. How could I know how a father felt. I was sad, as well. Mary and I had hoped so much to start a family before her untimely death.

"I am sorry," I said. "It was a thoughtless remark."

He nodded in acceptance of my apology. "It even occurred to me," he continued, "to comply with their demands. But a moment's thought set me to rights again. Even if they released Philip, I should be their creature thereafter. They would hold what I had done over me. If I confessed to my superiors, my career would be over. I can imagine how much Lestrade would crow over that."

It was well known that the two men were rivals, sometimes bitter ones.

"You did well to come to me," Holmes said. "It is quite true that once you have compromised yourself with these people, even if your son is returned safe and well, you will henceforth be in their power."

"Exactly." Gregson shook his head. "You are my only hope, Mr Holmes. Please say you will help me."

The poor man looked abjectly at my friend, who sat back in his chair, closed his eyes and made a steeple of his fingers. After a few silent seconds, he leapt to his feet,

"When are you to hear further from these people?" he asked.

"I cannot say. Soon, I am sure."

"Of course. I only hope that you were not followed here. You must know that they are likely to be watching you."

"I took precautions and left my house in the early hours by the back entrance. I am sure no one came after me."

Holmes moved to the window and peered out.

"Nothing out of the ordinary there. All the same, do nothing further to arouse their suspicion, and do not return here until you hear from me that it is safe to do so. We can communicate by telegram. Let me know when they contact you again, recounting exactly what they tell you to do. You must of course agree to everything they ask of you."

Gregson started.

"I cannot," he exclaimed.

"Do not worry. I promise that you will not have to do anything against your conscience. Your agreement is only to buy time and ensure that Philip remains alive and unharmed. I suggest, too, that you demand he write a short message to you to that effect on a page of each day's newspaper. Meanwhile, I shall be doing my very best to hunt these animals down."

"How will you accomplish that?"

"Ways and means, dear Gregson, ways and means… First of all, you must tell me as much as you can about your visitor, and about Philip's habits and friends. And let us move away from the table over to the window, so that Watson may at last satisfy his appetite and eat his kippers before they get too cold. He has been eying them this long while."

Gregson cast a glance my way, as if reproaching me for my animal needs at such a time. My excuse is that I think less clearly when hungry, unlike Holmes, whose senses seem sharpened by lack of food.

"What do you make of that, Watson?" Holmes asked when at last our guest had departed.

"A nasty business," I replied. "You made great promises to the poor fellow. But how ever will you track these men down, with so little information?"

"On the contrary, I consider I already have plenty to go on… But perhaps you could ask Mrs Hudson for some more toast. This has gone quite hard. Oh, and another kipper would not go amiss."

I was surprised. Given the urgency of the situation, was he not planning to rush off at once? It seemed not. It was only after a leisurely breakfast, that he at last readied himself to go out. I admit that I was rather disappointed that he did not request that I join him.

"Better you stay here and await communications from Gregson," he said.

A long dull day ensued, with no developments. I perused so many learned articles from old copies of *The Lancet* and *The Times of London* that my head was become quite fog-bound. It was only in the late afternoon that a telegram at last arrived, addressed to Holmes. Since I was privy to the matter, I considered it fitting that I should open it. The telegram consisted of seven words: *Day after tomorrow. Caledon and Dunedin bank. London Wall.*

I gasped. The C&D was a well-established merchant bank, known to possess, as well as the usual sums of ready cash necessary for everyday purposes, a store of safety deposit boxes whose owners were rumoured to be among the richest men in Europe. A robbery there would shake the financial and political foundation of many states. But I wondered at the choice, at the same time: the bank was well guarded, its vaults said to be impregnable, thus posing a mighty challenge for thieves.

Soon thereafter, Holmes arrived back in that state of extreme exhilaration I recognised only too well. Like a bloodhound, he had picked up a scent and was tugging at the leash to race off after it. He hardly looked at Gregson's telegram before disappearing into his room only to emerge a while later transformed into one of those disreputable individuals that hang around low bars or places of ill fame.

"Do not wait up for me, Watson," he yelled as he ran out. "I have no notion how long I shall be."

It was all most unsatisfactory. Was I supposed to stay behind and simply hope for further messages from Gregson? Even if such arrived, I myself should not be able to act upon them or pass them on to Holmes. I decided, therefore, to go out, at least to clear my head.

Light was fading as I strolled towards the Regent's Park. Already summer was giving way to autumn, the leaves of the elm, beech and chestnut trees changing from green to motley shades of red, brown, yellow and gold, and soon to fall. A light mist hung over the lake, where swans and mallards glided sedately. Distant voices of children filled the air as nursemaids walked their charges. Old folk sat on benches absorbing the peaceful scene. Hard to believe in the villainy of man in such a setting.

I returned to Baker Street in the hope that Holmes would have returned in the meantime. However, there was no sign of him and I ate my supper in solitude. Reluctant to go to bed, I lingered over a glass of brandy and water. It must have been the second glass that lulled me asleep where I sat, for I woke with a start in the middle of the night, though could find no cause for it. The house was as still as ever. I could not help but worry for my friend. Holmes was forever placing himself in situations of danger, convinced that he could extract himself safely if necessary. But surely the day would come when this was not the case. Already he had escaped by the skin of his teeth at the Reichenbach Falls. If a cat has nine lives, how many does a consulting detective have? I sat in darkness, for who knew how many hours, brooding over this, watching eerie shadows dancing on the walls.

Eventually the sky outside started to lighten and the nocturnal silence of the street was broken by the comforting noises of early morning: the clanking urns of the milkman, the trundling of the breadman's wagon, the postman whistling, downstairs, Mrs Hudson and the household staff bustling about. I crossed to the window to look out, but there was still no sign of Holmes. Then came a sudden shriek of alarm. I raced down to find what was the matter, and discovered the scullery maid cowering in the passageway, and our landlady standing at the kitchen door eyeing what appeared to be a most disreputable-looking individual lying, apparently out cold, across the table. After a moment or two, the fellow raised his head, bleary-eyed, and grinned.

"Mr Holmes," said our landlady severely, "you'll be the death of me one of these days. And you have scared the life out of poor Phoebe here."

This was the maid, a young person of limited intelligence and capabilities, whom Mrs Hudson must employ out of the goodness of her heart, for the girl had no redeeming features that I could see.

"My sincere apologies," Holmes said. "I returned in the early hours with a terrible thirst on me and must have fallen asleep here."

Mrs Hudson sniffed the air. "It seems to me that it was more than water that was drunk."

In truth a powerful odour of strong liquor, as well as tobacco smoke, permeated the room.

Holmes laughed.

"Not much escapes you, Mrs Hudson. I admit I had occasion to take a glass or two of rum last night with some unsavoury types, solely in the line of duty, you understand. However, I can assure you that only the purest well water has passed my lips since I came home. And now a strong pot of coffee would not go amiss, if you can manage it. I am sure Watson would concur. He looks to have been up half the night himself."

I nodded. Relieved to find Holmes none the worse for his adventure, I was anxious to return upstairs and learn what he had discovered.

"Well, gentlemen," Mrs Hudson said, somewhat appeased, "I suppose that can be managed."

The maid was still in the passageway when Holmes and I proceeded back to our rooms. Now, while, in general, Holmes has little time for Phoebe – unless to complain about her – on this occasion he actually apologised for scaring her, an attention which, I rather suspected, terrified the poor child even more.

Despite my impatience to learn of his discoveries, Holmes insisted on cleaning himself up before all else, and so it was only when we were seated at the breakfast table with the aforementioned pot of coffee, boiled eggs and toast in front of us, that my friend allowed himself to describe his adventure of the previous night.

"Gregson having furnished me with precise details of his unwelcome visitor," he began, "I applied to one of my informants, who directed me to one of low gambling haunts of Limehouse, a so-called 'copper hell', which a person of that description was known to frequent. I soon recognised my quarry and settled myself down to observe the play for a while. A crowd of foolish youths were being cheated so cleverly, they never suspected a thing, which, I suppose, is how they netted young Gregson. Once I understood the set-up, I myself joined them for a hand of cards."

He smiled in satisfaction. I knew well the reason, for I had played against him myself and never got to the bottom of the fact that he invariably won, even in a seeming game of chance.

"My successes caused quite a stir," he continued. "Of course, one has to be careful and not antagonise men who might be inclined to take revenge, especially in a place like that. I won against those same poor young fools, addicted to the vain hope that sooner or later they would come out on top."

"So did you find the men who have abducted Philip?"

Holmes cut the top of his egg and regarded the contents with satisfaction.

"Mrs Hudson is learning. She has cooked this to perfection. A five minute fifteen second egg, Watson, near enough." He dipped a soldier of toast into the soft centre and ate it with relish. "What did you ask?" he said at last. "Oh yes, whether I had tracked down the men holding young Philip. As to that, Watson, you are looking at the newest member of the gang."

"What!"

"After I collected my winnings, I could tell that I was being watched closely and suspiciously by certain villainous-looking denizens of the place, including one that exactly matched the description of Gregson's unwelcome visitor, so I treated them all to a round of rum punch. Without asking me directly, they clearly wanted to know how I had pulled off such a coup. I replied that I was just lucky, winking at the same time, so that they knew I had a trick or two up my sleeve."

"Quite literally," I remarked.

"Good heavens, no, Watson! I should never resort to such a low dodge,"

"Hmm." I had often suspected it of him whenever we played together. His face, of course, remained a mask of innocence. "So what then?"

"I let it be known," he continued, "that I was but newly arrived in London, intimating that I had recently been detained up north at her Majesty's pleasure – I pride myself on mimicking a Lancashire accent with accuracy – and was now looking to make my fortune in the big city, far from where I was known. When the scoundrels ascertained, from various hints and remarks I dropped, that I was a man with no scruples whatsoever, and after I had plied them with more rum punch, they let on that they were looking for such a one as me to help out in a forthcoming enterprise. If I performed to their satisfaction, they said, they might even consider recruiting me to their exclusive club."

"Good heavens, Holmes! Who are these men?"

"The leader of the band is one Dudgeon, a dwarfish, greasy man built like a brick privy and quite as filthy, nicknamed Bulldog for his unfortunate facial resemblance to that beast. Then there is his deputy in devilry, Rogers, a long, skinny slippery sort of fellow, never at rest. And, finally, Crick, our friend who visited Gregson, a hefty, wall-eyed individual. You never know if he is watching you or if his attention is quite elsewhere. It is most disconcerting. A lucky affliction for us, though, for it was the description of him that was recognised by my informant, and enabled me to track the gang down with such little difficulty."

"So what now?"

"I have employed the latest scion of the Tribe of Wiggins, along with the rest of the Irregulars, to follow my new friends trusting that one or the other will lead us to where Philip is confined. For my part, or that of 'Jeremiah Cotter' – the name I gave to the gang – I am to meet them in the same copper hell tonight, presumably in order to proceed to rob the Caledon and Dunedin bank."

"Good heavens, Holmes. Then there's no time to be lost."

Holmes nodded. "Unless we have some luck, the outlook is certainly grim. If the men are arrested in the course of the robbery, Philip is doomed. Or if Gregson does what the villains demand, and distracts his men away from the scene of the crime, then he will be disgraced and most probably imprisoned himself."

"It is a pity he does not feel able to confide in his fellow officers. Would they not assist him under the circumstances?"

"Rightly or wrongly, he feels not. You yourself know well how he and Lestrade dislike each other, how jealous they are of each other's success, how happy with each other's failure."

I shook my head. "It's a sorry state of affairs when men in their position succumb to such petty rivalries."

Holmes smiled. "I think you will find, my innocent friend, that the self-same petty rivalries occur in all walks of life, even in the medical profession."

I nodded then, recalling a sorry instance, concerning two colleagues at Barts, that had recently come to my notice. "Especially in the medical profession," I said.

At that moment a violent hammering could be heard on the front door below, followed by a loud altercation between the housemaid, Clara and a child's insistent voice, after which heavy steps pounded up the stairs to our room. It was Wiggins himself who burst in, a raggedy boy of twelve, bearing such an extraordinary resemblance to the elder brother who had first assisted Holmes in his investigations, that I was quite transported back several years. The boots the lad was wearing were clearly several sizes too big for him, which accounted for the excessive noise they made. He was followed in by a ratty little fellow of about eight, his bare feet blackened by city filth. These same extremities seemed to fascinate the boy, for he stared down at them without raising his head.

"Mister 'Olmes, sir. We found 'im," Wiggins shouted. "We found 'im."

Holmes leapt up.

"Are you sure?" he asked.

"One hunnerd per cent, sir. Down by the river in one o'' them shacks on the wharf. It were Jimsy, 'ere, what follwered the skinny feller, what found 'im. Weren't it, Jimsy? 'E peeped through a crack in the wall and seed 'im, all tied up. Din'cher. Jimsy?"

"Yurs." The child's voice was surprisingly deep and hoarse. He continued to stare at his feet.

"So tell Mr 'Olmes 'ow it was, Jimsy."

Reluctantly the little fellow looked up, apparently did not care for what he saw, so looked down again.

"Go on," Holmes barked. "Has the cat got your tongue, young fellow?"

Jimsy lowered his head even further, while Wiggins cumbersomely hopped from one foot to the other.

"The boys look cold," I ventured, "Perhaps a nice hot cup of tea with some of Mrs Hudson's drop scones might not go amiss."

Holmes looked at me impatiently, but the two lads clearly approved of the suggestion, and I rang down instantly to place the order.

Perhaps Mrs Hudson had anticipated such a demand, for the comestibles arrived in record time, and soon the two lads, perched on the very edge of the couch, as if fearful of soiling it, were munching and slurping away.

"Milk AND sugar," Wiggins commented approvingly. "Yer Mrs 'Udson"s a real treasure, ain't she, gents, even if she 'as a sharp tongue on 'er."

Holmes made no reply, pacing restlessly, his frown deepening every time one of the lads reached for another buttery scone.

"So now, Jimsy," I said at last, considering that sufficient refreshments had been availed of. "Please tell us exactly what you saw."

The boy stared up at me, his eyes green as bottle glass. Perhaps it was my softer tone, compared to Holmes's testy one, but he seemed readier to confide in me.

"Yurs," he said, his mouth still full of pastry, "I follered 'im to the river, I did. 'E wuz a-lookin' back all the time, to see if he were follered, but din pay no 'eed to me. Soon enough, we gets to this broken old shack in one o' them wharves and in 'e goes... So I creeps up..." By now, Jimsy had relaxed into his account and was enjoying himself tremendously, "an" don' I find a broken plank where I can see in. An' what d'yer think? There's this young feller, all tied up, and a big stout, red-faced woman standin' over 'im. ''Ow's our guest, Molly?' sez the skinny cove. 'Behavin isself, is

206

'e?' She mutters some complaint about 'ow much longer she 'as to stay with 'im. "Not much longer. Molly,' sez he. 'one way or t'other,' sez 'e. "Untie 'is 'ands, will yer.' Then 'e pulls a newspaper from out 'is pocket and tells the lad to write on it. The booby starts to blubber then and the woman 'its 'im. Weren't nice ter watch, sir."

"No, indeed," I replied, "but you did well, Jimsy, didn't he. Holmes?"

Holmes nodded.

"But there's more, aint there, Jimsy?" said Wiggins.

"Yurs." Since, by now, the little chap had stuffed another scone into his mouth, we had to wait a minute or two before he was able to proceed.

Holmes drummed his fingers on the table, but it was not until after Jimsy had washed the crumbs down his throat with a slurp of tea, that he looked up at us again.

"The fat woman follered the skinny feller out. They din see me but I could peep round at 'em and 'ear 'em well enough, even though they was whisperin'."

"Jimsy's got sharp ears, 'avent yer, Jimsy," Wiggins put in proudly.

"Yurs," came the reply. "I 'ave."

"Yes, yes. Very good," said Holmes. "What did you hear?"

"So Fattie asks, 'You aint reely goin' ter let 'im go, are yer, Bill? Not when 'e knows our names and faces.' Skinny feller laughs. 'Doncha worry about that, Molly girl,' sez he. And then 'e done this."

With an unfortunate degree of relish, Jimsy drew a dirty finger across his throat.

"No honour among thieves," I remarked, with a shudder.

"Well, Jimsy," Holmes said. "I reckon you have saved the day. Well done, lad."

The boy regarded him with astonishment. I doubted he was much used to praise.

"Tell me," Holmes continued. "Was this Molly the only guard you could see?"

"Yurs," Jimsy replied. "Only she's a big "un, mister."

"All the same," Holmes said. "I suppose she'd hardly pose a threat to Watson here, armed with his pistol."

Jimsy looked dubious. "She's a big "un, she is," he repeated.

Now, I pride myself that I am not by nature a coward. and yet I see no good reason to place myself at an unnecessary risk.

"Can we not call in the regular police at this stage?" I suggested. "After all, it's a clear case of abduction."

Holmes shook his head. "In order not to alert the gang, and, as well, to allow Gregson the honour of catching them in the act of robbery, I deem it better not to involve Scotland Yard at this point."

"Doc an' us'll manage," Wiggins said, pushing out his chest in a manly way. "Doncha worry about that, Mr 'Olmes, sir."

"That's the spirit," my friend replied. "Because I myself need to be elsewhere. We must turn the tables on these villains and put them out of action for ever. In the meantime, I must send a telegram to Gregson, explaining what's happening."

To make sure that none of the gang members were hanging around the wharf, we decided to leave our expedition to release Philip until late afternoon, when Holmes was to join the rest of the gang at Limehouse.

Thus it was that twilight was already setting in when Wiggins, Jimsy and I made our cautious way to the banks of the Thames, to those miserable reaches of broken-down warehouses where flitting shadows signal the presence of individuals bent on activities of a dubious nature. I was glad of the reassuring presence of my pistol, and not just for the undertaking ahead of us.

At last, we arrived, Jimsy silently pointing at our goal. Of all the run-down edifices in the vicinity, this had to be one of the worst, a construction of rough planks set in a puddle of mud and stagnant water. Wiggins and I stayed in the shadow of an upturned fishing boat while Jimsy crept up to the hovel and peered through one of the many cracks in the walls. He then beckoned us forwards, whereupon I put my eye to the crack, but found it hard to see in: The space was dark and it took a moment or two for my eyes to adjust. Finally, I managed to make out a large woman dozing on a chair, a bottle in her hand. A shape on the ground, presumably the wretched Philip, lay stretched out beside her. This should be easy, I thought, especially if the woman, as it seemed, was drunk on liquor. We moved round as silently as we could, to the door.

My notion was a straightforward one: to enter, pistol at the ready, subdue the woman, and, with the help of the two lads, free poor Philip. Alas, for the best laid plans…

As I entered, there echoed an unearthly screech which almost caused me to drop my pistol. It was nothing supernatural, however, but came from a caged parrot rearing up on its perch, and fluttering its wings in excitement. The woman, awakened, jumped up.

"Oo are you?" she growled. "Wha' d'yer want?"

Jimsy had not exaggerated his description. This was a big woman indeed. As tall as myself, wide as a barrel, with the thick arms of a stevedore and a ruddy complexion to match.

"I am come to free the boy," I said. "Stand back, if you know what's good for you."

She might be big, but was not encumbered by her flesh, for "Oh no, yer don't," she uttered, flinging the bottle at me with so much force and so true an aim that it hit me on the side of the head, sending me reeling sideways. Taking advantage of my momentary confusion, she leapt forward and tried to grab my gun. We grappled and I felt her strength. She twisted my arm and I dropped the pistol. Laughing, she kicked it out of the way.

"Free the boy, is it? Not while Molly's in charge, mister."

She knocked me to the floor with her huge fist and set her boot upon my chest, pressing down so hard that I gasped for breath. All the while the parrot continued to screech frenziedly.

I have to admit, at that moment, I feared for my life. The woman was crushing my ribs, squeezing the breath out of me. Suddenly, however, it was she who was screeching. She lurched away from me as if electrocuted, screaming vile abuse. Raising myself up with some difficulty, I perceived an extraordinary sight. Somehow, Jimsy had managed to leap on to the woman's shoulders, his skinny knees gripping her head, and was pulling at her hair while she spun around trying to grab him.

"That's enough, Jimsy," a calm voice said. "Get down." Wiggins had retrieved my pistol and was jabbing it into the woman's side. "Now Molly," he continued, after Jimsy had released her from his iron grip. "I don't want to kill yer, but will if necess'ry. Be quiet, now, there's a good woman. Sit down."

I suppose she realised she was outnumbered, even if it was by one rather ineffectual adult man and two children. She sat back down in her chair, mumbling curses.

Rather ungracefully, I pulled myself up off the floor and crossed over to where Philip was lying. I took off his gag and loosened his bonds.

" 'Ere, doc," Wiggins said. "Give them ropes ter Jimsy. We can use them to tie up madam, 'ere."

"Who are you?" Philip asked, in shrill tones. "Are you going to kill me?"

The poor lad's eyes were wide with terror. I tried to reassure him, but days spent awaiting his fate at the hands of the gang had clearly affected his mind, for he shuddered away from me.

Wiggins had no patience for this behaviour.

"Be grateful we 'ave come ter save yer," he said. "At great risk and danger to ourselles."

The woman Molly, trussed up like a chicken now, gave a harsh laugh.

"Wait till my men come a-looking for yer," she scoffed. "Ye'll be right sorry for this night's work then, my laddies."

"I think not," I said, sounding more confident than I felt. "Inspector Gregson will have arrested the three of them by now."

"Oh. yurs. Where's that then?"

"Robbing the Caledon and Dunedin bank. Your men won't see the light of day for many years, no more will you."

"Is that so, mister?" The confident mockery in her voice gave me pause. Perhaps we were wrong, after all.

"Shut 'er up, Jimsy," Wiggins said. "I'm sick of the sound of 'er 'orrible voice."

The woman shook her head violently from side to side.

"Don't gag me, dearie," she said, apparently suddenly cowed. "I'd be afeared I can't breathe. I 'ave a weak chest, I 'ave... I promise to be quiet. Promise."

Jimsy looked at Wiggins for instruction.

"Do it," the latter said coldly. "Did she ever show mercy to this feller?" indicating Philip, sitting up now, tears rolling down his cheeks, rubbing his chafed wrists and ankles.

To get the gag on the woman was a mighty struggle, in which Wiggins and I had to hold her still, while Jimsy tied it tight round her mouth.

"And shut up that bleedin parrot, too, Jimsy." For the bird continued to screech. " 'E'd waken the dead, 'e would."

In case neck-wringing was in prospect, I hastily threw a moth-eaten blanket over the cage, silencing the parrot in an instant.

By now, Philip was assured that we were there not to harm but to help him. However, the lad was so weakened by his ordeal that there was no way he could depart the shack on his own steam. In any case, I was unwilling to leave Molly alone. Like Samson in the temple of the Philistines, weak chest or no, she seemed strong enough, once left to herself, to break out of her bonds, so I penned a note for Jimsy to deliver to the nearest police station, reckoning that, under the circumstances, it was permissible to enlist the support of the local constabulary. To this, I added a cryptic message, to be conveyed, with all possible haste, to Inspector Gregson, informing him that our endeavour had been successfully concluded, the inference thereby being that the arrest of the rest of the gang would no longer pose a threat to his son. The messenger, admittedly, was not of the sort to inspire confidence, but I hoped that my missive would overcome the lad's visible deficiencies.

Thus it turned out, for, in a short space of time, a couple of bemused constables arrived with a wagon in which to transport Philip, accompanied by myself, to hospital, and Molly, cursing and scratching, to prison.

I was, of course, agog to learn if Holmes's enterprise had reached an equally happy conclusion, while only too aware that my part in the lad's liberation was hardly distinguished. Nevertheless, Philip was free, and, even as I left him in the hospital, was awaiting the arrival of his mother.

Back at Baker Street, there was as yet no sign of my friend and colleague. No word, as Mrs Hudson averred, had reached her, but, shocked by my dishevelled and bruised appearance, the good woman started to fuss rather overmuch: I was sporting the beginnings of a formidable black eye, thanks to Molly's well-aimed bottle. Nothing would satisfy my landlady, even though I assured her that all was well, but that I would sit by the fire, with a blanket over my knees sipping a scalding brew of beef tea. In vain to suggest that I should much prefer to pace up and down with a stiff brandy in my hand, for I was restless and, as time passed, was growing more and more concerned about the fate of my friend.

Mrs Hudson was having none of it.

"Mr Holmes will come back in his own good time, as he always does. Meanwhile, you stay quiet, Doctor, and finish your tea."

I promised to do so. Luckily, she was far too busy to stand over me and make sure I did exactly as I was told.

It was after midnight and into the early hours before I at last heard the front door open, and steps on the stairs, halting steps, however,

212

not the firm tread I associated with my friend. Nevertheless, it was he, or rather 'Jeremiah Cotter', who fell into the room. To my chagrin, he burst out laughing at the sight of me, but my vexation soon turned to concern, as I saw how he winced.

"Are you all right, Holmes?" I asked.

"I am afraid the two of us might have bitten off more than we could chew this time, Watson," he remarked ruefully. "I rather underestimated the cunning and strength of our adversaries."

He sank into his chair. I reheated some beef tea on the Bunsen burner he habitually used for his medical experiments, and gave it to him.

"What the devil is this?" he asked, sniffing at it.

"Mrs Hudson's patent restorative," I replied. "It did wonders for me. Especially with the addition of a splash of brandy."

While he was partaking of the broth, I recounted my adventure.

"Without Wiggins and Jimsy," I said, "the outcome might have been very different. They were the heroes of the night."

"They shall be rewarded handsomely."

He then described his own experiences. He had gone to the gambling den, as arranged, to meet with the three villains.

"Huddled around a table, and already well-oiled with rum, they informed me that the plan that night was to rob a certain diamond merchants in the City."

"Not the Caledon and Dunedin bank, then!" I exclaimed.

"Apparently not. They had not trusted Gregson with the truth, and now I realised – noticing they were watching me very closely as they told me of the plan – that they did not trust me either. I do not know what had raised their suspicions. Or maybe they were just generally cautious. However, I think my blank look dispelled, for the moment anyway, their mistrust. Still, since there was now no way I could get word to Gregson, I realised I would have to thwart their enterprise on my own."

In fact, as it turned out, the establishment in question backed on to the Caledon and Dunedin bank, so that the orders to Gregson to distract the police from the area would still serve the men's purposes. However, the rest of the Inspector's plan, to install constables secretly inside the bank would now prove fruitless.

"Our destination was a back alley behind the diamond merchants," Holmes related. "On the way, the men joked how useful it was to have powerful friends. In addition to Gregson, whom they supposed to be obeying their orders, it turned out that they had another creature inside the merchant's establishment, another blackmail victim. This wretched man had provided them with keys and the combinations of the safe. The robbery would be, as Dudgeon laughed, like taking sweetmeats from an infant." Holmes shook his head. "When we arrived, I was left with wall-eyed Crick to keep watch outside, while Dudgeon and Rogers went within. Crick was wary, but surprise was on my side and I was able to floor him with some nifty baritsu moves. I then followed the other gang members inside and found them about to raid the safe. Telling them that the place was surrounded by constables, who had already overpowered Crick, I urged them to flee. Rogers panicked, but Dudgeon, frowning at me, said that Gregson would never have put his son's life at risk. He sent Rogers to look outside, to check if I was telling the truth, while I was to stay behind with him. I tried the same moves on him as on Crick, but he was ready for me, and the struggle was tougher, he being as strong as the bulldog he so much resembled. Rogers returned in the midst of all, shouting that Crick was laid low and that there was no sign of any constables. Now it was two against one and I feared that I would come off the worst and fail in my attempt, especially when Rogers drew a knife from his belt and thrust it into my thigh..."

"Holmes," I cried. "Let me see."

"A glancing blow, nothing more."

But now I saw a darker patch on his trouser leg. He waved me away.

"I have patched it up, Watson. It will surely keep until I finish my account." But noticing now how he was grey with pain I urged him to let me tend to the wound. He was stubborn. I had no choice but to let him continue.

"Luckily," he related, "I was able to grab the weapon and turn it on my assailants. Rogers at least will long bear the scars on his face and arms. However, my advantage was slight. Bulldog Dudgeon was coming for me again with a roar, and all looked to be lost, when suddenly the door burst open and two hefty constables appeared. They had given up on the bank raid and were returning to their beat when they heard the fracas, and come to investigate. At first, they handled me roughly, taking me for one of the gang, and imagining we had fallen out over the loot. However, after I mentioned Gregson's name and my own, they took better stock of the situation, and left me be, handcuffing the two crooks…"

Holmes looked downcast.

"I very nearly failed, Watson," he said, after a pause.

I felt for my friend, who liked to be in control of the situation at all times. At least, I mused, for once he could not chide me for my own shortcomings. On this occasion, both Holmes and I had been saved by others.

"I gained some satisfaction, however," he continued. "As Dudgeon was being led away, he sneered at me. "A hollow victory, Sherlock," he whispered. "When news of our arrest goes abroad, it will be all up with you know who. My friend will make sure his father never sees him alive again." Well, you can imagine how delighted I was to be able to inform him that Philip was safe and that his 'friend' had been arrested also."

"But you didn't know that," I said.

"I have the greatest faith in you, Watson, my friend," he replied, much to my gratification. But then he added, "Admittedly, Wiggins had dropped by the gambling den, before we set off, to give me a discreet thumbs up."

No doubt to Lestrade's dismay, Gregson and his men were crowned in glory at the apprehension of such a notorious and dangerous gang, while our own involvement remaining unrecorded, as Holmes wished it to be. The inspector himself, however, visiting us subsequently with his son in tow, was effusive in his thanks, and most concerned regarding the injuries we had sustained, minor though they turned out to be.

"How can I ever reward you sufficiently," he said, reaching for his wallet.

Holmes waved it away.

"No reward necessary for a friend and colleague," he remarked magnanimously, adding, "I am sure at some time or other there will be a *quid pro quo*."

The Inspector looked somewhat puzzled at this, but smiled his gratitude.

Philip, much restored since I had last seen him, assured us that he had learnt his lesson, that the horrors of his confinement had brought him to his senses and that he would never again cross the threshold of a "copper hell". It seems that he has kept his word, for the last we heard, he was back working for Mr Clarke, the printer, acquitting himself well and leading a quiet life.

Wiggins and Jimsy were amply rewarded out of the inspector's pocket, which was only right. I myself purchased two pairs of boots for the lads, though the last time I saw them, Wiggins was still wearing the overlarge ones and Jimsy was still barefoot, so I suppose they had pawned the good new ones. Ah well!

The Case of the Fatal Flowers

The early morning spring light that poured through our Baker Street windows so gladdened my heart that I was about to remark on it to Holmes, when I noticed he was drumming his fingers on the table impatiently, a frown darkening his brow. My trivial observation, as he would have deemed it, would only have irritated him further.

"What's the matter?" I asked, knowing the answer full well.

"Nothing," he snapped. "Where's that dratted woman with our breakfast?"

Poor Mrs Hudson. It was not her fault that Holmes had currently no enticing case in train to test his powers of deduction. Idleness did not suit my friend, and I feared that if something did not come up soon, he would resort to chemical means to escape for a while "the dull routine of existence", as he liked to put it.

"But here she comes," I exclaimed. "And bringing the post, along with our boiled eggs, I warrant."

Let there be something in the mail to distract him!

"Nothing for you today, Mr Holmes…. But there's a letter for you, doctor." She placed the tray on the table and passed me a pale blue envelope.

"A woman's hand," Holmes remarked, glancing at the inscription.

"How can you possibly know that?" I replied a little testily. "It is only cheap novelists, Holmes, who claim that a person's sex can be determined from their handwriting. A silly notion, disproved once and for all by a recent article in *The Lancet*."

"Yes, but just open the letter and tell me if I am not right."

At least his mood had improved with the challenge.

I tore open the envelope and took out an illustrated card.

"Yes, it is from a woman," I replied. "But that doesn't prove anything. You had a fifty-fifty chance of getting it right."

Mrs Hudson smiled as she poured out our tea.

"Does he ever get it wrong, doctor?" she asked.

By now, Holmes was positively jovial. "And who is this charming missive from, might I ask?"

"Surely you can tell?" I could not resist the jibe.

"The faint thumb print on the seal tells me it from a country woman used to working outdoors, and yet the quality of the envelope and inclusion of the card indicates she is a person of taste and breeding, so not a simple farmer. Other than that…" He shrugged.

"The card is very pretty," Mrs Hudson said.

"Yes," I replied, handing it to her so that she could see it better. "It's painted by my late wife's very good friend, Christina Godfrey. She is a botanical artist."

"You mean, she did this herself!" Mrs Hudson exclaimed. "Oh, doctor, you should frame it."

The card was indeed lovely, depicting a pale yellow flower I could not identify but which Holmes immediately recognised as sea sandwort.

"Very useful," he explained. "Helps to stabilise sand dunes."

"Beautiful as well." Mrs Hudson was still holding it.

"After I have read through the message," I told her, "You can keep the picture, seeing as how you like it so much."

Handing the card back to me, she thanked me more fervently than the small matter warranted, picked up the tray and left the room, a big grin on her face.

"Some people are easily pleased," Holmes said, attacking his egg. "So, does Mary's friend have anything interesting to say for herself?"

"Actually, yes," I replied. "She invites me down to Bromley for the day, and particularly requests that you come too, since she has a problem she would like to discuss with us."

"Oh dear." Holmes shook his head. "Must I come? I am sure you are well able to deal with her little vexation, Watson, whatever it is."

I should explain that Christina Godfrey, while a dear friend of Mary's, has, over the years since my wife's death, become a friend and confidante to me as well. We share the sad experience of having lost a dear one, her own husband having died young. Indeed, mutual friends often suggested in the past that she and I might one day become closer than friends, but the years went by and it never happened. I think we were both content with the situation as it was, and now that we were well into middle age, it hardly seemed relevant.

"I think a trip to Bromley might interest you, Holmes," I said. "Christina is a beekeeper."

"Ah," he replied. "I could tell she worked outdoors. And yes, that does make a difference."

In recent times, Holmes has rather surprised me by expressing the intention at some stage in his life of giving up detection altogether and settling in the countryside to raise a rare breed of sheep or goats, or perhaps keep bees. I could never see it happening, but of course Holmes always has the ability to shake one's assumptions.

Thus, it was that, on the following day, having replied to Christina's invitation by telegram, the two of us boarded an early train from Victoria Station to Bromley, where we were to be picked up by dog cart.

It was Christina herself who met us. Once a pretty slip of a girl, she had broadened into a true countrywoman, still handsome but weatherbeaten, with bronzed skin and eyes like ripe hazelnuts. Large, serviceable hands, unornamented with gloves or rings, held the reins firmly as we bounced through the countryside, through hedgerows filled with flowers I felt sure both Christina and Holmes could name easily, but which I simply rejoiced to see.

It was not until we were settled in her comfortably cluttered parlour over mugs of tea and slices of thickly buttered fruit cake, two large spaniels at our feet, did she broach the reason she had requested our visit.

"I make a good enough living," she said, "from sales of my honey and royal jelly, but friends seem also to like to buy my botanical art, which I started merely as a hobby."

"Yes," I replied, "the card you sent was beautiful. Our landlady intends to frame it."

"Well, that's good to hear," she said. "I can give your landlady more such pictures, if she would like them."

"She would love that."

"Your problem," Holmes interjected, "relates to your paintings, does it?"

"Correct." She looked at him in some surprise, as did most people, unused to his well-honed deductive powers. As for me, I assumed he had surmised as much from the fact that she had immediately mentioned her art preliminary to outlining the matter in hand.

"Some weeks ago," she continued, "I received a very generous commission to provide a series of botanical paintings. Of course, I was delighted. However, two aspects of the business struck me as odd. In the first place, the commission came anonymously. I was to send each piece as I finished it to a post restante address."

"A little strange," I said, "but hardly disturbing."

"More so, was that each of the paintings had to depict a poisonous plant, from a list supplied. I assumed my client to be an eccentric collector, of which there are quite a number, you know. Some of the requests I have received… well… can be unusual, to say the least. I don't mind the birds, bees and butterflies, or even the fairies and sprites – illustrations like that can be charming additions to children's nurseries. But one gentleman wished for the face of his dead wife to be depicted in flower form. I turned him down."

"And in the present case?" Holmes asked.

"As I said, I was provided with the names of six poisonous plants, all of which I have painted and sent off. So you can imagine my horror when I read in *The Illustrated London News* of the death of a man by aconite poisoning, aconite being one of the plants I had illustrated."

"Surely coincidental," I said.

"One might think so. However, it was mentioned as a curious fact that, among the man's possessions, was a painting of the very same fatal flower. The image was even reproduced in the article." She paused. "Gentlemen, it was my painting!"

"I see," I remarked. "Curious, indeed. Do you think he is the person who commissioned your work, and then chose one of the depicted plants to commit suicide?"

"No, I don't. Who would choose to take aconite? It causes a most unpleasant death as you, John, a doctor, must know."

I nodded. "Very true."

"I myself read the same story," Holmes remarked. "Wasn't the wretched fellow's body found by his wife? Didn't suspicion alight upon her?"

Christina nodded. "Initially it did. But she and their three children had only just returned from a week staying with her sister in Birmingham. She couldn't have been home when the fatal dose was administered."

"Unless," I suggested, "she had left it in some food or beverage for her husband to consume while she was away."

"The police have discounted that. The man in question, a Mr Francis Turvey, had been entertaining a visitor on the fatal night. Two wine glasses were found, one of which contained residue of the poison."

"You are very well informed, Christina," I said.

"I made it my business, given my unwitting involvement. You see, I am good friends with the local Superintendent here, and felt I should inform him that the Turveys, who, by the by, live quite locally, had somehow got hold of my painting. It was he who provided the additional details." She shook her head. "No one thinks I am involved in any way, and the authorities aren't pursuing the lead of the anonymous commissioner. They judge, as you did, John, that it is merely a coincidence."

"Hm!" Holmes grunted. "Typical of those plodding bobbies. No imagination." He made a steeple of his fingers and pressed them to his lips. "Well, Mrs Godfrey," he continued after a moment, "you have presented us with a most tantalising puzzle. I should very much like to investigate it for you, starting with an interview with Mrs Turvey if she is up to it, to discover how and when exactly the painting came into their possession.... But now, how about you show me your bee hives?"

Mrs Turvey was a tired-looking woman I judged to be in her late thirties. Of course, she was mother to three small and very demanding children, added to which her recent bereavement must have contributed to her worn looks, and yet I rather felt she had let herself go before that. Her dress was dowdy and somewhat slovenly, her hair caught up in a loose chignon, from which strands hung down like rats' tails. Her manner was resigned, and, while she had no problem answering Holmes's questions, it was as if she was performing yet another burdensome duty. Only when he got on to the subject of the painting did she display some animation.

"The man from the papers was very interested in it," she said. "He took a picture and put it in the news."

"Yes, I saw it too. I am wondering when did you acquire the work?"

"Francis brought it home. He gave it to me."

"A present?"

"I suppose, although it would have been most unlike him to do that.' She frowned. "I don't know where he got it. He would hardly have paid good money for it. Probably one of his many friends gave it to him and he didn't want it for himself." She sniffed. "I liked it well enough – those blue flowers are quite pretty, aren't they?" She glanced up at the painting, still hanging on the wall. "But I had no idea the plant was poisonous until the man told me. I don't think Francis did, either, or he would have said. It's just the sort of thing he would have found amusing…. Bernardine, leave that be. You'll break it." The child had picked up a dusty china shepherdess. "Take your brothers into the garden while I'm talking to the gentlemen. And don't pick anything or go near the stinging nettles…."

The garden that was visible from the parlour window was hardly endowed with any evidence of a horticulturalist's care, being overgrown with large weeds. I imagined that the police must have had a busy time searching through it for evidence of aconite.

The interview left me overcome with depression, thinking of this wretched woman locked into what seemed to be a loveless marriage, with a man who cared so little for her he wouldn't even buy her a present. She informed us that she had no idea who might have visited him on the fatal night, man or woman, and appeared indifferent. Her main preoccupation was wondering how she would manage with the family breadwinner gone. However, her sister in Birmingham, had suggested she sell up and move in with her.

"That's what I'll probably do," she said, without enthusiasm. "It's our family home, you see, my late parents' home, I mean. Cecily was looking after them there 'til they died. Now she's rattling round in it on her own."

"Well," I remarked to Holmes as we made our way out, "that was rather a waste of time."

"On the contrary, Watson. Mrs Turvey revealed something useful without realising it."

"Did she, indeed? What precisely?"

"As to that," he replied, smiling, "you'll have to wait until I have investigated further. Meanwhile, why don't you return to your friend's house and quiz her on who knew she painted flowers?"

"You think it's someone close to her then?" A horrid notion.

"Quite possibly. After all, she doesn't advertise her art widely, and the fact that Mrs Turvey is also local is telling, don't you think?"

I tried to be discreet in my questioning of Christina, but she is a smart woman and caught my drift at once.

"So the great detective thinks one of my acquaintances murdered the poor man," she said.

"Not exactly. Someone you know might have mentioned your art to someone else, giving them the idea to link your picture to a poisoning."

'Whyever should they do that?'

'I don't know." I sighed. "Who, apart possibly from Holmes, can truly penetrate the workings of a twisted mind? But there has to be some sort of a connection."

"Hmm," she was prepared to concede as much. "Well, as you can see, I display my paintings all over the house, and so anyone who visited me at any time could have viewed them. Some I give to friends or occasionally sell them: if a friend wants to give them as a present, for instance, and insists on paying."

"Did anyone ask recently if you fulfilled commissions?"

She thought about it. "Now you mention it, there was someone... Oh, I don't know. Who was it?" She stared at me as if I might provide the answer. "It'll probably come back to me in the middle of the night."

"In that case, let us know at once."

"Oh John. I do hope it has nothing to do with anyone I know. That would be extremely troubling."

Later that afternoon, I made my solitary way back to Baker Street, as Holmes had instructed me to do if he didn't turn up in the meantime. Christina had laden me down with pots of honey and more cards of flowers she had painted, to give to Mrs Hudson.

She gave me a hug, too, as I was leaving, saying, "I do hope you and Mr Holmes get to the bottom of this nasty business."

How typical of her generous nature, I thought, to include me as one of the investigators. And I confess, the thought flitted through my mind of how pleasant it would be to come home after work to a woman like that, instead of to the somewhat desiccated and unemotional being that was my current housemate.

To compound the impression, I found Holmes already back home, and awaiting me impatiently.

"You took your time, Watson. I trust the bonny widow imparted plenty of useful information for us."

I recounted what she had told me. He was not impressed.

"Names would have been useful, Watson," he said.

"I could hardly ask her for a list of her visitors."

"Whyever not?"

"All are probably quite innocent of this business."

"Probably?" He raised his eyebrows.

"So what if anything did you discover?"

He sat back, looking irritatingly smug.

"Ah well, I thought it might be a good idea to consult with Mrs Godfrey's friend, Harry Bradfield, the local Superintendent of police. I asked him about other sudden deaths in the locality resulting from poison. At first, he shook his head – not the most imaginative of men, I must say. It's no wonder he hasn't progressed up the ladder of success. I asked then about fatal heart attacks or similar among men seemingly healthy enough up until that time. He conceded that a certain Colonel Levitt popped off of a sudden…."

"Popped off?"

"The Superintendent's own words." He grinned. "Anyway, the son insisted the police look into it but they were reassured by the

225

man's doctor that a heart attack wasn't unexpected, given the Colonel's habits of over-indulgence and idle habits."

"So that was that."

Holmes's face continued to display that insufferably superior expression. "Anyone else might think so, Watson. However, I decided to pay a visit to Mrs Levitt, and what do you know? What did I see hanging on the wall…?"

"Not one of Christina's paintings!"

"The very same."

"What flower did it depict?"

"The purple foxglove."

I nodded. "Digitalis. Known to cause heart failure if imbibed in sufficient quantities. Yet the taste is so bitter that it would seem an unlikely cause of death. Colonel Levitt would hardly have consented to ingest enough to kill him."

"Except, as his wife informed me, he had lost his sense of taste following an infection."

"Very convenient for a prospective murderer."

Holmes looked grave. "And suggestive. The murderer, if such there be, must be close enough to the victim to know of this condition."

"The wife, then?"

"I very much doubt it. Mrs Levitt is a loud, stupid woman, not especially regretful at the passing of her husband, admittedly. But neither did she strike me as someone who would have plotted his demise."

"Yet poison is generally held to be a woman's weapon."

Holmes smiled. "Yes, Watson. *Cherchez la femme*, as the French say."

"A woman wronged by both Levitt and Turvey?"

"Perhaps…." There was a faraway look in his eyes. Then he pulled himself together. "Yes, we must search for a woman who knew both men. There's no time to be lost."

"Before she strikes again, you mean?"

"If she hasn't done so already. Bradfield said that he would make enquiries among his staff regarding other sudden deaths of middle-aged men, and let me know the results.... I think it rather tickles him to be assisting Mr Sherlock Holmes."

"The great detective," I added.

"You said it, Watson. Not I."

Over the course of the next day, we waited for some new communication from the Inspector, but in vain. However, we were pleased to receive a note from Christina to say that she had at last recalled the person who had enquired about commissions: a woman who had come to buy some honey.

"I didn't know her," she wrote, "and cannot remember her name. However, she arrived with my friend, Belinda Montague. They were certainly well acquainted. I remember the woman admired my paintings, and asked me if I ever worked to order."

Efficient as ever, Christina provided us with Mrs Montague's address, in case we wished to follow it up.

"Most certainly we do," said Holmes. "It may be a slim lead, but it is the only one we have at the moment."

A telegram requesting an interview was duly dispatched and a positive reply came back almost immediately. The following afternoon at two would suit the lady.

We arrived promptly at the Beckenham address, a fine villa near the church, to find Mrs Montague out in her sunny garden, cutting bunches of daffodils and narcissi.

"Such happy flowers, I always think," she said, leading us into the house.

She was a comfortably plump woman in her forties, small of stature and still pretty, with curly auburn hair, a porcelain skin and a delightful smile. She gave the blooms to a maid to put in a vase.

"I shall arrange them properly later," she told us. "Now, gentlemen, please come into the parlour. I hope you will take tea with me. Sally will bring us some."

It was a bright room, tastefully furnished, facing the street. Our hostess invited us to take seats on a well-padded sofa, and sat down facing us across a low table. Then she leaned forward, looking at us both with eager grey eyes.

"So, gentlemen, I confess I am most intrigued," she said. "Whatever brings a detective here to my humble abode?"

Holmes made no reply. He was staring over her head at the wall, as if transfixed. I followed his gaze, and made an involuntary exclamation of surprise.

"What is it?" she asked.

"The painting," Holmes said. He stood up and went over to study it more closely. "May I ask, Mrs Montague, when did you acquire it?"

"Oh… that picture." She in turn was surprised. "Very recently, in fact."

"And who gave to you?"

"Well…" She laughed. "To tell the truth, I don't exactly know. I presume it's from Christina Godfrey, since it is one of her botanical pictures, you know. It arrived already framed, but without any accompanying card. I must get around to thanking her for it."

"Do you know what it depicts?" Holmes looked grave, as well he might.

She gave a little shrug. "Not really. I am not well up on my wild flowers," she replied. "Some sort of cow parsley perhaps."

"It is hemlock, and highly poisonous."

She was clearly taken aback. "What a strange choice of subject matter, then, although the flowers and leaves are attractive enough."

Holmes remained standing.

"Where is your husband, Mrs Montague?"

Now she also stood up, her pale skin become flushed.

"You haven't yet explained your presence here, Mr Holmes, and instead are plaguing me with strange and alarming questions? I have to say, I don't like it. Not at all."

"I apologise, madam, really I do. But it is most important that you tell me where your husband is."

She responded to his urgency.

"At work. He is a solicitor with an office near the Beckenham Junction station."

"Can you telephone him right away?"

I, like Holmes, had noticed the instrument in the hall.

"For God's sake, why?"

"I suspect he may be in great danger."

She swayed on her feet. Fearing she might fall in a faint, I leapt up to support her.

"Danger...?" she repeated. "Yes, of course, I'll telephone him at once.... But what shall I say?"

"I should like to speak to him," Holmes replied.

"Very well."

She rested on my arm as we went out into the hallway. I noticed the sweet scent of lavender in her hair. It reminded me of my late wife, and made me feel even more protective towards little Belinda Montague.

"He's not there," she told us in a shaky voice, after speaking for a moment to someone on the end of the line.

"Let me?" Holmes took the receiver from her, and asked where Mr Montague had gone? When? He then replaced the receiver, shaking his head at me, unnoticed by the lady.

I led her back into the parlour and sat her down. The maid had just arrived with the tea and had placed it on the low table. I poured a cup for Mrs Montague. She sipped it automatically, then grimaced at the sweetness, for I had sugared it.

"Drink up. It will do you good," I said.

She took another sip, then raised those lovely eyes to me, now welling with tears. "Where is he? He should be there."

"Mrs Montague, I have another strange but important question for you so please answer it."

Holmes actually knelt on the floor in front of her and took her hand. "Do you remember going to visit Mrs Godfrey with a friend to buy some honey? It would have been some time ago."

She was clearly trying to order her thoughts.

"Er... I suppose you must mean when I went there with Cora Devine," she said at last. "Cora's not really a friend, more an acquaintance – someone I know from church – but she was most insistent on accompanying me. And then in the end I don't think she actually bought any honey, which I found strange."

"Do you know where she lives?"

"Yes, of course... at the vicarage.... She's the vicar's sister." Mrs Montague gave a little laugh. "We all find it amusing you know, that the vicar is a Mr Devine – D-E-V-I-N-E – so nearly divine, don't you see." Her laugh turned into a sob. "But why do you want to know about her?"

"Come, Watson. Not a moment to lose." Holmes was already half-way out the door.

I held back, feeling the need to give some reassurance. "Don't worry too much, my dear," I said to the lady in my most soothing doctor's voice. "I expect all will be well, and promise to let you know what we discover as soon as we know it ourselves."

The pleading look she gave me nearly broke my heart, but I hurried out after Holmes, calling to the maid to take care of her mistress.

From the street, we could see the church at the top of the hill, and beside it what surely had to be the vicarage, a solid, redbrick edifice that seemed the very embodiment of respectability and trustworthiness. Our knock on the door summoned the vicar himself, a dishevelled fellow in early middle age, who clearly spent a lot of time running distracted fingers through the pepper and salt locks that stood up stiffly from his crown, giving him a permanently astonished look. He regarded us vaguely, uttering the cryptic words, "I thought you were the men about the roof. But you're not, are you?"

Following our assertion that we most certainly were not the men about the roof, and asking for his sister, he called for her, and then, since there was no reply, came at last to the conclusion that she must be out.

"Fancy," he shouted. "Where's Miss Cora gone?"

A very undersized maid with an overlarge head materialised from the shadows in the hallway and declared that Miss Cora had "gorn on a pickanick with a pickanick basket."

"Do you know where would that be, Fancy?" Holmes asked gently.

The girl shook her head, then added, "If twere me, I'd be going to the common with the common folk, but Miss Cora, she aint common, and being as how she teaches at the school, she probably went to the park."

"My sister," the vicar explained, "teaches embroidery and cookery at the Kepplestone school for the Daughters of Gentlemen which is situated in the nearby grounds of Kelsey Park. Yes, that would be a charming spot for a picnic, by the lake I suppose."

"It's most important we find your sister," Holmes said. "Would you or Fancy be able to take us to this park?"

"Have to be him," Fancy put in. "The likes of me wouldn't be let through the gates. Common folks go to the common, like I said."

"Now Fancy, don't be cheeky. Surely you could show the gentlemen the way... You see, I am afraid," Mr Devine added, "I am far too busy wrestling with Samson and the Philistines. For my sermon, don't you know." Glancing at Fancy, "On the wickedness of temptresses." She in turn looked back at him stonily, surely the very opposite of a temptress.

"I s'pose, if I'm ordered I'll have to do it," she said finally.

"Good girl." The vicar was already retreating back to Samson and Delilah.

Fancy grabbed a coat that was almost too long for her, the hem brushing the street as we went.

"Him and his old sermons," she remarked disparagingly. "Samson, indeed."

It was hard to think of a reply to that. Instead, Holmes asked what sort of a person was her mistress.

"Her!" came the reply in equally dismissive tones. "She's a hard nut, she is. A queer one. Rules the roost. Rules him. Still, if I don't bother her, then she don't bother me."

It seemed that was as much as Fancy would or could say on the subject, so we hurried the rest of the way in silence. In truth, it was not far. The wrought iron gates at the park entrance were indeed locked shut, but we were able to ring a bell to summon the warden from his lodge.

"We understand Miss Cora Devine is here somewhere. We come from her brother, the vicar, and need to find her urgently." Holmes was speaking in the authoritative tones that usually made underlings spring to attention. In this case it had the required effect. The man nearly saluted, before opening the gates for us.

"Yessir. She's down by the lake, I reckon. Her and her friend."

As we walked in, the man gave a second glance to Fancy, but, since she was clearly with us, let her through, much to the little maid's satisfaction.

"Only for you gents being with me," she whispered loudly, "or old potato face would have given me me marching orders."

I found myself liking the girl more and more. Her attitude to life, despite her own physical shortcomings, was refreshing. And her description of the man's physiognomy was exact.

The park was a charming place with manicured flower beds and winding paths under overhanging trees. Given other circumstances, it would have been a pleasant and peaceful place to linger. We, however, could not delay and hurried down to the lake, where we spotted ducks and moorhens aplenty, two gliding swans, as well as a lady of extremely advanced years throwing broken bread to the birds.

"That aint her," Fancy said, in case we might have thought it was.

In fact, there was no sign at all of Miss Devine and the friend both Holmes and I suspected to be Mr Montague. We looked about ourselves, wondering what to do next.

"They must be here somewhere," I remarked.

"Thank you for that enlightening contribution, Watson," cam the dry reply.

"Will I ask the old girl?" Fancy asked. "She might have seen her."

"Good idea."

The girl bounded off and was soon deep in conversation with the lady, who looked our way and then gestured with her hands.

"She says they headed for the waterfall," Fancy reported, out of breath, having raced back, nearly tripping over that long coat. "It's that way, she says." And pointed.

A waterfall! I wondered if Holmes's thoughts returned to Reichenbach and his near tragic experience there. Would we find Miss Devine and Mr Montague wrestling to the death atop a mighty cascade?

In the event, the waterfall in question was hardly worthy of the name, being no more than about ten feet or so in height. Stone steps led up to a bridge over it, and on the bridge we discerned two figures, a man and a woman, evidently engaged in some sort of an argument, verbal not physical. Before we could approach closer, the man broke away and hastened down towards us, the woman gripping the parapet and staring after him, fury written on her face.

"Mr Montague?" Holmes stood in the man's way.

The man stopped. He was a fine-looking fellow, dark with a trim beard.

"Who's asking?" His tone was abrupt.

"Sherlock Holmes, on behalf of your wife."

"Sherlock Holmes!" The man gave a bitter laugh. "Surely Belinda's not having a detective follow me?"

"Not at all. We are merely concerned for your welfare."

The man relaxed a little.

"Thank you, but I don't need protection from that she-devil." He looked up at the bridge on which Miss Devine still stood, listening to us. "I can manage by myself."

"May I ask," I put in, "if you have eaten anything recently?"

"Eaten? Whatever do you mean?"

"I understand Miss Devine brought a picnic for you both."

"She did and all," Fancy put in. "I saw her pack it."

Mr Montague gazed at the odd little maid in wonderment.

"What is all this about?"

"I think she meant to poison you," Holmes said. "I just hope we are not too late."

"Do I look poisoned to you?" the man replied. "No, we hadn't got at far as the picnic. In fact, we might have done so, only an elderly lady turned up, near to where we were sitting, to feed the ducks, do you see, and Cora – Miss Devine – said that we should go somewhere more private." He paused. "I know how this might look to you, but I can assure you I was brought here under false pretences. The woman had sent me a message indicating that she had some very serious news to impart regarding Belinda. I feared that my wife might be mortally sick, and was reluctant to worry me – something I could well believe of the dear soul – so I duly came. Then Miss Devine… well…" he glanced again at Fancy, "can I say she tried to make love to me? She gabbled all sorts of rubbish. That she felt we had an unspoken understanding, that she had seen the way I looked at her. All complete nonsense. I had hardly noticed the woman before, except as someone my wife knew."

"Very strange," I said. "Then why should she try and poison you?"

"Exactly…. Perhaps I should add that she tried to embrace me and I pushed her away, quite forcefully, telling her I loved my wife, which seemed to infuriate her…. Did you hear that, you old hag?" He called up to the woman on the bridge. "I love my wife."

Whereupon Miss Devine ran off in the opposite direction.

"Maybe,' Montague continued, "she planned to poison me if I spurned her advances."

He was still taking the whole thing as a joke. Of course, he could not know of the earlier murders.

"Hmm." Holmes was deep in thought. "That hardly makes sense. You would surely not have remained to have a picnic under the circumstances."

"I reckon it's all on account of Mr Trevor," Fancy said.

We looked at her.

"Who?"

"Mr Trevor. He was curate here a while back, though not a very godly man in my experience. Far too fond of hisself." Fancy pursed her lips. "Anyway, they was supposed to be engaged, him and the mistress. Wedding arranged and all. Big cake ordered and all. Then mistress found out how he'd got our Gladys – the scullery maid, you know – in the family way, and that was the end of Mr Trevor."

"What do you mean?" I asked, shocked. "Miss Devine killed him?"

Fancy burst out laughing. "Would have, I 'spect, sir. Only never got the chance. He did a runner, didn't he. Leaving poor Gladys holding the baby, like they say. So she went back to her mum in Wales and got lucky there. Married a miner who took on her and the baby. Well, she were pretty, were Gladys." Fancy looked wistful. Then perked up again. "Only mistress has never got over Mr Trevor. Keeps his picture and sticks pins in it."

Suddenly, we heard harrowing screams from somewhere up ahead of us. Holmes, Fancy and I hastened to the place, followed more slowly by Montague. Having raced across the bridge to a clearing just beyond it, we were confronted by a terrible sight, the same woman writhing on the ground, in agonised convulsions. Her eyes were rolling in her head and she was vomiting. Beside her, a picnic basket lay open, its contents strewn over the grass. From the vomit, it appeared that she had stuffed a salad of leaves, hemlock leaves, into her mouth, the salad presumably originally intended for Montague. If I'd have brought with me my doctor's bag, I might have been able to allay her sufferings, but as it was, there was nothing I could do.

"That's her," Fancy said dispassionately and unnecessarily. "That's Miss Cora Devine."

She died in my arms. Stark staring mad was the general opinion when the details became public. After all, who in their right mind would do what she had done? To kill innocent victims in such a terrible way and then kill herself likewise! Mad as a hatter, quite clearly, if not possessed by the devil. The vicar was more circumspect, reckoning his sister killed herself in a fit of remorse, adding that he hoped God in his mercy would have pity on the poor tormented soul. I, however, dismissed the remorse. I think Cora Devine simply realised the game was up. Her last words, spat out, were "Well, I least I got rid of five of them, the lying, cheating rats...."

"Five!" Holmes exclaimed, when I told him. "But we only know of two."

It was Superintendent Bradfield who subsequently enlightened us. Yes, indeed, his researches had revealed that three other men had died suspiciously, and all were recipients of works by Christina Godfrey depicting treacherously beautiful plants, oleander, angel's trumpets and belladonna.

So had Cora Devine successfully seduced these men? It seemed unlikely. To me she had appeared only slightly less plain than Fancy, and certainly much older, though, admittedly I had hardly seen her at her best. Perhaps, like George Montague, her other victims were blameless, and the badness she saw in them was all in her head, as it was with Miss Haversham, the abandoned bride so vividly depicted by Mr Dickens in his novel *Great Expectations*. Sadly, Miss Devine left no written account, no diary, so we shall never know exactly what was behind it all. Just the portrait of Mr Trevor, pockmarked with multiple pinpricks.

Sitting with Christina Godfrey some time later, when the matter had been resolved as much as it could be, I explained what I knew for sure. She of course was shocked to have been involved in such a tragic business, even though innocently.

"I still cannot fathom,' she said, 'why Cora needed my paintings. Were they warnings to the men involved, do you think?'

"More likely it was from some perverted sense of humour. Perhaps she thought the wronged wives would enjoy contemplating images of the flowers by which their unfaithful husbands had met their ends."

Christina shuddered. "At least dear Belinda has been spared that. I encouraged her to destroy the painting, you know, but the Montagues have decided to keep it as a reminder of their very narrow escape. 'Too pretty to tear up,' they said." She smiled. "Nevertheless, I shall certainly think twice before engaging in any further commissions. In fact, perhaps I should give up painting altogether and concentrate on making honey."

"Please don't do that," I replied. "You have a wonderful gift, Christina. In fact, I should like to commission you myself. A painting of forget-me-nots, favourites of my Mary…. As long," I added, "as they are not in any way poisonous."

"They aren't." She nodded. "Yes, I should love to honour your wife in that way. She was a dear sweet friend to me."

I have to say the look she gave me then caused my heart to flutter just a little, but at that moment Holmes trudged in from the garden.

"Your bees!" he said. "I must congratulate you, Mrs Godfrey. They're very well set up. I wonder would you be willing to give me some hints, for I have a mind to keep hives myself?"

"In Baker Street?" she asked, wonderingly.

"Not at all. There a little farm down in Sussex I've had my eye on for some time. For my retirement, you know. But I shall need something there to keep me busy."

"Busy as a bee," she said, and we all laughed.

Titbits from the Dining Table at 221b Baker Street

Breakfast

Well, here's a fine how do you do, Watson." Holmes was meticulously cutting his buttered toast into soldiers to dip into his morning eggs.

"What's happened?" I asked, envisaging yet another knotty problem to unravel.

"It's Mrs Hudson," Holmes replied.

"Mrs Hudson?" Had she burnt the toast? Overcooked the eggs? Forgotten the marmalade?

"Hasn't she gone behind our backs, Watson," Holmes said, "and written another book."

He gave me what I can only describe as a searching look.

"Remember those stories she published last year?"

"Yes," I replied. "*Mrs Hudson Investigates*. As I understand it, she'd had some lucky chances to solve a few mysteries. She asked me to write them up for her but I told her I was far too busy."

"Quite right too, only then didn't the woman go and write them up herself. Some reviewer chap even described them as 'a triumph'." He frowned deeply. "And now, if you please, she has produced a novel."

He chopped the top off an egg with rather more force than warranted.

"A novel?"

"Indeed, Watson, a novel of 80,000 words or more. You'd think she had nothing better to do." He shook his head. "She even has an editor of her own these days. Someone called Susan Knight. And a publisher too with the cryptic name MX. Has to be a code of some sort, don't you think? " He put down his knife. "And they're employing something called Kickstarter to get it going. Kickstarter. Do you know what that is?"

"Sounds like a boot up the…"

"No, Watson. It's a way of encouraging people to support the publishing enterprise, 'to help bring creative projects to life'."

"Sounds like a good idea."

"Oh, you think so, do you? Anyway, Watson, that's hardly the point. The point is when have you ever written up any of my adventures in more than 80,000 words?"

"Er…"

"She took flagrant advantage of my absence, Watson, thinking me dead and the coast clear after the contretemps at Reichenbach, to go off on some adventure of her own. And this is the result! *Mrs Hudson Goes to Ireland!*" He shook his head and sprinkled salt onto the decapitated egg. "Women, Watson. You can never tell what they're going to get up to. Ha! They'll be asking for the vote next!"

We both laughed merrily at that.

"But really, Watson, what are you going to do about this?"

"What can I do, Holmes?"

He picked up a soldier and plunged it into the yolk.

"As you know, we are going to Devon shortly, to sort out this business of the Baskervilles. I expect a novel, Watson. A novel, do you hear? Nothing less."

And he popped the eggy soldier into his mouth.

Another Breakfast

"Hey ho, Mrs Hudson!" Holmes said jovially. "I suppose commiserations are due."

Our landlady put down the tray she was carrying on a side table, preparatory to serving us our breakfasts.

"Whatever do you mean Mr Holmes?"

He chuckled. "Your book," he replied. *"Mrs Hudson Goes to Ireland,* or whatever it's called. I believe you were trying to get people to pledge money to support it through something called… What was it again, Watson?"

"Kickstarter," I said.

"Ah yes. Presumably you couldn't find anyone interested enough." He shook his head sympathetically. "That's a pity but after all, let's be realistic. Who'd be interested in a landlady's adventures?"

Mrs Hudson placed two steaming dishes on the table on front of us.

"On the contrary, Mr Holmes. I am delighted to say that after less than two weeks, we have already raised double what we were asking for. Over £1000 instead of £500."

"That's wonderful news," I exclaimed. "Congratulations, Mrs Hudson."

She looked down modestly.

"Yes, it is most gratifying… Now gentlemen, eat your breakfast before it gets cold."

"What's this?" asked Holmes, gazing with some distaste at the dish before him. "It looks like porridge."

"It's called stirabout," replied Mrs Hudson. "A recipe I picked up in Ireland."

"Stirabout!" exclaimed Holmes. "What kind of a name is that?"

"Presumably," I replied, "it is so called because it is stirred about when you prepare it."

"Exactly," said our landlady.

I laughed at the expression on Holmes's face.

"It hardly requires the insightful brain of the world's greatest detective to work that one out," I added.

"It's a silly name and I don't like porridge."

"Just try it, Mr Holmes," Mrs Hudson urged. "It's not it all like your regular boiled oatmeal."

My friend still refused to pick up his spoon, so nothing loath, I plunged in.

"It's really quite good," I said, and had another taste. "In fact, it's delicious."

"What at those black things suspended in it?" Holmes asked, poking about in the dish.

"Those are raisins, Mr Holmes. Dried fruit, you know."

"I know what raisins are, Mrs Hudson."

"Go on, man. Just taste it," I said. "It won't kill you."

With a deep sigh, Holmes raised his spoon to his lips and allowed a small amount to pass into his mouth. We both looked at him expectantly. He took another larger spoonful.

"I grant it is not entirely unpleasant," he allowed at last. "In fact, it is considerably better than I expected."

Our landlady watched, a little smile on her lips, while we demolished the lot.

"Not so bad then?" she asked.

"There's cream in it. And honey," Holmes said thoughtfully. "Along with a strange flavour that I cannot quite identify." He reluctantly put down his spoon. There was nothing left on his plate to scoop up.

"I agree," I said. "A pungency of some sort. What is it, Mrs Hudson?"

She burst out laughing. "Just a little secret ingredient," she said.

"Come tell us. You must."

"A dash of something you won't get on this side of the Irish sea," she told us at last. "It's called poteen."

Something stirred my memory.

"Home-made spirit made in illicit stills!" I was horror-struck.

"I only added the merest drop," she said. "Something I brought back with me, along with memories of my adventures. You must admit it gives a nice kick. A kickstarter, you might say."

With that she swept out of the door.

We looked at each other.

"I dread to think," said Holmes shaking his head," what else she may have brought back from that benighted country." He ran his forefinger round his dish to pick up the very last smidgeon.

Teatime

"Happy Halloween," said Mrs Hudson brightly, bringing in an unusually delectable tray of cakes and biscuits.

"What!" said Holmes, looking up from his paper.

"It's October 31st," explained our landlady. "When the dead walk the earth, you know."

She poured out the tea.

"Mrs Hudson, what new superstition is this?" Holmes reached for a slab of fruit cake. "Some foolish notion you brought back from that benighted Ireland of yours, I suppose."

"I believe it is indeed a Celtic feast," I said, partaking of the delicacies as well.

Holmes gave me a crushing look.

"I surmise from your sparkling eyes and merry gait, Mrs Hudson," he went on, "you have more 'good news' to impart about your book."

His ironic tone was quite lost on that worthy woman.

"Yes indeed, Mr Holmes. How very very kind of you to mention it."

Suddenly I had misgivings. Mrs Hudson's tone showed she understood perfectly how Holmes felt about it all. That there was even perhaps the tiniest hint of envy… I should not like my dear friend to know it, but I had secretly read the manuscript of *Mrs Hudson Goes to Ireland* and was well impressed with the lady's adventures in the Emerald Isle and the lively style with which she described it. The woman was no fool.

"As of today," she continued, "we are 293 per cent funded through Kickstarter with just four days to go. It is most gratifying."

"Well done," I exclaimed. "And might I add that this cake is absolutely delicious."

"Thank you, Doctor," she replied.

"It isn't bad," conceded Holmes, reaching for another slab. "Some new recipe, I detect."

"It's even better with a smear of butter," she told us.

Holmes spread a pat on the dark fruity cake

"Four days, you say, Mrs Hudson. I trust then that will be the last we hear about the whole dratted business." He took a big bite of the confection.

"Not at all," she replied. "That is just the beginning, you know."

Holmes shook his head in exasperation and then let out a cry. "Good heavens! What is this! I nearly broke my tooth."

He withdrew an object from his mouth and placed it on the plate.

"Oh, Mr Holmes," exclaimed Mrs Hudson. "You got the ring!"

"What! Are you trying to kill me, woman!"

"Not at all," she replied. "The cake is called barm brack. It is served at Halloween in Ireland and whoever gets the ring baked inside it," her eyes twinkled, "will be wed within the year. Congratulations, sir."

To spare everyone's blushes, I shall not relay what Holmes said in answer to this, but just that Mrs Hudson and I had a great laugh over the matter.

Suppertime

"Well, Mrs Hudson," I asked as that good woman entered with a steaming pot of something that smelt different. Appetising enough, but certainly different. "How did your book launch go?"

"Thank you for asking, Doctor," she replied. "It went very well indeed. A pity you couldn't be present."

"Alas, I had an emergency to see to. A sick patient, don' t you know." Which was at least half the truth.

"Yes," she continued. People took part from all over the world. From England, Ireland, the United States of America, Israel, Malaysia. It was amazing."

Holmes let out a cynical chuckle. "Certainly too amazing to be true, Mrs Hudson. I suppose you waved a magic wand and they all appeared."

"Oh no, Mr Holmes. Not magic. Technology. The Internet, you see. It can connect people from all over the world."

Holmes burst out laughing for real. "Mrs Hudson, now I know you are pulling our legs! This is 1895. Whatever are you talking about?... And what in heaven's name is this?" He poked distastefully at the bowl placed in front of him by our landlady. "Is that… is that a sausage?"

I looked at my own bowl. It seemed to contain a thick soup of some kind. A sausage was bobbing in it, a pale sausage.

"I know how much you gentlemen have enjoyed tasting Irish dishes," she said (not quite accurately as previous readers of my accounts will know), a merry smile upon her face. "So I thought I would treat you to some Dublin Coddle."

"Dublin Coddle?" I said. "Before we venture to eat it, please explain?"

"Sausages, rashers, potato, carrots, onion and barley steamed in broth. It's a way of using up leftovers before Friday when Catholics can't eat meat, you know. But it's also very tasty and nourishing on a winter's day. It'll put hairs on your chests, gentlemen, if you'll pardon the expression."

"I don't want hairs on my chest," Holmes said firmly, laying down his spoon. "This Irish business has gone on long enough, Mrs Hudson. Some boiled eggs and toast and marmelade, if you please."

"Just try it, Mr Holmes," she urged. "It was a favourite of Dean Swift's, you know."

"Dean Swift, be d....d!"

Meanwhile I had taken a tentative spoonful to humour our landlady and pour oil on waters that looked to become somewhat troubled. "Not bad, not bad at all," I commented. "Not for every day of course, But certainly interesting for a change. And it IS a cold day." I looked out at the falling snow.

"I'll leave the rest of it here, in case you gentlemen feel like seconds," Mrs Hudson said. And as she went out the door, she turned. "Oh and I am surprised, Mr Holmes that you expressed disbelief at the international nature of my launch. Seeing that you were there yourself."

I looked askance at Holmes. His jaw had, for once, dropped.

"How the devil did you....?"

"Why, didn't your name pop up on my screen," she said. as she left the room.

"Holmes?" I asked.

But he was too busy lapping up his coddle to reply.

246

Luncheon

"Watson!" Holmes cried as I entered the room." Whatever has got into Mrs Hudson? Ever since she came back from Paris she has been behaving in a most peculiar way. I caught her humming the Marseillaise this morning."

He was sitting at the dining table, staring down despondently at the fare in front of him.

"What's wrong?" I asked.

"I asked her for a quick snack," he said, "to stave off the hunger pangs, you know, and she brought me up this, whatever it's supposed to be."

"It looks like a sandwich," I said.

"Yes, it looks like one. But is it?"

There was bread, there was cheese, there was ham…

"You're the detective. You tell me," I replied.

"It's French," Holmes said. "The bread has been dipped in egg and fried up. Utterly disgusting."

"Have you even tasted it?"

"I have no intention of so doing. I have sent her down to bring me up some soup."

"This enthusiasm for all things French must surely be connected with her recent trip. I understand she has even written a new book about it."

Holmes frowned up at me.

"Another book!" he exclaimed. "So why am I the last to hear this?" adding darkly, "No wonder she has no time to prepare proper food. A new book, indeed!"

"Yes, apparently she had quite a time in Paris. There was a murder, you know."

He looked up at me sardonically. "I'm sure there was. More than one, indeed."

"No, but one involving Mrs Hudson personally."

"I'll murder her myself if she keeps producing this foreign muck."

"Come now, Holmes Be adventurous. It looks rather tasty."

"You be adventurous, then." He pushed the plate towards me. I sat down a took a bite.

At that moment Mrs Hudson entered with a steaming bowl of soup and set it in front of my friend. She smiled across at me.

"Enjoying your croque monsieur, Doctor?"

"Yes, indeed, Mrs Hudson. Most delicious."

Meanwhile Holmes was staring in disbelief at his soup. A round of crusty bread and cheese was floating on a dark brown liquid.

"Whatever do you call this, for goodness sake!"

"Soupe à l'oignon," our landlady replied. "French onion soup, to you. As eaten in Paris."

Grinning broadly, she swept out of the room.

Mrs Hudson Goes Bananas

It being four in the afternoon, and tea time, I entered the parlour to find Holmes already at table, playing gloomily with his tea spoon, taking up grains of sugar from the bowl and letting them drop back in.

"What's the matter?" I asked.

"I just don't know what's come over Mrs Hudson," Holmes replied, shaking his noble head.

"In what way," I asked.

"Well, when I complained just now that her rock buns might as well be real rocks they were so hard, she quite turned on me. "So waddayer goin to do about it, Buster?" she yelled."

"Buster?"

"I believe it's a term of address on the other side of the Atlantic."

"Astonishing."

"And then when I remonstrated with her further, she simply walked out on me, muttering something about a second-rate gumshoe..."

"A what?"

"Exactly... She has become impossible, Watson, ever since she went off solving crimes on her own. It has quite gone to her head. In my humble opinion, she should stick to what she's good at, like looking after us properly, instead of mucking about in things beyond her ken. "

"Oh now, that's a bit rich. She's had quite a bit of success in the detecting business, you know."

I couldn't help wondering if Holmes was just a little bit jealous.

"Defending her now, are you?" he asked. "You should have heard what she called you."

"Me?"

"A half-witted dolt of a sidekick, I think it was."

"Oh!"

I had no opportunity to react further for at that very moment the lady herself burst in upon us, waving what appeared to be a blunderbuss. Her eyes were rolling in her head and manic grin spread across her usually demure face. She was clearly demented.

"Yippee-kai-yay, motherflickers!" she bellowed, directing the blunderbuss in our direction, with the clear intention of blasting us off the face of the planet. But luckily, before she had a chance to put her plan into action, she fell forward, flat on her face, out cold.

"I see what you mean, Holmes," I said, as he picked up the weapon, while I attended to the poor mad woman.

At that moment, Clara, the maid, ran in, a bottle in her hand.

"Oh, sirs, is Missus all right?"

"*She's* all right," Holmes replied. "It's us you should be worrying about. She nearly blew our heads off."

The girl nodded. "Poor Mrs Hudson," she said. "She's not been herself ever since the Absence."

"What absence? Of her wits, do you mean?"

"No, this, sir." She held out the bottle. "One of her French artist friends sent it over. Missus reckoned it was a cure for her rheumatism and took a great swig out of it."

Holmes took the bottle. Instant enlightenment dawned on his brow. He even laughed, then, and handed the bottle to me.

"Absinthe!" I said reading the label.

"The green fairy... Watson. Or should I say the green devil. A much-loved tipple over the channel, I believe. Causes all sorts of bizarre hallucinations. Mrs Hudson should be back to her old self when the effects wear off. Probably won't remember a thing. And meanwhile..." he took the bottle back from me, "I shall retain this for safe keeping."

He locked the stuff away with an enigmatic smile... And, strange to say, I never saw nor heard of it again.

Teatime

"Well now," said Holmes, buttering his drop scone with satisfaction. "I must say it is good to have Mrs Hudson back from her travels. Adequate as Clara might be in most respects, she is not a patch on our exemplary landlady when it comes to the kitchen."

Clara is the maid servant who takes over when Mrs Hudson is away. I have always found her pleasant, obliging and more than adequate in fulfilling her duties, but perhaps I am not as fussy as Holmes. Or perhaps Clara is less willing to indulge his little foibles, such as the precise time (five minutes fifteen seconds) that he requires his egg to be boiled. He had complained most morning that it was either too hard or too soft, to which Clara, I suspected, was within an inch of retorting, "Well, cook it yourself, then."

"I trust," Holmes now continued, "that Mrs Hudson had a nice restful time with her daughter in... where was it again, Watson?"

"In Kent, Holmes, and no. Weren't you listening when I told you? The poor woman went there for rest and recuperation after her ordeal in Paris, only to be caught up in yet another murder mystery, and nearly getting herself killed in the attempt to solve it."

"Good gracious! That would have been most inconvenient," my friend replied. I am afraid empathy is not one of his stronger characteristics.

He wiped melted butter from his chin.

"You say *attempted* to solve it. The poor woman failed, I suppose."

"Not in the least. She brought the culprit to justice. In fact, she has written of it in a new book, *Death in the Garden of England*. It is most thrilling."

"Hmm." Holmes frowned. Did he feel threatened, I wondered, by Mrs Hudson's success in solving crimes? Surely not. And yet...

"I hope," he said, "she has no plans for any future adventures, although..." he reluctantly fingered a letter he had received that very morning, "there is something she might be able to assist me with."

I looked askance. Holmes wishing for assistance, and not from me?

"It's a new case, Watson, a case that needs very delicate handling, and, I rather think, a woman's touch."

He folded up the letter and replaced in in an envelope embossed with a seal that I recognised. It was the seal of the Ottoman Sultan.

Were we all then heading to Turkey?

ACKNOWLEDGEMENTS

Thanks as ever to my wonderful publisher, Steve Emecz and his team. Special thanks to David Marcum, exemplary editor of the *MX Anthologies of New Sherlock Holmes Short Stories*, for his encouragement as well as his encyclopaedic knowledge of the canon that saves me from falling into embarrassing errors.

Thanks to my readers, Ann O'Kelly, Phyl Herbert and Bernie McCormick for their helpful comments, Pat Jackson for her impeccable proof-reading, and to Pete Morriss for his unfailing ability to identify anachronisms.

Thanks and much love to my family, Karl, Jenny and Leo and their partners and children, for keeping me grounded.

Susan Knight has written five Mrs Hudson books: *Mrs Hudson Investigates,* a collection of short stories (2019) and the novels *Mrs Hudson goes to Ireland* (2020), *Mrs Hudson goes to Paris* (2022), *Death in the Garden of England* (2023) and *Death in the Harem* (2024), all under the imprint of MX publishing. In addition, she has contributed sixteen stories to the *MX books of new Sherlock Holmes Stories*, nine of which were previously published in the collection, *The Strange Case of the Pale Boy and other mysteries* (2023). The other seven can be found in this volume. Another story, *The Case of the Reluctant Footman* (*The Discoveries of Sherlock Holmes, Book 7*) is part of the Kindle Unlimited Project, (2025). She has written three other non-Sherlockian novels and two short story collections, as well as a non-fiction book of interviews with immigrant women in Ireland. She lives in Dublin.